HOTEL

Sacher

A NOVEL

HOTEL

Sacher

A NOVEL

RODICA DOEHNERT

Translated by Alison Layland

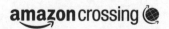

Previously published as *Das Sacher: Die Geschichte einer Verführung* by Europa Verlag in Germany in 2016. Translated from German by Alison Layland. First published in English by AmazonCrossing in 2018.

Published by AmazonCrossing, Seattle

www.apub.com

Amazon, the Amazon logo, and AmazonCrossing are trademarks of Amazon.com, Inc., or its affiliates.

ISBN-13: 9781503904040 (hardcover)
ISBN-10: 1503904040 (hardcover)
ISBN-13: 9781503904033 (paperback)
ISBN-10: 1503904032 (paperback)

Cover design by Shasti O'Leary Soudant

Printed in the United States of America

First Edition

*As I write, I think of all those who have joined me
in weaving this story.
It belongs to us all.*

PREFACE

The Original Sachertorte

Cream together 140 grams of softened butter, 110 grams of confectioners' or icing sugar, and the caviar from half a vanilla bean. Gradually add six egg yolks (reserve the whites), and beat until the mixture is thick and foamy. Melt 130 grams of dark chocolate in a bain-marie. Add to the mixture. Whisk the six egg whites with 110 grams of superfine sugar until the meringue forms stiff peaks. Place on top of the first mixture, sprinkle 140 grams of sifted flour over it, and fold in using a wooden spoon.

Line the base of a springform pan with parchment paper, grease the sides with butter, and sprinkle with flour. Pour the mixture into the pan, smooth the surface, and place in an oven preheated to 170 degrees Celsius. Bake for just under an hour (during the first 10 to 15 minutes, leave the oven door slightly ajar). Test for doneness by lightly pressing a fingertip on top of the torte; when the torte is ready, it will spring back. Leave upside down in the pan to cool. After about 20 minutes, remove the parchment paper, and—while the torte is still in the pan—turn it back over. When the torte has cooled completely, remove it from the pan and cut in half horizontally. Warm some apricot jam and stir until smooth. Spread the jam over both halves of the torte, then place one half on top of the other. Coat the torte's sides with apricot jam, and leave to dry out slightly.

For the icing, dissolve 200 grams of sugar in 120 milliliters of water, bring to a boil, and simmer for 5 to 6 minutes, then allow to cool. Melt 150 grams of dark chocolate in a bain-marie, then slowly add to the sugar solution and beat to a smooth, thick consistency. While the icing is still warm, but not too hot, pour over the torte and smooth with a few strokes of a knife or cake spatula. Allow to sit until the icing has hardened. Serve with whipped cream.

Sachertorte was created in 1832 by a young Franz Sacher as a dessert for Prince Klemens von Metternich. Metternich supported the restoration of the Austrian monarchy and was an opponent of all progressive citizens' movements that threatened the status quo of the Austro-Hungarian Empire. But he was also one of the initiators of the 1814–1815 Congress of Vienna, during which the participating states and their representatives saw the deep-rooted turmoil that followed the Napoleonic Wars as an opportunity to negotiate peaceful solutions. This coming together of the European powers showed that cooperation among them was possible despite national and political differences.

It was an early attempt by European states to resolve a crisis on the continent through reason and diplomatic negotiation.

A hundred years later, however, the irrational desire for destruction surfaced again in the First World War, the emotional and political consequences of which are still with us today.

And yet!
We could have been everything to one another.
Everything.

PROLOGUE

Fog hung damply over the city. In the pale light from the gas lamps, it rose up from the Danube, spreading along alleyways and squares and over innumerable building sites, enshrouding the Hofburg—the imperial palace on the Ringstrasse—forcing its fingers into the coats of the horse-drawn-cab drivers, and settling damp and heavy on the hats of passersby.

The lithe form of Death stalked the streets purposefully, his skinny limbs clad in a black suit, an unlit cigarette at the corner of his mouth.

At the same time, Love passed coquettishly from the noise and grime of the city into the golden glow of the foyer of the Hotel de l'Opera, which would soon come to be known as the Hotel Sacher. Her light dress seemed inappropriate for the season and the day.

It was the evening of November 22, 1892. They would meet that night, not for the first time and not for the last in this city, in this very place. And their meetings were always significant.

Love had time and was prepared to wait. She took a seat on one of the sofas in the hotel foyer, while Death climbed a low wall by the rear entrance. In a practiced movement, he swung himself up to the second floor of the hotel, where the owner, though not yet fifty, lay on his deathbed. The flu had robbed him of every ounce of the strength he would need to survive this encounter.

A cab bringing the dying man's father from the station drew up before the main entrance. Franz Sacher quickly pressed the fare into the coachman's hand and entered the hotel, where the doorman greeted him reverentially. Sacher senior nodded a greeting to the hotel employees who had gathered upon his arrival, before hurrying up the stairs.

While Death swung along the sills of the facade in search of the right window, his gaze fell on the girl who was leaving the rear door of the hotel, hugging a pot of soup to her breast. Marie Stadler had been wiping the floors of the kitchen and the cake shop for four long hours. The eleven-year-old, the oldest of four children, came three times a week to do this work, her pay contributing to her family's household. And there was always a pot of soup for supper.

Death remembered that he had been meaning to take a closer look at the little girl. Maybe he could take the man and the child in one go? Save a bit of time. But this night was probably too far advanced to start rearranging things. After all, the girl wouldn't run away; he could turn back to her at any time. The man, the hotel proprietor, was more important. His death would be of interest—make history, even. That was what this night was all about.

BOOK 1
DEATH

1

The air in the kitchen was heavy with sugar, chocolate, and preserves. Anna Sacher, a little over thirty, breathed in the sweetness, reveling in the certainty that she had finally escaped the death that featured so strongly in her childhood—the shrill cries of cattle and pigs, calves and lambs that accompanied the morning slaughter at the abattoir.

Casting an eye over the finished cakes, Anna matched the tortes to the orders—still half a dozen to be taken over to the opera house. The performance was sold out, and Sachertorte—enriched with plenty of cocoa, with apricot jam spread lavishly beneath the chocolate icing— was to be served during intermission. Her father-in-law's recipe. Once Anna was sure that all was running smoothly in the kitchen, she decided to go to her husband's bedside.

From the sofa in the foyer, Love watched Anna approach. As she passed, the lady of the hotel straightened her dress, which emphasized her voluptuous figure, and looked sternly into the questioning eyes of her employees.

"Make sure that nothing interferes with the guests' enjoyment. I'm relying on you, Mayr," she instructed the doorman, marshal of her troops, before sweeping up the staircase to the private rooms on the second floor.

Love didn't follow her, but ran her hand over the smooth fabric of the seat and waited.

And then they arrived, Martha and Maximilian Aderhold of Berlin. A handsome pair, young and vibrant. He wore a fashionable coat and a hat that partly concealed his face. Martha's slim figure was complemented by a midnight-blue velvet coat adorned with intricate embroidery.

"Welcome to Vienna. It has come to our attention that you're on your honeymoon." The doorman's features betrayed not a hint of his inner turmoil and uncertainty regarding what might happen to the hotel, and his own position, after the death of its owner. In the next few hours, his whole life might change.

Maximilian Aderhold put an arm around his beautiful wife. A radiant smile reflected the proprietary pride of a newly wed man.

"May I extend the very best wishes of all of us here at the hotel? Now, please, would you kindly complete the formalities for me?" The doorman slid the registration form across the reception desk.

Martha Aderhold took a step back and gazed around the entrance hall. Comfortable seating was arranged around thick Persian rugs. On the wall hung a beautifully woven Gobelin tapestry depicting three nymphs frolicking with a personification of night. The parquet floor and wall paneling were exquisitely crafted, and the carpet was a rich imperial red with woven patterns.

Only a few days earlier, Martha and Maximilian had founded the Aderhold Press in Berlin, and now they were searching for authors to whom they could offer contracts. Vienna seemed to be a promising starting point.

Love looked over at the young publisher with sympathy, knowing her life would not be an easy ride, before moving her gaze to take in the young woman's husband, whose face was dominated by a high forehead —the brow of an artist and a man who aspired to greatness.

From him, Love's eyes moved across to the staircase, where Princess Konstanze von Traunstein was descending on the arm of her husband, Prince Georg von Traunstein, on their way to the opera.

The seventeen-year-old princess, herself newly wed, looked at Martha Aderhold in surprise, as if catching sight of an old friend. A smile flitted across Martha's face. She was more impressed by the other pair's arrival than she cared to admit, and hoped the princess would not notice.

Prince von Traunstein nodded politely to the Aderholds, then moved toward the doorman.

"How is our dear Sacher, Mayr?" he asked discreetly, seeing the sad truth in the man's eyes. "You have my sympathy," he murmured, clearly moved.

At the door to the street, where His Serene Highness Georg von Traunstein and his princess were met by a page, Traunstein felt an impulse to turn back with a consoling glance for the doorman. As he did, he saw Martha Aderhold removing her hat in an unselfconscious movement, without a trace of vanity. A wave of dark hair flowed out over her shoulders, framing the delicate features of her face. Georg von Traunstein regarded her with fascination. Martha Aderhold returned his gaze in surprise. The moment passed before it had begun. Georg left the hotel with his wife, and Martha turned to her husband.

It was now perfectly obvious to Love that these four people were about to embark on a stormy journey. What wouldn't she have given at that moment for a cigarette?

2

Meanwhile, on the floor above the scene playing out in the foyer, Death had entered the sick man's bedroom. His cold breath permeated the room, just like the fog blanketing the city.

Anna Sacher came in. Her father-in-law, Franz Sacher, still in his traveling clothes, gently laid his son's hand on the eiderdown and went over to his daughter-in-law. They kissed each other's cheeks in greeting, and then Anna went to the bed and leaned over her husband.

"I'll go and fetch the grandchildren," Franz Sacher said, leaving the room.

"Anna, my darling . . . Anna," the dying man whispered, fighting for breath.

"Everything's running as it should in the hotel, Eduard. Don't worry." Anna dabbed the beads of fever sweat from his brow.

Death sat in the armchair by the window, enjoying the calm.

~

Two streets away from the hotel, a man was sheltering in a doorway: cold eyes; coarse, pockmarked skin.

A coach sped toward the dark figure, who emerged from the shadow of the building. A velvet pouch fell at his feet. The man in the coach, which never slowed its pace, remained hidden in darkness, although his hand could be glimpsed for the briefest moment, and with it the coat of arms on a signet ring: a two-headed vulture.

The figure reached down for the midnight-blue pouch, weighed it in a hand, and tucked it in a coat pocket.

The girl, Marie Stadler, hurried down the alleyway, her gaze lowered. The pot of soup warmed her pleasantly as she moved between the milky cones of light from the street lamps.

As another coach, this one bringing the Traunsteins the few yards from the hotel to the opera house, whisked past her, Princess Konstanze von Traunstein caught a fleeting glimpse of the hurrying child.

Marie was thinking of the coins the housekeeper had paid her for her work. She would be allowed to keep one, and she imagined herself adding the coin to her money box. She had saved sixty-four   only four more weeks and she would be able to buy the hair ribbon she had seen in the window of the shop around the corner from the hotel.

Marie had worked since she was six. At first, she had helped her mother with the laundry she took in for wealthy ladies and gentlemen, but recently Marie had been deemed old enough for her own job. After just a few months, she now earned more than her mother. People were keen to hire children. They weren't paid as well as adults, yet a child could get as much done.

The steps behind Marie grew louder. She smelled cigarette smoke and drew closer to the wall of the building to let the man past. But he stayed behind her. Marie quickened her pace. A little soup spilled from the pot, running down over her dress and her wooden clogs. Her mother would be cross with her.

A hand suddenly grabbed her shoulder. The other covered her mouth. The pot of soup fell to the cobblestones with a clatter, spilling the contents into the gutter. Marie struggled fiercely.

"Keep still or you're dead," the stranger hissed, pressing her face to his breast. His coat smelled musty. As he tried to press a handkerchief soaked in ether over her mouth and nose, she bit his hand. He cried out with rage and pain and quickly dragged her into the back doorway of one of the neighborhood's many brothels.

The air inside the house was heavy with perfume. On the stairs, Marie tore herself free. She staggered away in a daze, looking for a door, lost. The stranger followed her. She found a door and emerged into a vault-like space between sheets hanging out on a line to dry. Marie felt the cold breath of the night air. The door behind her opened. Only the linens stood between her and the man. Marie saw another door, ran to it, and grasped the handle, terrified. The door was unlocked; behind it, pitch darkness. Marie stumbled down a few steps, caught herself, and felt her way forward. Behind her a match was struck but immediately went out. The brief flare had been enough to show her the way. Her pursuer stumbled in the darkness, cursed, and lit another match. Marie found a dilapidated wooden door and ran along a cellar passage weakly illuminated by electric bulbs. She tried to cry out for help, but her voice cracked in fear. He came closer.

Würtner, the opera's music librarian, was busy delivering the orchestra's sheet music backstage for the next day's rehearsal when he heard a muffled scream. Abandoning his wheeled cart, he hurried to the metal cellar staircase and descended the stairs, cautiously but swiftly. He saw a shadow on the wall and quickly turned to see a man carrying off a girl by force. Würtner set off in pursuit. He knew his way around down here; he was only a few paces away from the alcove where the firemen kept their axes.

The abductor dragged the girl toward the back of the cellar, to a passage that led from the opera house to one of the adjacent buildings. Instinctively, Würtner grabbed an ax. Later, he would be unable to recall where he got the strength from. He soon caught up with the man carrying the frantically struggling child and brought down the ax on the back of his head. The sharp blade buried itself in bone and split his skull.

The man stopped, his hands loosened their grip, and the girl was released—and then, after what seemed an eternity, the kidnapper collapsed. The blue velvet pouch fell from his pocket.

Marie looked down at the blood around her feet. She slowly raised her head, looked into Würtner's uncomprehending eyes, and fainted.

~

Death's legs were slung casually over the arm of his chair, the tips of his shoes gleaming in the light of the candle that Anna Sacher had placed on the dying man's bedside table. Death thought of the girl.

The clock ticked remorselessly. The opera would soon be over, and audience members would be making their way to their reserved private booths at the hotel. Anna wondered whether word about her husband's condition had got out. Would their guests stay away out of piety or superstition? She wondered whether she should ask her father-in-law to watch over the dying man, and go down herself to make sure everything ran smoothly.

Anna felt her husband's hot hand and recalled their wedding in the Votive Church. She had been twenty-one at the time; the widowed hotelier had been considered a good catch in Vienna society. Eduard had respected Anna from the start and gave her free rein. Their marriage had lasted for twelve years, although she had never been in love with Eduard Sacher—it was the hotel and the responsibility she loved. She thought about it clearly and rationally.

These reflections drew a respectful smile from Death. He liked people who could think clearly; most people were too caught up in the muddle of their emotions. Death would have liked to tell them about the room their souls would enter when they left the world, the room to which he would soon take Eduard Sacher. This room, Death knew, was a pure blessing. There, being was the only state. Being, with no future and no past. A room of the deepest possible rest. A comforting nothing from which the self was born—all the fulfillment necessary. Death also knew that almost all those he had brought to this threshold entered the room full of longing, as though they had been waiting for this, and only this, all their lives. He always hung back respectfully at the door.

Franz Sacher arrived with the children. Ten-year-old Annie was hit hardest. Eduard, a year younger, had his mother's pragmatic disposition and viewed his father's death as a fact that had to be dealt with.

Annie clung to her dying father as though by doing so she could keep him alive. And then, as she fought for her father's life, the mists parted. Annie looked at the armchair by the window and saw the man tapping his shiny shoes. She looked directly into Death's eyes. It lasted only a split second; even the memory would soon vanish in the fog of forgetfulness. But the feeling, that feeling of having peeked behind the curtain, would remain with Annie from that moment on.

A last breath escaped Eduard's lungs, and with it, his life. Death rose and greeted the man's soul. He wrapped the tails of his coat around that deepest of human mysteries and took it from the room.

Anna Sacher closed the eyes of the corpse, then folded his hands. She reached out and stopped the clock's pendulum. She felt a kind of relief, like the relief she had felt as a little girl when her father died and they left the abattoir.

Franz Sacher looked at his son's body and realized what it was about Eduard that he had never quite understood: his fear of life.

Franz felt the small, damp hand of his granddaughter, Annie, clutching his. The girl looked at her father, her face wet with tears.

~

Marie raised her eyes and found herself looking into a man's face. Dreadful afterimages of her abduction washed over her, and she began to tremble.

"No need to be afraid, little bird," Würtner said, imploring her with his eyes as he held a spoonful of sugared water to her lips. "He can't hurt you anymore."

Würtner had brought her to his quarters. Behind the archive shelves was a little chamber he used when he spent the nights copying orchestral parts until daybreak and was too tired to go home, and he had laid Marie down on a threadbare sofa there. The distant sounds of music and singing drifted in.

"You're such a sweet little girl. No one should be allowed to hurt you." His voice was high and clear, ill matched to his thickset body.

Würtner moved close to Marie, so close that she could see the yellowish scalp beneath his thinning hair. He didn't stop circling the spoon in front of her face, and out of terror she opened her mouth.

It tasted sweet and cool. Her strength returned with every swallow. Once the glass was empty, she wiped her mouth and asked in a small voice, "Can I go home now?"

When the man said nothing, she slipped from under the blanket, stood, and walked toward the door.

"Why do you want to go home?" he asked sharply.

Marie turned fearfully. "My mama's waiting for me."

"Your mama certainly isn't waiting." He barked out a coarse laugh. "Your parents sold you."

Marie stared at Würtner.

"Where do you think that man was taking you? Men want a cure for syphilis. That's why they grab little girls like you—virgins—off the streets."

Marie began to cry.

"You've been lucky!" He steered her away from the door, back to the sofa. He sat down next to her and took her hand in a fatherly gesture. She could smell his sweat. "But now I'm going to look after you," he said. He really meant it. He would never let the little girl, his little bird, out into the big bad world outside. He would protect her, just as he would have liked someone to protect him when he was a little boy.

The distant music swelled to a finale.

~

Powerful chords united the singers, the musicians, and the audience one final time. The dying echo of the instruments had scarcely faded to silence when a storm of applause burst out. Moved, Konstanze von Traunstein closed her fan. Music always stirred the princess and made her feel wistful. She wished she were an artist, or at least the muse for a great genius. She looked at her husband's profile, watched his hands clapping enthusiastically. She would be sharing the rest of her life with him. The thought filled her with discontent.

Georg felt Konstanze's eyes on him and turned to his wife with a smile. She was a stranger to him, even after six months of marriage. Constanze Nagy-Károly, as she was known in Hungary before her marriage, was a jewel among the eligible young women he had considered for his wife. The Traunsteins had always considered age and title as the criteria for marriage, with special consideration given to those with a fortune who wanted to buy into the family's pedigree. Georg had no doubts when he asked for her hand in marriage. He needed a wife. He wanted a wife. The fewer complications in his home life, the better. Georg was determined to lead a meaningful life, following his calling to make the world a better place. That was the mission he wanted to devote himself to.

Georg breathed in the delicate scent of Konstanze's perfume, which blended with the smell of her thick, dark hair. The scent triggered desire. He was surprised. He had the right to desire his wife, but he had been brought up to believe that a certain distance—cool, disciplined relations—was essential in a marriage. Passion was something for brothels and affairs. Emotions were the biggest threat to a marriage. They were unpredictable. Georg looked down on people who were unable to keep a cool head; he preferred those he could rely on at any time and in any situation. In fairness, he judged himself by this standard more than he judged anyone else.

3

The coffin containing the body of Eduard Sacher was taken out in the half-light as day dawned. The staff had gathered in the courtyard to pay their last respects to their employer. The official notification was to be given that morning, and then his body would be given over to Viennese society and its obituaries. The staff could do no more than hope for the improbable—that Anna Sacher would be able to carry on running the hotel.

Anna looked into the faces of her employees. She heard suppressed sobs and knew that they all feared for their jobs and their futures. Some of them had only recently started families. These people needed her, and she needed them.

"So, to work! Our guests should know that nothing has changed." Her voice had a new register to it.

She turned back into the hotel, mentally going through the preparations for the day.

As she entered the office she had shared with Eduard, she saw her father-in-law in her seat, looking through the books.

Anna caught her breath. "Are you at the papers already?"

"We'll appoint an administrator until I've found a buyer who'll give us a good price," Franz muttered. "At least we'll be able to pay off the mortgages. As for my own money that I invested in the business . . ." He waved a hand in dismissal.

Anna stood next to him. To sit in Eduard's place would have been to give in to her father-in-law. She wanted him to leave her seat.

Anna was not normally one to keep her needs and wishes quiet, but this situation called for shrewdness. With the death of her husband, she had lost the license to operate the hotel and restaurant. She was also no longer entitled to use the designation Purveyor to the Imperial and Royal Court. She was a widow with a young family. It all meant she had to win over her father-in-law as an ally, prevent the sale of the hotel, and obtain his help to convince the authorities.

"Eduard would . . ." She paused, deciding not to add *perhaps*. "He would have wanted things to be different."

Her father-in-law, refusing to respond, merely remarked good-naturedly, "I'll be pleased if I can keep the family's losses to a minimum."

Franz took Anna's silence as agreement and turned back to the papers, their rustling amplified by the quietness of the room.

"*I'm* going to run the hotel from now on," she said.

Franz Sacher looked up. "The licenses are in Eduard's name. They won't transfer the title of Purveyor to the Imperial and Royal Court to a woman," he said with irritation. Surely Anna couldn't be so naïve?

"They should let the business keep the title. They don't need to transfer anything to me."

Before he could object, there was a knock at the door. The doorman entered, followed by a young man in a threadbare suit.

"I'm sorry to interrupt"—Mayr would have liked to protect Anna Sacher and her father-in-law from the visitor—"but this gentleman is from the police."

"Good day to you! My name is Lechner, police agent," the young man said with a brief bow. "I offer you my sincere sympathy, Frau Sacher, Herr Sacher. Please forgive me for disturbing you today of all days. It's about the Stadler girl, Marie. She didn't come home yesterday. We found her soup pot but no other sign of her. And there was a dead body in the vicinity. I need to interview your staff." The man's baby face was a thin veneer that barely concealed his determination.

"Yes, yes, go ahead." Anna had little patience for this. "Mayr, will you please show the policeman out through the tradesmen's entrance afterward?"

Lechner winced, barely perceptibly. He was no lackey. He had started a week ago as a criminal-investigation recruit with the Vienna Police, and this was his first case.

"I bid you good day." Giving no further sign that he had taken offense, Lechner gave another slight bow and left the room.

Anna turned back to her father-in-law. "This hotel's my life, Franz. I won't give it up."

"The children are your life, Anna. They've just lost their father."

Franz Sacher turned back to the documents. Was he really against allowing his daughter-in-law to continue running her husband's legacy? But try as he might, he was unable to imagine how a young mother, alone in Vienna, could run a hotel—especially while maintaining the quality its guests had come to expect. And he had no intention of leaving his home in Baden to take his eldest son's place. Franz Sacher was over seventy and was enjoying his retirement just under two hours' drive from the hustle and bustle of the capital. He loved his solitary walks, peaceful lunches, and the smell of coffee at four every afternoon. Nothing in the world could induce him to return to the world of hospitality. He had played his part and given his sons a good start in life. Eduard had been running the spa hotel for more than ten years now.

Anna had no idea what her father-in-law was thinking; all she saw was his severity. She mustn't weaken now. She had to concentrate on what she wanted.

4

Martha and Maximilian Aderhold, the young Berlin publishers, were at breakfast.

Martha dug in with gusto. Maximilian felt sluggish this morning and would have liked to spend longer in bed. But the two of them had an appointment at the Café Griensteidl, just five minutes' walk away, where they were to meet Hermann Bahr, star of the Viennese literary scene. Maximilian loved Bahr's essays and works of literary criticism. They were hoping to gain some advice for their publishing house and to enlist his help in enticing some promising young writers to publish with them.

From the Berliners' perspective, it seemed that Vienna, the capital of the Habsburg Empire, positively glowed with the artistic individuality of young authors, poets, painters, and architects, none of them older than thirty. These artists seemed to be on a quest, working at a level of creative perfection—at least this was Maximilian's enthusiastic analysis as he dragged Martha along in his wake.

On one of their evening walks through Tiergarten Park in Berlin, they had decided not to set any limitations on their publishing house. They wanted to embody an expression of modernism, to be at liberty to make whatever aesthetic decisions they wanted, to experiment and see where their inclinations and talents took them.

Martha and Maximilian had met six months before in the reading room of a university in Berlin, where Martha, who as a woman could not be admitted as a student, had turned to books for the knowledge she was unable to obtain in the lecture hall.

From the moment they first met, Martha had been attracted to the bright-eyed man. She waited patiently until he invited her to walk with him. Their books under their arms, they strolled along the avenue Unter den Linden, through the Brandenburg Gate into the Tiergarten. Maximilian told her about his own writings and promised to bring her a sample the next day. They walked up and down the winding paths until darkness fell, when Martha took a hackney carriage home.

Drawn to Berlin, where her mother was born, Martha Grünstein had left her parents' home in Bremen.

Arthur Grünstein allowed his daughter a period of time free from marital and family obligations. He deemed it a foregone conclusion that he would eventually find his daughter a husband who was a worthy successor for his import business. Until he did, Martha was free to follow her whims. But Grünstein's plans did not consider the possibility of her falling in love and making her own decisions.

Martha did not feel at all guilty about spending her time with Maximilian, mapping out their future together. By the side of this gifted young man, she felt that her life had meaning. Her father had grown rich from foreign trade, and a considerable portion of his wealth would form her dowry—enough to establish their own press and to provide them with a comfortable living until the money ran out.

Once Martha had read all of Maximilian's unfinished texts and given him her critical and appreciative appraisal, he felt noticed and understood by this woman three years his senior.

Martha, who had until then always been so sensible and rational, suppressed the idea of her father's disappointment. He had his business, which he had established when he was young, and she wanted her own. And besides, her father was in excellent health. This way, he would be able to live out his vision instead of handing over his business operations to a son-in-law who probably wouldn't have the same aptitude. In fact, Martha soon realized, Maximilian was completely unsuited to business. If her father really wanted to hand over the reins, he should find a successor who could pay his way. He shouldn't feel any guilt about that as far as she, his only family, was concerned. So Martha had worked out a plan, setting the wheels in motion before any scruples or second thoughts could divert her from her intentions, and before her father could intervene.

As Maximilian was Protestant and Martha Jewish, they had a civil wedding ceremony. Neither religion was to play a part in their lives.

The concept of atheism had become fashionable, yet they did not feel godless. On the contrary, they wanted to be open to the spirituality that they believed was best reflected by art. After the wedding, they traveled to Vienna to begin to build something that as yet had no clear shape, no content, but was merely an idea.

Martha explained this in a letter to her father that she composed on the train as soon as it left the station. When she handed the envelope over the post office counter in Dresden, she was overcome by a guilty conscience.

And now! On this first morning, Vienna was enshrouded in fog. Everything looked harsh and impenetrable.

Maximilian sniffed at a croissant and laid it back in the basket. He couldn't eat. It was a weakness of his to build up dreams in advance of a situation, only to be disappointed. At such moments, Martha always felt it was her place to maintain a degree of optimism and keep their objective in sight. She was determined not to return to Berlin empty-handed. Her father was a businessman and would be best convinced by results.

As they sat there in silence on that first morning in the strange city, each wrapped up in their own thoughts, a waiter approached and poured coffee. Maximilian saw deep sadness in the man's eyes.

"Are you all right?" Maximilian had no desire to be served by a man who was not doing so of his own free will.

"Last night . . ." The waiter's voice cracked. "Herr Sacher Jr. . . . our employer . . . he died."

"My God," Martha exclaimed.

"What was the cause?" Maximilian suddenly wanted to know the details—after all, it could have been a murder.

"The flu," the waiter replied. "Of course, we don't want our guests to be upset by it. Can I get you anything else?"

Maximilian and Martha shook their heads in unison. How could they order anything else, given the circumstances?

The waiter withdrew with a bow.

"We're in a mortuary." Maximilian stared at Martha, truly horrified. "They should have told us when we arrived that the proprietor was on his deathbed."

"But we wouldn't have moved to another hotel, would we, Max? It's just as well that we didn't know." Martha spoke in the clear voice she always used to inject a ray of hope into critical moments. But deep down she, too, was shocked. They had spent the first night of their married life only a few yards away from where a man had died.

Love had come to sit at the table across from them. She was no match for Death. People's fear of Death always overpowered their experience of Love. Death excited and upset them. People saw power in Death. And yet—Love rumpled her brow thoughtfully—didn't people talk of the power of Love? And wasn't it said that people were powerless in the face of Death? Nevertheless, Love felt inferior to Death, at least in this moment. But now she was finally going to liberate herself! For she was life itself, and Death the alpha and omega of a life lived in Love. That was how it should be. That was how people should ultimately feel. It was in this spirit that she would carry out her purpose.

5

Konstanze von Traunstein examined fabric samples that various Viennese interior designers had sent to her at the hotel.

"Everything will carry on as normal here, Flora. Why shouldn't it?" the princess said, attempting to reassure the chambermaid.

Flora, who had come to the suite to clear the breakfast things, was close to tears.

"I want to use this fabric to cover my little sofa," Konstanze said cheerfully. She wanted to impose at least a little of her own taste on the interior of the mansion where she lived with her husband and father-in-law.

"It's beautiful!" said Flora, forgetting her tears.

"What do you think of this wallpaper?" Konstanze held up a sample of blue paper with stylized gold flowers. Narrowing her eyes, she looked across at the elderly maid who sat embroidering in the window seat and who had been following every word her young mistress spoke. She had angular, joyless features, and her gray hair was scraped back into a tight bun. She had been in the service of the Traunsteins for decades. Konstanze didn't like the maid and was determined to get rid of her at the next possible opportunity.

"Beautiful . . . it's all so beautiful." Flora sighed, moved by the elegance of the samples and sketches.

Konstanze changed the subject, asking with a shudder, "This girl who's gone missing—Marie Stadler—do you know her?"

Konstanze noticed how the old maid gave a barely perceptible wince.

Flora nodded eagerly. Marie Stadler's disappearance had been a source of gossip among the hotel staff, and she had mentioned it to the princess earlier. "Her mother's a laundress. Her father's a coalman. The police have been to see them. But no one knows anything."

"She simply vanished on her way home?" Konstanze mused.

Forgetting her station, Flora whispered, as to a friend, "They also found a dead body."

Konstanze crossed herself in shock.

"The madam of the establishment across the street from the opera house found him, right by her cellar door. There are secret passages beneath the streets, leading from one side to the other." Flora's voice quivered with excitement. "They say there are people in the city who catch little girls, and then at night . . ."

The maid looked up, disapproval across her face. Flora fell silent.

"Go on," Konstanze urged.

"They sacrifice them in demonic rituals," Flora finished.

Konstanze turned pale. "I've never heard such ridiculous talk."

There was a knock at the door. Without waiting for a reply, her father-in-law, the elderly Prince Josef von Traunstein, entered the suite. "Hello, Stanzerl, dear!" Calling her by the pet name he always used, her father-in-law kissed her hand a little more intimately than necessary.

Her eyes lowered, Flora curtsied, quickly gathered up the breakfast tray, and left the room.

"Your son's at court." Konstanze turned her attention to her fabric samples with an air of preoccupation before adding quietly, "Did you hear about the abduction, Father? And the dead man?"

Despite the horror in Konstanze's voice, the old man ignored the question. "I've already sent our condolences to Frau Sacher," he said as he picked up one of the fabric samples.

Konstanze looked at him, a question in her eyes.

"Leave it, Stanzerl," he said, sharply.

She recoiled, shocked by his tone.

Josef von Traunstein shot a warning glare at the maid, who was looking at them in curiosity, then turned his attention to a careful examination of the fabric. He said in a jovial voice, "So, you're furnishing a doll's house for yourself?"

Konstanze felt his powerful body close to hers and took refuge in the demeanor of a pouting child to keep him at a distance. "Your son says renovating the castle rooms is an unnecessary luxury."

"Georg will say such things," her father-in-law replied caustically, and went over to the sideboard to pour himself a brandy. "I'll have a word with him." He emptied the glass in a single gulp and poured another. "And apart from that? I hope my son's fulfilling his marital duties?"

Konstanze blushed in embarrassment and busied herself arranging fabric over the plans of her future home.

Her father-in-law watched her with a smug expression.

After the death of his wife almost ten years earlier, Josef von Traunstein had searched for a suitable new bride who could improve his troubled financial situation with an ample dowry. A number of profligate generations had squandered the family money, and his mansion and its grounds were in urgent need of a fresh injection of cash. But he had failed to find a suitable arrangement.

A few years later, things had gone differently for Georg. He was young, and in his case the Traunsteins' immaculate pedigree was valuable. By marrying off his son, the old man had also succeeded in providing for himself.

6

Johann was waiting for Flora in the dark corridor that led out to the courtyard, where the young bellhop and the chambermaid could have a moment to themselves. Johann grasped Flora's hands and held them tightly in his own.

"I've written to my aunt," he whispered with excitement. "Maybe she'll give me the money now? I'm the only heir, after all." He kissed her, full of hope for their future together.

They had come together a little over a year ago, shortly after Flora started working at the hotel. It was Johann's seventh year as a bellhop there; he had started working at fifteen. "We could have our own inn, Flora."

She looked at him doubtfully. She was nineteen, with no means of her own. Why should a woman she didn't know do her such a favor? She didn't want to even entertain such an idea—it could lead only to disappointment. "But not yet, Johann . . . the time isn't right."

Johann refused to be swayed from his optimism. "If everything goes wrong here, I know she'll help us," he said firmly.

Flora smiled, though she was not really reassured. They jumped apart at the sound of their mistress's stern voice.

"No chatting! Back to work! Nothing should be allowed to affect our guests," Anna Sacher called out severely. She had eyes in the back of her head. Johann and Flora quickly parted.

~

Anna's children had eaten lunch with some of the staff—beef goulash with a dessert of yesterday's cheese strudel and custard. The staff were clearing up so everyone could get back to their work as soon as possible.

Little Annie was still eating, stuffing a spoonful of strudel into her mouth, swallowing, and stuffing again. Eduard Jr. was swaggering about the kitchen, hands in his pockets. Even at this tender age, he was well aware that, as the only son, he had a claim to all this.

Anna entered the kitchen and turned to her chef. "The royal Schwarzenberg family has booked a meal for thirty guests this evening."

The chef had already thought about the menu, and handed her his suggestions. She skimmed the page with satisfaction. Nothing to correct or delete—as good as ever. The kitchen staff hurried to their work. As the housekeeper took charge of the children, Anna looked on gratefully.

"If the children are good, you may take them for a walk."

"Schoolwork first. But then, if you can spare me, Frau Sacher, I'll take them out," the housekeeper replied.

"Is there any news of Marie?"

The housekeeper shook her head. "None of us can tell the police a thing."

"Perhaps she's simply run away?"

"Marie is such a lovely, good-natured girl." The housekeeper had always been the one to give the little girl her money and her soup. She was at a loss to explain what had happened.

"Please tell Frau Stadler how sorry I am. If she needs anything, she mustn't hesitate to let us know," Anna said, bringing the subject to a close.

As they talked, Annie reached out for the dessert plate.

"You've had enough! You'll give yourself a tummy ache, Annie, and then you'll have to go to bed and stay there," Anna scolded.

Eduard teased her spitefully from the sidelines. "Like Papa."

"But I'm hungry." Annie took another spoonful.

"Enough!" Anna gave her daughter a clip on the ear. She waved a kitchen helper over to clear the table. Annie, crying, gripped the plate tightly with both hands.

"You're disgusting." Eduard was relentless.

"I'll see to it," the housekeeper said calmly.

Anna left the kitchen gratefully. The children should do as she told them. Surely that wasn't too much to ask. How else would she be able to devote herself to securing their future?

～

"Darling, I've just heard. I'm so sorry." Katharina Schratt, actress at the Imperial Court Theater and friend of Emperor Franz Josef, had returned from a vacation on Corfu in the early hours of that morning.

Anna hugged her friend.

"There's only one topic of conversation at court: Where shall we go from now on after dining with the Emperor?" Kathi Schratt asked animatedly. She was referring to the Emperor's habit of eating so quickly that a course was cleared away even before the dishes had reached the far end of the table. Most of the Emperor's guests, therefore, left a meal still hungry. It had become the custom to dine at Eduard Sacher's hotel before or after a meal with the Emperor. There, they could enjoy delicacies that hardly came to rest on His Majesty's table, and even if they did, they were rarely so skillfully prepared.

Anna led Katharina Schratt to one of the sofas in the foyer, where they could talk undisturbed. The head waiter, Wagner, came and served the actress a glass of her favorite wine.

"Some restaurants are already confident they'll be able to fill the gap." Kathi Schratt sipped her wine.

Anna picked up on the irony in her friend's voice. "It's long been a thorn in the side of the Bristol and the Imperial that a butcher's daughter could be running Austria's leading hotel."

Kathi Schratt laid a hand on Anna's. "I can't believe your lovely husband has died of flu. He wasn't even fifty," she said, her voice subdued. "What a tragedy."

With her friend, Anna could at last speak freely about her feelings. "Life was too much for him. You know why?" She didn't wait for a reply. "Because I took everything away from him. He couldn't bear to play second fiddle to a woman. He preferred to die. Makes me feel guilty." Anna paused, having acknowledged the indignation she felt over her late husband's weakness for the first time.

"Men only need us when it suits them. Franz wants me around, but heaven forbid I should so much as mention politics. He's the Emperor, after all, and won't listen to a word from me."

Kathi Schratt's relationship with the Emperor had been arranged by Elisabeth, the Empress herself, so she would know her "little man," as she called her husband, was in good company whenever she traveled for months on end. Elisabeth avoided the court as much as she could.

Kathi Schratt drank a last mouthful of wine and stood. "I have to go. I'm due at the dressmaker's—I've been told I have an audition with Viktor Kutschera at six." Kathi Schratt's eyes shone as she thought of her colleague. She rushed off, leaving Anna to her own stage, the hotel foyer.

7

Martha sat in the hotel café, reading one of the first manuscripts entrusted to her and Maximilian.

She was enjoying it and felt pleased that she had found the courage to marry Maximilian and establish a publishing house with him.

The café windows looked out onto the street. Outside, Konstanze von Traunstein was getting out of her carriage. She saw the young Berlin publisher, handed her purchases to her maid, and went in.

A waiter was about to show the princess to her usual table, but she quickly decided on one nearer to Martha. The waiter helped her into her seat.

"The usual, Your Serene Highness?" The princess nodded, then looked over at Martha, who was absorbed in her reading.

"Are you an author?" Konstanze asked her, leaning eagerly across her table.

Martha looked up. Her surprise mingled with a slight irritation at the childish obtrusiveness of this pushy young woman.

"My husband and I have recently founded a publishing house," she said, and then introduced herself. "Martha Aderhold."

"I'm Izabela Constanze Nagy-Károly, since my marriage, the Princess von Traunstein." Konstanze quickly moved over to sit at Martha's table. "Do you publish novels?"

Martha nodded.

The waiter arrived, bringing Her Serene Highness a portion of Sachertorte with whipped cream, accompanied by a coffee, also served with cream, and a chocolate liqueur. Faced with the sight of the princess cheerfully tucking into her gateau, Martha also ordered a coffee, this time with cream.

"How exciting!" The waiter had hardly left before Konstanze continued. "I love stories, especially long ones with happy endings. I particularly like making my own up. I've always done it, ever since I was little." She spoke without pausing for breath, glad to have Martha listening. "But I'm married now. My husband and I live on an estate in the country. Well, I haven't lived there long, myself. My husband is regularly obliged to visit the Hofburg, and I'm to be presented at the imperial court tomorrow. My services as a lady-in-waiting will then be required from time to time. It will be quite a change. But you know what she's like."

"Who?" Martha's head was spinning from this rapid salvo.

"The Empress," Konstanze replied. "She's always traveling—Corfu, Madeira, her beloved palace at Gödöllő in Hungary. I only hope she doesn't choose me to accompany her on her travels. I hear she goes for dreadful walks, miles at a time. At her age!"

Konstanze sighed as though she'd personally witnessed these exertions on several occasions.

Würtner, the music librarian, entered the restaurant. He was met by a wall of warm, stuffy air, the scent of freshly ground coffee mingling with the rich smell of spices. The babble of voices was too loud for his ears. He would never have entered this room if it had not been for his little bird.

Würtner looked at the array of cakes in the glass display cabinet and decided on a Sachertorte. The sales assistant packed up his slice with a flourish, smiling conspiratorially as she did so. She clearly assumed he was buying the cake for himself. Würtner paid the exact amount and stowed the torte away carefully in his briefcase. He could hardly wait to present the little girl with the sweet treat. As he was leaving, he bumped into Maximilian Aderhold, who was hurrying into the café. Würtner rubbed his bruised arm in surprise and darted out through the half-open door into the fresh air.

"Excuse me, sir," Maximilian murmured. He took no further notice of the man with the shabby briefcase, as he was preoccupied with looking for Martha. The hotel doorman had told him where to find her. Martha caught sight of Maximilian and waved to him.

The princess was moved as she watched the young couple greet each other with a kiss.

"Maximilian Aderhold, my husband. Princess von Traunstein."

Konstanze extended her hand to Maximilian. He bowed with perfect elegance but did not kiss her hand, then turned back to Martha. "Darling, we should get ready for the journey right away."

"Are you leaving Vienna so soon?" Konstanze sounded disappointed.

"For now," Martha replied cheerfully, gathering up the manuscript she had been reading.

"But you're on your honeymoon, aren't you?"

"We've yet to stop off in Prague and Leipzig."

Martha looked tenderly at her husband, who returned her gaze.

"I'll order a cab to the station." Maximilian bowed again to Konstanze. "I bid you farewell, Princess."

His eyes caught Konstanze's for a moment before moving down to her lips. He turned to leave the restaurant, the moment immediately forgotten.

"We've had far too little time to get to know one another," Konstanze said to Martha. "May I write to you?"

Martha leafed through the manuscript until she found a blank page, on which she jotted her details. "This is our address in Berlin."

She paid her bill and took Konstanze's hand. "Goodbye."

"I hope we meet again!"

Konstanze watched Martha leave. Sitting there, in a dress clearly too big for her, the princess looked like an abandoned child.

"Another coffee, Your Serene Highness?" The waiter was more than attentive.

Konstanze nodded, but changed her mind. "No! Bring me some paper and ink. I need to write a letter immediately. I hope it will be waiting for her when she returns to Berlin."

8

Music drifted from the stage as Würtner hurried along the corridor to the opera's music library. Two stagehands nodded to him as he passed. He returned their greeting briefly and disappeared behind his door, locking it once he was inside.

Marie was sitting on the worn sofa in Würtner's inner office, leafing through music scores that meant nothing to her. Würtner had given them to her to look at, saying he would be back soon and she should not be afraid. Amazingly, she wasn't. For the first time in her life, she had time to herself. She had done a lot of thinking, including about whether her parents really had sold her. She trawled her memory for possible signs of the truth but found nothing. Nothing in favor of her parents and nothing against them. She had been scolded and she had been praised. Sometimes she had been struck. Marie had simply let it all happen. She had protested only where her little brother was concerned; he had only just begun to walk, after all. If her parents really had sold her, they'd have money now. Maybe her brothers would at last be given warm jackets? And her mother could go to market and buy enough food to satisfy all their appetites. Once, her father had said something strange. He had remarked that she should be pleased that he treated her like his own flesh and blood. Her mother had protested quietly but had been unable to look him in the eye.

Würtner opened the door to the room and pushed in his wheeled cart. With a flourish, he drew back a checked dish towel to reveal the piece of cake, the wrapping paper partly drawn back.

"Sachertorte," he announced, proudly presenting his gift. "I'm sure you've never tasted anything so delicious in all your life."

Marie said nothing.

Würtner encouraged her: "It's all for you."

When Marie remained motionless, he picked up the fork, cut off the tip of the cake slice, and held it up to her mouth. Marie recognized the smell from the bakery in the hotel.

"You can eat what the posh folks eat," he said gently.

Marie opened her mouth. With relief, he pushed the morsel in. The Sachertorte melted on her tongue into chocolate and jam. He offered her the fork. She took it and began to eat, tears running down her cheeks. She ate piece after piece, crumb after crumb, until the wrapper was empty.

"It's not nice to be alone." Würtner fished a handkerchief from his pocket and wiped her tears away. "But now we're no longer alone, my little bird. You're my little bird, aren't you?"

As Marie savored the sweetness on her tongue, she could hear voices singing in the distance.

Würtner pointed in the direction of the music. "Listen!"

Marie listened.

"They're rehearsing *Figaro*." Würtner abandoned himself to the melody, entranced. "Do you like it?"

Marie didn't know. She was still spellbound by the taste of the chocolate.

"It's Mozart," Würtner explained with reverence. "Wolfgang Amadeus Mozart."

Marie swallowed saliva that tasted of chocolate.

"Young Wolfgang was immersed in music from when he was just a little boy. His father taught him, you know."

"Is he here?" Marie asked, her eyes shining with hope.

"Wolfgang? No, he's dead."

Marie jumped with shock. Würtner tried to reassure her.

"He's been dead a hundred years. But he's famous for his music." Würtner carefully folded the wrapping paper, which still smelled of chocolate. "Do you want me to teach you a little about music?"

Marie nodded. She would stay here for a while longer and then go home.

~

"File the girl's case away, Lechner," the central inspector of the Vienna criminal police told his new inspector. "It's a credit to you that you're taking your first case so seriously, but there's plenty going on in this city for you to make your name with."

He clapped Lechner on his shoulder.

"Very well, sir." Lechner gave a slight bow to his superior and walked past the crowded rows of desks where criminal inspectors were writing their reports, until he reached his own, right at the back against the wall. He saw Sophie Stadler, Marie's mother, sitting there waiting for him. Dark shadows beneath her eyes told of the sleepless nights she had suffered worrying about her daughter.

"Good day to you, Frau Stadler," Lechner said, in a very commanding tone for his age, as he took a seat opposite her. Marie's mother looked at him, her eyes filled with hope. He didn't have the heart to disappoint her, and drew a pile of papers toward him.

"How often did Marie work at the Sacher?"

"Three times a week. She sometimes helps me with the laundry, as well." Sophie Stadler stared at the page on which Lechner was making detailed notes of what she told him.

"Did you ever notice anyone with their eye on the girl?"

Sophie Stadler shook her head.

Lechner looked around to see whether they were being watched. "A gentleman caller, perhaps?"

Sophie looked at him, horrified. "For goodness' sake!"

"Your Marie isn't in any of *those* establishments—you can rest assured about that, Frau Stadler."

"Rest assured?" Marie's mother said in despair.

Lechner thought of his own mother, who had also been a laundress. She had spent her life slaving away, and her children were her hope, the only meaning in her life.

He pulled himself together. "Marie's date of birth?"

Lechner had made quite some progress on the trail of the vanished girl. He had identified the dead man as a pimp who supplied brothels with girls, especially underage virgins. Lechner had combed the brothels making inquiries, but none had yielded so much as a trace of Marie. He had talked to the few prostitutes who were prepared to talk to a member of the police. Most of these women wanted nothing to do with child prostitution, and he was confident that he could believe them when they said Marie had not been seen.

The morning when, under Lechner's supervision, the pimp's corpse had been brought out of the basement corridor, he had taken the opportunity to inspect the scene of the crime and had followed the corridor to the metal door that led into the opera house. It was locked. Lechner had not thought it necessary to have it opened or to speak to the staff at the opera house; he had been too fixated on the fact that the dead man was a pimp. The popular superstition that intercourse with a virgin could cure the insidious syphilis was a lucrative one. The disease had spread through all strata of Viennese society, including the nobility. Lechner was sure that those men in particular would be immoral enough to buy an untouched little girl for themselves. And he was not convinced that they seriously believed it would cure them of syphilis. They were simply child molesters. The very thought filled Lechner with rage. He would stick with this case, regardless of his boss's expectations.

9

The Aderholds' travel bag was set down on the cobbles next to clumps of still-steaming horse manure. Maximilian paid the cab driver who had brought them home from the station.

Berlin was one big construction site. Beyond the Schlossinsel parkland, new streets lined with multistory houses and cramped backyards were spreading through the Charlottenburg, Mitte, and Prenzlauer Berg districts of the city. The Aderholds lived on the fourth floor of a town house, near the River Spree, that Martha's grandparents had built. Her grandfather had grown rich from the cloth trade, and his assets had passed to his only daughter, Martha's mother, Ella Blumenthal.

Martha was looking forward to being back in the cozy atmosphere of her apartment and hoped that Hedwig had prepared for their arrival.

The cab driver handed Maximilian the carryall. "What on earth have you got there? It's as heavy as lead!"

"A few lead ingots, in fact," Maximilian said with a poker face as he took the bag.

"Seriously? Lead? You're pulling my leg!" Like most people, the cab driver fell hook, line, and sinker for Maximilian's deadpan humor.

"So what d'you think? Books, perhaps? A cold winter like this, you need lead in your pencil, and a good wad of paper could be worth its weight in gold if the fire goes out," Maximilian replied in perfect Berlin dialect.

Martha winked at the cab driver to suggest he shouldn't take any of it seriously. She moved to take a handle of the bag, to share some of the weight with her husband, but he waved her away with a dramatic grimace and said playfully, "If I break my back, my dear lady, I'm doing it for you."

He reached for the front door with one hand, the bag in his other, and bowed low as she passed, greeting her in a nasal imitation of the Vienna accent. "After you."

Shaking his head, the cab driver climbed onto the box seat. "Would you believe it?" Martha heard him mutter. "Lead pencils? Books worth their weight in gold? What's he talking about?" The whip cracked, and the horses stepped out.

As Maximilian carried the bag to the middle floor, he observed between gasping breaths that women might well be demanding increasing equality and independence, but it was still the men who carried the bags around.

"I hope that's something that will never change," Martha replied. "After all, we need to keep ourselves pretty for you."

She gathered up her skirts and, with a swing of her hips, sashayed up the stairs in front of her husband.

The maid opened the door before they could ring.

"Hello, Hedwig." Martha handed over her purse and gloves as she entered.

Maximilian dropped the carryall and paused to catch his breath before announcing, "We're back, Hedwig. And with a bag full of books, too."

Martha gratefully noticed the warmth of the rooms. They were home.

"My wife and I are now going to recline on the sofa and read through the contents of the bag." Maximilian took Martha's hand and pushed her and the bag together into the dining room. "And we're dying for a cup of coffee like we brew it at home. No cream, no frills. Just fresh black coffee! With precisely the right amount of water."

In the excitement of their homecoming, Martha and Maximilian had failed to notice that Hedwig had something to tell them. But it was too late. Arthur Grünstein rose from an armchair in the living room.

"Father!" Martha took a shocked step back. "Why didn't you wire us?"

"I did, my girl." Grünstein indicated the telegram that lay unread on the sideboard, then turned to Maximilian and weighed him up with a critical expression. "So this is the man who has the audacity to marry my daughter?"

Grünstein, a thickset man, moved toward Maximilian.

Martha stepped between them. "Father, please! I—"

She was trying to explain herself, but Grünstein would have none of it, not right then.

"Behind her father's back!" he thundered as he pushed his daughter aside.

Maximilian kept his composure, introduced himself with perfect civility, and extended his hand to Martha's father.

"Behind her father's back!" Grünstein repeated. "And without a rabbi."

He refused to shake his son-in-law's hand. Martha was wounded. Her words of defense came out more strongly than she had intended.

"It's my business, Father. Anyway, we're atheists."

"As far as I know"—Grünstein jabbed his finger at Maximilian—"he's a Protestant." He'd been making inquiries. He turned to his daughter. "It's one thing to get yourself hitched without a word, but it's another thing entirely to send me a letter demanding that I pay you your inheritance."

Martha's objection came out in a small voice. "I *asked* you, Father."

Arthur Grünstein left it at that; he wanted not to argue with his daughter but to challenge this Maximilian Aderhold. "Can you provide my daughter with a home? Will you keep her to an appropriate standard throughout her life?" he demanded sharply.

"I don't think Martha's a woman who wants to be kept."

Grünstein looked at Maximilian, trying to tell whether he meant what he was saying.

"You underestimate your daughter, Herr Grünstein, if you believe she wants to be dependent on a man. We have other ideals to pursue."

As Max talked himself into a sticky place, Martha regretted her failure to prepare for this first encounter between the two men.

"Please, Father, let's have breakfast before we go any further." Martha gave Hedwig a signal as she tried to lighten the atmosphere. "Max and I have been sitting on a train for the last two days."

The maid hurried off into the kitchen. Martha went over to the sideboard and took out a bottle of port and three glasses, signaling to Maximilian behind her father's back that he should hold his ground.

But Grünstein was relentless. "I'd be interested to know what he means by 'other ideals.'"

"Your daughter and I intend to establish a publishing house," Maximilian replied, as self-confidently as he could. "Martha and I have just returned from Vienna and Prague, where we made some very promising contacts."

Martha handed her father a glass of port. Grünstein tipped it back without raising his glass to them.

Martha had to keep a clear head and work out how to wind her father around her little finger so she could sell the idea to him. She had learned this strategy by watching her mother, who had always won any argument with Arthur Grünstein.

While Hedwig set the table and Grünstein drank a second and then a third glass of port, Martha told him about Vienna and Prague and outlined their plans. They wanted to publish young authors and poets from these capitals. The initial investments would be manageable, and should one of the young unknowns prove to be a great discovery, the profits could be considerable.

Grünstein was not yet ready to take an interest in the details of the business, but turned once again to his son-in-law. "What experience do you have of the book trade, young man?"

"None." Maximilian held up empty hands nonchalantly. "But I'm sure I'll pick it up as I go along."

He felt as if he'd been whisked back in time to the moment when his math teacher made a fool of him in class because he'd misquoted Pythagoras's Theorem.

"Maximilian's going to write some of the books himself," Martha said in an attempt to rescue her husband.

Silence fell over the room as Grünstein realized his daughter intended to lead her life on the unsteady foundations of artistic self-fulfillment. And he could do nothing but give her the money to do so. He reached his empty glass out to Martha without a word. She poured him a generous drink.

"Well . . . mazel tov!" Grünstein said drily, and drank the glass down in one swallow.

Hedwig opened the sliding door into the dining room. The table was laid, and the smell of coffee and a fried breakfast filled the air. Just as her late mother had done before her, Martha affectionately put her arm around her father's neck. "I can smell bacon and eggs. Come, Father, I've never known you to refuse that." In diet, as in several other respects, Grünstein was not a strict adherent to Jewish practices. He was a man who did whatever he liked. As Martha ushered him toward the dining table, she exchanged a look with Maximilian. *Hold your ground! Don't take it personally!*

The conversation at the table was strained. Martha and her father talked about old acquaintances and discussed the news from Bremen. Grünstein told them that in recent months he had been doing well trading tea from abroad. Maximilian sat in silence, feeling superfluous. He ate too much and began to smoke even though the meal was not yet over. He ignored Martha's critical glare and withdrew, saying he had work to do.

After the lavish breakfast, Martha persuaded her father to go for a walk. They walked through the Tiergarten Park, at first in silence. The November sun was struggling to peek through the clouds, and the air was pleasantly mild.

Even though Grünstein thought his daughter had a sharp mind and a talent for business, he nevertheless balked at her idea of establishing a publishing house, from the commercial perspective, at least. Grünstein had nothing against books—on the contrary, he was an avid reader. But he doubted it was possible to make money from them.

Martha broke the silence. "We had some very fruitful meetings on our travels, Father. Maximilian has good powers of persuasion. He's already found some writers willing to entrust their manuscripts to us for consideration."

"Publishing by no means guarantees sales. There are any number of small presses. It's the big ones who get all the business."

"But imagine how it would be if just a few of our books did well!" Martha grasped her father's hand, as she had always done when something excited her.

Grünstein was silent, torn. Since receiving his daughter's letter, he had been brooding about how to set her future on a healthy, successful foundation. She was married now, and there was nothing he could do about it, but he wanted to see her secure, to know she was happy. And besides, this was a question of his investment, Martha's inheritance, her financial security.

"I could have retired from business a long time ago, my girl, but I want to see you well provided for—that's why I've involved myself in the tea trade recently."

Grünstein cleared his throat, as he always did when he was deceiving himself. The truth was that he loved the import business and in particular trade with the German colonies. So he worked first and foremost for pleasure, with his and Martha's assets only a secondary consideration.

Martha took her father's cough as a sign of disapproval. "You've always hoped I'd come home and let you find me a husband who'd continue your business."

When she was planning to marry Maximilian, Martha had justified herself by means of endless imaginary conversations with her father and her dead mother. She wanted to be free to make her own decisions. All or nothing.

Grünstein knew this Maximilian Aderhold was the wrong man. His instincts told him so. And his experience told him that an unhappy man couldn't make a woman happy, but he could make her dependent.

"Parents see their children's futures differently. They watch them with the eyes of love, concerned only for their happiness and well-being." He was only too aware of how old-fashioned and sentimental his words sounded.

"Not to mention their own well-being," Martha retorted.

"A family is a family," Grünstein replied.

Silence descended between them again as they walked around the park, where a few ducks were fighting over bread crumbs thrown to them by a nanny, to the delight of her little charge.

Martha steered their talk in a different direction.

"Max is a law graduate. When he showed me his manuscripts I knew he couldn't spend his days in a courtroom. It would stifle him. He needs to make something of himself."

"And so you want to establish a publishing house for him?"

"What's wrong with that?"

"What's wrong is that you're doing everything for him. What's he doing for you?"

Although she was reluctant to pursue these kinds of thoughts, her father's words hit home. Was it important that Maximilian did something for her? He was there for her. He read his manuscripts to her. He was fun. She could laugh with him. He made her life complete.

"He loves me," she said passionately. "And isn't what *I* do more important? I can work alongside him, build up my own business, promote artists."

"It's a husband's duty to provide for his wife, not the other way around," Grünstein insisted. He knew he was upsetting his daughter, but he had to have his say. He didn't want to regret having said nothing before it was too late.

Martha drew her arm from her father's and moved a few steps away. Grünstein knew it was time to stop, before they both dug themselves in too deep. He followed her. They began walking together again.

"Mother would have liked Maximilian," Martha said.

Grünstein relented. "She'd be happy that you're building your own business. Yes, she'd like that."

Martha was relieved. Her father was yielding. "Do you like it, too? A little?" she said, a note of gentle teasing in her voice.

Instead of replying, Grünstein stopped, dug into his coat pocket, and brought out a little parcel wrapped in tissue paper. His hands were shaking as he held it out to his daughter. Martha unwrapped it and looked at the chain with the blue stone in her hand.

"Mother's lapis lazuli," she said, moved.

Grünstein fastened the chain around his daughter's neck. "She instructed me to give it to you when you married."

"Mother would never have instructed you to do anything," Martha said tenderly. She wanted him to accept her decision and her love for Max.

Grünstein loved his daughter too much to bear the tension any longer.

"If only you knew the half of it!" He squeezed her arm. "I hope you . . . you'll both be just as happy as your mother and I were."

Martha was about to thank him, but he didn't give her the chance.

"At least promise me that you won't casually throw the money to the wind." Grünstein blew his nose. "You have your mother to thank that I can even begin to tolerate this Maximilian Aderhold at my daughter's side."

Martha snuggled up to her father. Arm in arm, they walked along the lake, where the ducks were still squabbling, past the nanny in her prim uniform and past the little boy in her care, who was already showing signs of becoming the head of the family he would someday have. The sun, which had been doing its best for a November day, grew weaker and eventually disappeared behind the thickening clouds.

∼

Martha was sitting in the armchair by the window, reading. As she did so, she carefully separated the edges of the pages with a letter opener.

Max was pacing nervously up and down, smoking. He had been agitated since her father's visit and was particularly unsettled by the chain with the blue stone she was now wearing at her throat. Her family heirloom was a visible sign that he didn't belong.

Maximilian was the son of a Prussian official and a mother who had abandoned him and his father when he was still a little boy. He could hardly remember her, and his father never spoke about her. A nanny had raised him. Shortly before his fourteenth birthday, she had told him in confidence that his mother was an actress. His parents' marriage had turned into a catastrophe just a few weeks after it had begun.

"Your mother simply had to leave, Maximilian."

It was no consolation to him. He had set his heart on achieving something great.

Martha quietly cut open the pages of the book. "Father caught us off guard. I should have known he'd come. We should have prepared ourselves for his visit."

At last she had given Maximilian an opening, and an opportunity to vent his annoyance. "You mean we should have rehearsed the scene?"

"Perhaps." Martha refused to respond to his mood. She indicated the book by Friedrich Spielhagen she was holding and read aloud, "If the poet, indeed the artist, is the inventor, the creator, of something new, something never seen before, that has only come about through him, that without him would never have existed, then it is right and proper that he should be looked up to with due respect and awe as a chosen one, divinely gifted and inspired; if, on the other hand, he is the discoverer of something that is there for anyone to see, that anyone could find if he makes the effort to look for it and in the course of so doing gets lucky, favored by fortune as anyone could be, then if it comes to it, he is to be envied but in no way excessively admired."

Maximilian reached over and examined the book's cover. *"Essays on the Theory and Technique of the Novel,"* he read. "If you can't write, you invent the theory of writing, Herr Spielhagen."

He pushed the book away in disgust.

"Oh, Max, stop being so bleak about everything." In an effort to cheer him up, she said, "I'm wondering what niche we can find to ensure we can be profitable."

"You're talking like your father."

"I want you to be able to write without having to be concerned with money."

But Maximilian was spoiling for a fight.

"I need you to trust me, Martha . . . Trust!" His eyes flashed. "The ability to bring to light a work you carry around in your head is destroyed by outside demands. I need peace and quiet; I have to concentrate. But your father comes in here and steals my breath away, puts me under pressure. And here you are, continuing where he left off, telling me that I shouldn't think of money, that I shouldn't worry. Thank you so much." Irony flooded his voice, which had grown louder and more forceful as he spoke.

Martha, who had never seen Maximilian like this, set the book and letter opener aside on a coffee table and stood. "I'm going for a walk so you can write in peace."

She was unsettled by his outburst; it reminded her that they had known each other for less than a year.

As Martha reached the door, Maximilian came to his senses. "I'm sorry. I know you understand me. You're the only one who really knows what I feel," he stammered.

She kept her distance. This kind of outburst, too, was new. He kissed her and took her by the arm. She could smell the tobacco on his jacket, his aftershave. She felt his body as he pressed against her. She became aware of what it was that separated them. He wanted to resolve the situation with wild desire, but the more passionate he became, the more she felt distanced. He shoved her skirt up and forced himself into her, as though he could release himself in her, with her.

10

Konstanze had vomited yet again. The maid appeared with a towel.

"I think you're expecting, Your Serene Highness."

"Expecting?" Konstanze echoed in shock. The news pulled the earth from beneath her feet, and she had to sit down.

"You should call the doctor to confirm it."

"No, no doctor." Konstanze couldn't face anyone right then. She had to come to terms with things herself first.

"Your husband will be delighted." The maid was enjoying the younger woman's helplessness.

"Don't you dare say a word to anyone," Konstanze commanded desperately.

The maid left without replying. She had been there for Georg's birth, and knew full well to whom and when she should speak.

Konstanze sat on the bed, tears running down her face. She looked over to the window, where it had begun to snow, and heard shots in the distance. Her father-in-law was out hunting with his cronies. He was no substitute for her own father, however much she had thought he might be at the start. He had misinterpreted her need for security, and now she regretted ever having confided in him.

A fire crackled in the grate. The serving girl was waiting for her mistress with fir branches and colorful ribbons. Konstanze had planned to decorate the house for Advent that afternoon, but she had lost interest and merely gave the servant a few halfhearted instructions. Her thoughts circled around the baby she was expecting, who would bind her to the Traunsteins forever.

The mansion was dark and gloomy. She had devoted her time and energy over recent weeks to the upstairs—her rooms. Their marital bedroom and the gallery had been newly renovated and decorated to her taste. But downstairs it was still dark, the furniture in the drawing room and the dining room heavy and worn. Dark stains were visible on the wallpaper above the fireplace. Many of the walls were paneled and cluttered with hunting trophies.

Two Bohemian maids were setting the table for dinner. When they saw Konstanze coming, they stopped chattering in their own language, greeted the princess with a curtsy, and continued their work in silence. Konstanze straightened a fork. There was nothing else for her to do. Before, when she was a child, she had looked forward to life as mistress of a big house, imagining having servants on hand to fulfill her every wish, hosting parties, or appearing in glorious evening dress at court balls. That was all part of her life now, but it brought her no joy.

The dining room led through to the windowless library, its shelves stuffed with old books that had been there for generations. Her husband's study was the only room on the ground floor that stood out from the rest. His desk stood in front of a large window with a southerly view that looked out over the extensive grounds. On Georg's desk were a T square, pencils, pages of writing, and blank paper. On the wall hung a reproduction of da Vinci's *Vitruvian Man*: a naked man, arms outstretched, echoing the Crucifixion, standing inside a web of circles and squares. Konstanze thought the picture looked like a mathematical equation. She went over to the globe that stood in the middle of the room and spun the sphere.

She didn't like this room, either. It made her jealous. This was where her husband pursued his dreams. It was where he gave life to his visions. It was where his heart beat.

"What delightful news, darling. I hope it will be a girl." Still in his coat, Georg strode into the room, bringing a breath of cold winter air with him. "We've plenty of time for a boy." He kissed her brow and took her hands. "Lots of girls first."

The maid entered behind him. With a self-satisfied smile, she helped her master from his coat. Konstanze threw her an indignant glare that rolled over her with no effect. The maid left the room with the prince's coat over her arm.

Radiant, Georg unfolded an architect's drawing.

"I've just come from the village. I was talking to the architect and our priest about the modernizations." Using the drawing as a prop, he gave her an enthusiastic description of his plans. "A school will be built here. We're going to renovate the house next door for a doctor to live in. And we'll create an apartment for the midwife."

Georg looked enthusiastically at his wife. "A modern village, Konstanze. Perhaps our children can even go to school there!"

"Surely not, Traunstein; not with the peasants' children."

Georg's optimism was undimmed. "Let's see what kind of place the world is in five or six years."

Konstanze took her husband's hand and led him to the sofa in the drawing room. She wanted to use the situation for her own ends. "Will you do me a favor, Traunstein?"

"Anything you wish."

He was in a good mood. He had always wanted a sister, but Konstanze was more than that. She was his wife. He had married well.

"I'd like Flora, the maid from the Sacher, to come to me here. The maid here is old."

His smile faded. He was loyal to his staff.

"And spiteful!" Konstanze continued.

"Frau Sacher won't want to let the girl go," Georg said.

"That's my point! It speaks well for Flora." Konstanze beamed at him with an innocent smile. "And I'd feel so much less lonely when you're not here."

She looked at Georg beseechingly. A moment's silence, and then she had him. He smiled. Konstanze clapped her hands playfully. "But there's something else."

"Darling?" He saw in her a child's impulsiveness.

"I'd like to ask my husband's consent to invite a friend here."

Georg looked at his wife in surprise. He wasn't aware that she had any friends.

"You know her."

Georg shrugged helplessly.

"Martha Aderhold from Berlin. I've told you about her," Konstanze said, pouting at the possibility that her husband hadn't been listening when she had told him so excitedly about the Berlin publisher.

Of course Georg remembered the beautiful woman who had walked so confidently through the hotel foyer.

"It would be polite to invite her husband as well," he said, a little too matter-of-factly.

Konstanze was disappointed. She had hoped to be able to spend a few days alone with Martha. She was about to try again when her father-in-law burst into the house with the hunting party. The men were hot, their coats and jackets steaming.

"We've heard there's some good news," the old prince rumbled without pausing for breath.

Konstanze sighed. The news was out.

"I hope it's a boy. I can make up for what I missed out on with my son," Josef von Traunstein bellowed to his friends as they all moved through to the dining room.

He sat at the head of the table, and Konstanze and Georg took their places on either side of him.

While old Traunstein tucked his napkin into his collar, he made fun of his son. "Instead of going hunting with us, my son has recently been nurturing an ambition to sink our assets into the village, that bottomless pit."

Georg stayed calm. "The school and the hospital facilities have long been promised to the villagers."

"Promises are exactly that: promises!" Prince von Erdmannsdorf broke in.

Josef von Traunstein laughed approvingly.

Encouraged, Erdmannsdorf continued, "The lower classes are grateful to their prince for their security. Make them equal and they'll oppose you."

"That moral principle has fallen out of fashion," Georg said, as coolly as he could manage.

"You think so? I'm with the great Heine on that one—fashions come and go," Erdmannsdorf replied, looking down his nose at Georg.

Georg ate in silence, wishing he were master of the house. He'd throw them all out.

"I heard you'd be only too keen to hand over your service as His Majesty's chamberlain to someone else?" As always when he came to visit, Erdmannsdorf was doggedly supporting old Traunstein's efforts to show up his son.

"Ever since Rudolf's death, the court has been a mere facade. I don't have a role there. So I like to work where I can make a difference—here on our estate." Georg kept his voice steady, suppressing the emotions he always felt when talk turned in this direction. Georg thought of Crown Prince Rudolf, who, before taking his own life three years earlier, had represented such hope for the country's renewal.

The conversation continued in the same vein, with the same aggressive undertones, repeatedly underscored by unpleasant, derisive laughter.

Konstanze took no notice. She was thinking about what she would say in her letter to Martha Aderhold and whether she should mention her pregnancy. The fear that the Aderholds might turn down her invitation was gradually tarnishing her joyful anticipation.

After the meal, the men retired to the drawing room to smoke. Georg accompanied his wife to the stairs and kissed her hand to say good night. Konstanze quickly ascended the stairs to her rooms. Glad to be alone again, and hoping to be left in peace with her plans and dreams, she immediately locked the door.

Josef von Traunstein drew his son aside. The other men were already in the library.

"You're making a laughingstock of yourself, Georg."

"I'm amazed, Father, to hear you talk of our assets." Georg struggled to suppress his outrage. "It's my money to spend as I wish."

"It's your wife's money." Josef von Traunstein lit a cigar in a puff of smoke that hit his son in the face. "I'll give you some advice: go hunting. A man who doesn't hunt has no balls. Your estate workers will sense it—and they won't be the only ones!" The old man walked away, having lost interest in his son.

Georg went into his room and shut the door. Peace reigned here. He sat down at his desk and turned to his work.

Since the death of Crown Prince Rudolf, Georg had withdrawn into himself. He had no confidence in the politics of the heir to the throne, Franz Ferdinand; the Emperor's nephew lacked Rudolf's vision. He was a tactician, too often motivated by his own personal interests.

Georg had decided to concentrate on the region for which he was responsible, creating the kind of order in his village he would have liked to see in the whole Austrian Empire. He was inspired by the idea of mutual respect between people, of people living together in harmony. This didn't involve abolishing the aristocracy; on the contrary—the upper classes should lead the way, performing the most noble deeds in society. If individuals led by example, virtues would multiply. Georg followed the ideals of the Freemasons. He regularly attended open lodge meetings in Pressburg, since the Freemasons' work was forbidden on Austrian soil and they had withdrawn from the crown lands, establishing lodges in cities over the border.

11

The gold could not be washed from her finger. Mary's Child had disobeyed the orders of the Holy Virgin; she had used the key to enter the thirteenth room, where she saw the Holy Trinity. Father, Son, and Holy Ghost. Entranced, she had reached out and touched their radiance. Now her finger had turned golden, betraying her guilt. That was the story in this book of Grimms' fairy tales with its ornate illustrations. The Virgin Mary's hair flowed into the lines of the frame around the picture and mingled with wreaths of flowers around its edge.

Every time she looked at it, Marie saw something new.

Würtner had brought her the book. "You're a clever girl, my little bird; named after the Virgin Mary, too. And I'll make sure no one can harm you. Practice your reading," he added sternly, "like the posh folks do. It can only be good for you."

So Marie had read the story of Mary's Child again and again. The fairy tale drew her in and at the same time repelled her.

Würtner sat bent over his lectern. He copied out music seven days a week, rising from his place only to eat. By now, Marie was more familiar with his back than with his face—the gray-brown jacket tight across his shoulders, and the black sleeve protectors on his lower arms.

Würtner felt her eyes on him. "The sheet music tells the musicians what each instrument should play."

Marie went across and looked over his shoulder.

"Each note relates to the next like the letters in a word." He looked at the sheet, which was almost complete. "The words form a sentence. And the sentences give us music."

Marie would have liked looking at the sheet of music if she had liked the man who was copying it. But as things were, the lines and circles, the curves, and the Italian instructions left her cold.

"I'm hungry," she said.

"We'll eat later. Sit down and practice your reading."

Marie didn't want to.

"D'you want to go back to cleaning floors for the ladies and gentlemen at Frau Sacher's place?"

Marie knew by now that she would never have to do that again. She had thought about it during the nights spent lying on the worn-out sofa in the little room. She had also wondered whether she really had been better off in the coal yard where her father slaved away, or in her mother's laundry room . . .

Marie wandered farther into the library and leafed aimlessly through orchestral parts lying neatly on tables.

"If you pick up a score, you must put it back exactly as you found it," Würtner said from behind her.

Marie mimicked him silently, then dropped a notebook. Würtner appeared not to notice. She picked up the book and dropped it again. Then she tiptoed to the door and pressed the handle. She had never got this far without him calling out. She was about to slip through the opening when she heard his voice.

"Did you drop something?"

"No," she replied quickly.

Then she was out in the corridor.

The opera house lay silent in the night. She stopped by one of the rails of freshly laundered costumes and breathed in the scent of soap. She was suddenly overcome by homesickness so strong that she let out a sob. She quickened her pace, hurrying along the seemingly endless corridor in the hope of finding a staircase. She spotted a metal door that looked different from the others. Marie pressed the handle. It was locked. A side passage led in a different direction. She followed it. At the end she saw another door and ran up to it, pressed the handle, and heard voices coming from the street.

Würtner grabbed her shoulder. "What do you think you'll tell them at home when they ask where you've been?" He turned her around to face him. "And if they put two and two together, it won't be long before they think of the dead man."

Gently but firmly, he led her back down the passage.

"I saved your life, Marie," he said imploringly. "And now I'm going to make sure you're safe from the world."

Würtner felt Marie resist and thought feverishly of ways to regain her favor. An idea occurred to him. "It's the premiere of *Figaro* soon, and the Empress will be here," he said with the voice of a magician.

Marie grew animated again. She had heard of the Empress, how beautiful and kind she was. She must be something like the Holy Virgin.

"Sisi?" Marie's voice cracked with excitement.

"And if my little bird's a good girl, you can see Sisi for yourself." There was a hint of triumph in his enchanter's voice. "We'll go to the opera together."

He held his hand out to Marie. She took it and they walked back to the music library.

"Very few understand the wonder of music," Würtner mused. "You do, because you're a very special girl."

Yes! She was. She could feel it herself, as she could feel her connection with the fairy tale, with the music she heard drifting from the stage, and with the invisible music on the sheets. And now she was going to see the Empress.

12

Anna had her first few months as a widow behind her. Her husband had provided for her and the children in his will and had decreed that a lawyer should be appointed, along with an administrator, to assume responsibility for the affairs of the hotel and the family. As long as her father-in-law remained in Vienna, he would hold all the decision-making powers.

Anna was determined to cooperate with the old man until she had steered the situation to suit her own interests. But they were still waiting for the authorities' decisions, and the uncertainty of the situation was playing on Anna's nerves. Their creditors and suppliers were fearful for their payments and insisted on being paid on the spot. From a business point of view, Anna was under pressure from all sides, and on top of that were the children, who demanded her time and attention. Every day she worked well into the night to ensure she kept on top of things. When she finally managed to fall asleep, she would often wake, sweat drenched, after only a few hours. Fear robbed her of her sleep—fear that she would fail, that her trading license would be refused, or that she wouldn't be able to maintain the quality demanded of a Purveyor to the Imperial and Royal Court. Anna tossed and turned in her bed, fully aware that she needed to be up by five in the morning with the strength to face the day.

This morning, she was no sooner up and about than the fears came crowding in with her first coffee of the morning. Not because she had been suppressing her doubts, but because she kept taking on more challenges.

The staff had reported in for duty. Wide awake now, Anna Sacher moved along the row of employees, Mayr at her side, checking the cleanliness of hands and nails, shirt collars, aprons, and gloves.

The hotel and restaurant inspection board had given notice of an inspection, and they could be there at any moment.

"The inspectors will peer into every corner. If they see fit, they can look into every room. I want to make sure they have nothing to criticize," Anna impressed upon her staff. "Absolutely nothing! And Archduke Otto has informed us he'll be arriving soon—private dining room number five, as always. The British ambassador will be dining in private dining room two. To work!"

The staff hurried to their places.

"Johann, Flora, I need to talk to you." Anna indicated with a nod of her head that they should come to the office.

Flora looked at Johann. Had they done something wrong? Had their behavior somehow upset their employer? Frau Sacher could be merciless.

"It concerns a request from Prince von Traunstein. He's asked me if I can send Flora to Traunstein House," Anna began as she leafed through the mail lying on her desk.

Flora sighed with relief. Not a reprimand.

"You'll be well paid, Flora," Anna continued. "I've agreed with His Serene Highness that you should be given a two-year contract. After that, you'll be free to return."

Johann could stay silent no longer. He turned to look at his sweetheart. "Traunstein House? You don't want to go there!"

Anna Sacher responded. "I know you two are planning to marry."

Flora could manage nothing more than a hesitant "Yes . . ."

"I'm doing it for Prince von Traunstein, but it will also be better for the two of you. It's not easy for me to lose a capable chambermaid." Anna Sacher had no time to discuss the matter. "The princess has to come to court regularly, and you can meet here on those occasions."

She stood, clapped Johann on the shoulder, and left her office, well aware that the young couple would need a moment alone to digest the news.

Flora and Johann stood there like schoolchildren. Johann could tell from his sweetheart's expression that she liked the proposal.

"Flora?" he asked, his face fearful.

"Listen, we're penniless, and your aunt's not likely to give you anything just like that," Flora said in an attempt to conceal her guilty conscience—she was actually pleased by the offer. "If I become a lady's maid, I won't have to clean up after strangers."

"But I love you. I can't be without you for that long."

"I love you, too, of course. And that's why I can put up with it," Flora said decisively.

She thought of the beds she had to make every day, of the guests' chamber pots, and of the dirt and disarray they left behind. The future promised silk sheets and the jewelry and finery of a princess's entourage. She was eager to see the mansion and its rooms, especially since she'd been shown the plans for their renovation. In her imagination, Traunstein House was a fairy-tale castle, run by a princess with a good heart.

～

As ever, the arrival of Otto von Habsburg, nephew of the Emperor, spread a wave of agitation through the foyer. With his loud voice, he kept everyone on their toes. Anna leapt to Mayr's side and accompanied the archduke to his private room. He was an imposing man in his midthirties, a man who lived life to the fullest in every respect.

Head waiter Wagner stood to attention and opened the door to a discreet dining room, where the table was laid for eight.

"Will your guests be arriving soon, Your Imperial Highness?" Anna asked politely.

The archduke laughed heartily, and at that moment Mitzi, a ballet dancer from the opera house, appeared as if on cue. She had been sprucing herself up in the ladies' powder room.

"Oh, madam . . . I'm as hungry as a wolf and want as much as you can give me of everything," she cooed.

The archduke grabbed his sweetheart around the hips. "I'm the wolf!"

"So, we're not expecting anyone else?" Anna Sacher kept her tone professional.

"My darling can eat for three and I can eat for six, so you've set one place too few, Frau Sacher," the archduke boomed.

"Very well, Your Imperial Highness. I'll have them come to take your orders."

Anna gave Wagner a subtle hand signal. No need for words; he would keep a special eye on this private dining room.

No sooner had Anna closed the door than Mayr appeared with the two hotel inspectors. Anna already knew the senior of the two, since she had visited him shortly after Eduard's death in connection with her application for a license. The official had been most dismissive about her inquiry. "Do you have any idea how many people in this city are applying for licenses? And a woman at that!" Anna had insisted that she was entitled to apply for a license, and had signed the form *Frau Eduard Sacher*.

The other inspector, responsible for recording their findings, was substantially younger, with an arrogant expression.

Sounds of frivolity were already drifting from the archduke's private room, making it necessary for them to raise their voices.

"We're expecting the British ambassador and his wife at any moment," Anna said in a loud, commanding tone to Wagner, who was approaching with two assistant waiters laden with plates of hors d'oeuvres.

Wagner replied equally loudly, "Very well, ma'am!" and directed the assistant waiters so skillfully into the archduke's room that not a glimpse of the carryings-on was revealed.

Anna turned with a friendly smile to the two hotel inspectors. "Maybe you gentlemen would like to view that room, to gain an impression."

Mayr gave the inspectors an obliging smile and, with a flourish, opened the door to the private dining room in which the ambassador would be having dinner. They looked in at the exquisitely prepared room.

Anna knew that her doorman, like she herself, was hoping that nothing more would be heard from room five.

"Let's continue our tour in the kitchen," the senior inspector finally decided.

"After me," Anna replied courteously, working hard not to betray her nerves by fidgeting. With a friendly gesture, she bade the gentlemen follow her.

"Changing of the guard!"

Franz Sacher entered, interrupting a chambermaid who was reading to the Sacher children from *Grimms' Fairy Tales*. Having spent a long weekend in Baden, he had returned in an excellent mood.

Eduard jumped up, ran to his grandfather, and pressed his face into the older man's thigh, giving Franz no choice but to ruffle the boy's hair. He nodded to the chambermaid. "I'll stay with the children now. You can go back to your work."

His tone was more respectful than would normally be used to address an employee—he considered himself a guest in this establishment. The chambermaid curtsied and left.

Franz sat in the armchair and picked up the book to continue reading. But it would take more than a fairy tale to distract the children from their worries; they were more concerned about the obvious strain their mother was under. Annie rose and smoothed her dress. She had become a serious girl over the recent weeks, taking pleasure only in her food.

"I hope the inspectors will order us to leave," she said with conviction.

"Annie! Your mother's doing everything to make sure the business can continue," Franz said in surprise.

"If we stay here, Mama will never have any time for us," Annie replied.

Franz Sacher's objection was cut short by the next line of attack, this time from young Eduard. "Perhaps you could marry Mama, Grandpa?"

"I've been married twice before." Franz Sacher snapped the fairy-tale book shut. "In any case, I'm a bit old for all that."

The boy was not about to let it go. "What happened to your wives?"

"I'm a widower, like your mother's a widow."

Under the children's penetrating gaze, he suddenly felt like a latter-day Bluebeard.

"Widower and widow, that makes sense," Eduard remarked.

"And Mama's already being a bit nicer to us again," Annie added.

Franz Sacher caught sight of himself in the mirror behind the sofa and straightened. He thought he looked quite good as he sat there surrounded by the children. "Why don't we have ourselves driven around the city in a cab?"

The children whooped with delight—Eduard with enthusiasm, Annie a little more reserved. She saw her grandfather's suggestion of going out to enjoy themselves for what it was: a distraction. Things would never again be as they were when Papa was alive. Perhaps she should follow him, instead of hoping for better times?

Franz Sacher noticed Annie gazing into the side room where her father had died.

∽

Anna sat at a desk piled with papers. She felt unable to tackle even the simplest correspondence. Toward the end of that crazy day, the British ambassador's wife had fainted just as the inspectors' tour had finally seemed to be drawing to a welcome conclusion. One particularly alarming stumbling block had been overcome painlessly, when the senior inspector asked for a napkin and held it in front of the keyhole of the kitchen door while his colleague blew through it from the other side.

"A sly trick they learn in the military," Mayr had whispered to Anna as they both held their breath. The napkin stayed spotlessly clean.

"Gentlemen, do you think His Majesty's ministers would come here to dine if they ran the risk of being spied on through the keyhole by vermin?" Mayr protested in a loud voice.

"You wouldn't believe what we see in a day's work," the younger inspector retorted. It was obvious how much he was hoping to find a fault for his records.

Yet they had found nothing to complain of.

As if they would! This was no brothel. The private rooms might be inviting places for cozy assignations, but their guests knew how to behave in a way that avoided scandal. They were all masters and mistresses of discretion.

Nevertheless, the archduke had refused to be kept in check. When his second bottle of champagne had failed to arrive quickly enough, he had stormed out of the room clad in nothing but his sword belt, complete with saber.

"I get hot when there's no champagne," he roared, drawing his sword and waving it around in front of Mayr, who was desperately trying to control the situation.

The ambassador and his wife were on their way to dinner when they were confronted with the commotion around the naked archduke.

"Shocking!" The lady fainted into Mayr's arms.

The sword-waving archduke now stood, naked and inebriated, right in front of the hotel inspectors. Mitzi cheered from within the private room and called for her playmate.

Anna turned hot and cold when she thought about the incident and its possible consequences. Her father-in-law came and sat down opposite her on the guest chair. She looked tired, and he noticed her beauty, maybe because of it.

"They won't find anything they can use against you, Anna. After all, they were confronted with no less than His Imperial Highness, Archduke Otto of Austria."

Anna nodded, not entirely convinced. Franz laid his hand on hers, and a warmth flowed through him. Coming to his senses, he cleared his throat, keen to turn the conversation to his grandchildren and their longing for an intact family.

While they were out in the cab, the children sitting on either side of him, Franz had recalled his feelings from his own boyhood and felt the old chill. It no longer seemed such an outlandish idea that he should be involved in their family life in the role of father to his grandchildren. Why not? Who said he had to spend his old age in Baden, every walk he took bringing him a mile closer to death? Fate was offering him an alternative; he simply had to decide whether he wanted to grasp it.

Franz Sacher felt more clearly than he would ever have thought possible that the decision lay in his hands. And in Anna's, of course.

She stood and smoothed her dress. "The children were so good today, Franz. I'll go upstairs and say good night to them."

At the door of her office, Anna paused and called Wagner over. "Please bring my father-in-law something good to drink, Wagner." She turned and looked at Franz. "Are you all right?"

He nodded with a smile. He liked her.

13

The Aderhold Press was located among other commercial premises around a courtyard surrounded by reddish-brown brick walls. A young chestnut tree grew in the middle of the courtyard. It seemed determined to take over the whole courtyard one day, but in that summer of 1893 its leaves were still sparse enough to count.

Martha and Maximilian had spent the previous few months establishing their publishing house. Kurt Menning, the employee they had inherited along with the printing press, was still waiting for things to take off. He had busied himself with the printing machine for weeks, taking it apart, replacing worn parts, and smothering it in lubricating oil. Then he had taken apart the type cases, polished the lead type, and arranged it back in the cases. Now he was sitting, eating a sandwich and reading the newspaper.

Two rooms away, Maximilian sat at his desk in his shirtsleeves. He scribbled a couple of lines, then frowned as he crumpled up the sheet of paper, threw it in the bin, and began again. He repeated the process. Throwing the balls of paper was the only thing Maximilian seemed to be improving at. He felt wretched. The more he tried to write at least half a page that had some meaning or, even better, substance, the less successful his writing became. After hours of fruitless activity, he finally turned to reading through the manuscripts that had been submitted to them, as Martha had asked him to do. She wanted them to decide jointly which they should publish.

"Good day, Menning." Martha was back from a shopping trip. She enjoyed the process of equipping their premises with everything she deemed necessary to ensure that their publishing business ran smoothly and to produce a creative atmosphere.

Menning rose from his wooden stool and doffed his peaked cap. "G'day, Frau Aderhold! Well, I'm getting on with it."

His greeting had become a daily ritual that Martha scarcely noticed by now.

"Excellent!" When Menning looked at her expectantly, she added, "Be patient with us for a while longer."

"You telling me there's still nothing? The floor's covered in stories." Menning had more than fifteen years' experience printing books, and his outlook was pragmatic.

"We're still sorting through them," Martha said, attempting to justify their indecision. She was still hoping their first publication would be Maximilian's novel. "And my husband's hard at work as ever."

"I heard that," came Maximilian's voice from the office. He concealed the awkwardness of his situation by affecting a casual air.

Menning addressed them both. "You need to leap in with both feet. Won't do you any good just to hang around waiting for good luck to happen your way. You have to grab it by the horns, close your eyes, and ride into the fire."

Martha laughed. "You're a real poet, Menning. Why don't you try your hand at writing?"

"Get away, Frau Aderhold. You know I'm more of a practical man."

"And a good one at that." Martha gave him a cheerful nod.

Menning sighed. "All right, I'll carry on getting the workshop ship-shape. It'll keep me busy, at least."

"You'll soon be longing for these quiet times. When things get going it'll be riding into the fire for sure."

Martha walked cheerfully past the overflowing wastebasket in the office and greeted Maximilian with a kiss.

Menning remained skeptical about what was to become of the business.

"Well, so long as they pay me," he muttered. He replaced his cap on his head, poured himself another coffee from the metal pot, and began to read the newspaper. It wouldn't be right to simply go home.

Martha put her purchases down.

"The carpenter wants to start installing the shelving next week." She walked up to one of the untouched walls. "Just imagine your books here: Aderhold, Maximilian!"

He went along with her. "I'll write a whole shelf full."

"And the critics will rave about them." Martha threw her arms around her husband playfully and adopted the nasal tones of a literature critic. "Herr Aderhold, in your next work, you describe . . ."

"A great love." Maximilian took up the thread in the same voice. "Where did you get your deep emotional insight?" He grasped Martha's shoulders, looked her in the eye, and said softly, "I have a wife who raises me to such giddy heights of emotion."

His doubts vanished for a moment, leaving him feeling free and independent.

"By the way, there's a letter from Austria," Martha said as they drew apart. She took an envelope from her pocket.

"Ah, the little princess." Maximilian sat back in his chair and lit a cigarette.

"She'd like us to finally visit her and her husband at Traunstein House," Martha said as she removed her coat and began unpacking her shopping.

"She's not one to give up easily." Maximilian shook his head with a smile before turning back to his papers.

The Aderholds had already turned down several invitations from Konstanze, as they had been devoting all their energy to building up their publishing business. But it was summer now, and Martha wanted to leave the city for a vacation.

"We could combine it with a few days in Vienna," she suggested, knowing better even as she spoke. Maximilian would refuse to go anywhere until he had at least a first draft of his book down on paper.

His reply duly came. "You go," he said decisively. "Leave me here to sweat it out, to cook up something really good."

She watched him bend enthusiastically over his writing. Lost in thought, she laid a hand on her mother's chain and forbade herself from allowing the slightest doubt to creep in.

~

Martha enjoyed the journey through the summer countryside.

A carriage bearing the von Traunstein coat of arms had collected her from the station at Linz. Konstanze had sent her apologies with the driver, saying she would have loved to come herself but was not able to leave the house because of her advanced pregnancy.

The manuscript Martha had been intending to edit on the way rested in her lap. She had laid her pencil to one side and was now looking through the carriage window at the ever-changing landscape. Plains became hills without any noticeable transition. Only a few minutes later, ravines came into view, only to disappear from sight just as quickly. The forests seemed endless and untouched. They traveled through small villages where the houses seemed to have grown beside the stables and barns.

The Traunstein mansion and its extensive estate lay in a valley, its tower topped by a blue flag showing the family's coat of arms—a two-headed vulture.

Konstanze, heavily pregnant, came out onto the steps to greet Martha.

"I'm so pleased you've come," she said breathlessly. The child Martha had met in the café had grown into a young woman. They joined in a spontaneous embrace.

"My husband sends his apologies. He's working on his novel," Martha said.

"And mine's still at the imperial court in the Hofburg," Konstanze said with delight.

Martha sensed the unconditional kindness radiating from Konstanze, which enfolded her like a fine, glowing veil as the princess took her hand and led her up the steps.

The servants were lined up at the front door, and Martha was surprised to see Flora.

"I talked Frau Sacher into letting her come here." Konstanze gave Flora a sign to follow them and babbled on without pausing for breath. "Your room is at the end of the corridor on the second floor. Fortunately, I've managed to redecorate the whole story by now." Konstanze laid her hands on her belly. "I dread to think what it would have been like if I'd been forced to live among all that old junk in my condition." She made a leap to the next train of thought without interrupting her flow. "Of course, I'll put Flora at your service for as long as you're here." She turned to the butler. "Anton, see to the luggage," she ordered before continuing her ascent of the staircase alongside Martha. She seemed to be having some difficulty.

The room allocated to Martha was large and bright.

"I hope you'll stay for a while?"

Konstanze noticed with pleasure that Martha was impressed. She took Martha's hand and said, "I want you to feel at home here, as if we were old childhood friends."

Martha squeezed the other woman's hand, which was small and delicate and made her feel years older. "Martha."

"Konstanze." She shook Martha's hand effusively. "We'll drink champagne at dinner tonight, Martha. Now, you go and freshen up."

Konstanze called for Flora. Martha protested.

"I can manage fine by myself."

But Konstanze would not be persuaded. "Flora, make sure you spoil Frau Aderhold enough to make Frau Sacher turn green with envy."

Flora curtsied and immediately began unpacking Martha's suitcase. Protest was futile.

Later, the two women were sitting across from one another at the long table in the dining room, eating their dessert. A servant topped off Martha's champagne flute. Konstanze had limited herself to a single glass.

Martha felt how different this all was from her own life, and was beginning to enjoy the distance.

"You wrote me so many lovely letters," she said to Konstanze.

"I can write beautiful things to you because I know you read them in the right spirit." Konstanze acknowledged Martha's praise with a grateful smile before turning serious. "What else is there to do here other than put pen to paper?" Sobered by this thought, she pushed her dessert aside, barely touched. "My husband wants to fill the house with children."

Martha looked at the princess in her place at the long dining table. Hunting trophies hung above her, from a mountain goat to a six-point pair of deer antlers. Skull after skull.

Konstanze followed Martha's gaze and felt compelled to defend her position.

"You have a good life; you're free. You're founding a publishing house; you can travel independently," she said.

"I'm not as free as all that. At the end of the day, I'm responsible for our money and for the business."

Konstanze was impressed but still couldn't empathize with Martha.

"If my father had still been alive, I could have asked him to give me a few years of freedom," Konstanze said brightly, as if it were still an option. "My mother wanted to see me in safe hands. She lives in a convent and has devoted her life to our Lord God." Konstanze's eyes darkened. Abruptly, she clinked her empty champagne glass against Martha's and said cheerfully, "We're unhappy women and yet the others envy us."

Martha drank.

"But when I write, I can transform my life into anything I please. I can fall in love and then get divorced. I write a little every day." Konstanze placed her hands on her belly. "It's moving!" She took Martha's hand and laid it next to her own. "The midwife says it's due any time now."

Konstanze's thoughts seemed to scatter like a butterfly flitting from flower to flower. Martha felt the baby moving.

"Can I read something?" she asked abruptly. When Konstanze hesitated, she added, "One of your stories."

Konstanze looked at her, truly amazed. "One of mine?"

Martha nodded. The publisher in her had awoken.

~

Flora was brushing the princess's hair and braiding it for the night. Lost in thought, Konstanze gazed at her reflection in the mirror. "Do you have a close friend, Flora?"

"Yes, Your Serene Highness, but I haven't seen her for over a year."

"What is it that makes you friends?"

Flora thought for a moment. "We can talk about anything."

Konstanze was surprised. "Anything at all?"

She had never been able to talk to another person about her innermost thoughts or feelings. Konstanze was an only child. Her mother had suffered from life and her marriage. Plagued with migraines and bouts of depression, she had spent most of her time in bed. Her husband, Istvan Nagy-Károly, had been the opposite, full of joie de vivre and business acumen. With a keen eye on the future, he had bought up land around Budapest, and when, a few years later, the city had begun to grow, the value of his land had multiplied.

Konstanze took after her father, inheriting her lightheartedness from him. He had given her all her heart desired.

Shortly after her sixteenth birthday, her father had died of a heart attack during a picnic by Lake Balaton as he relaxed in a deck chair, a glass of red wine in his hand. Partly to cope with her grief and loneliness, Konstanze had begun to write poetry and stories on his blue writing paper.

At the end of her year of mourning, Konstanze's mother had suddenly revived, sorted through their assets, and employed the services of a marriage broker for her daughter. The choice, from among many suitors, was Georg Maria von Traunstein. The Traunstein family had been involved in the Vienna court for generations, and Konstanze would be guaranteed a place as lady-in-waiting for the Empress. Constanze

Nagy-Károly married Georg Maria von Traunstein not long after her seventeenth birthday.

14

They were out in the park.

Martha was sitting on a bench, reading the first few pages of Konstanze's story, while the princess leaned against a nearby tree, watching her. Dandelion seeds floated by on a light breeze, and dappled sunlight filtered down through the leaves of the trees.

Martha turned the last page over. Unable to contain herself any longer, Konstanze blurted, "Of course it's nowhere near as good as something by a proper author."

"What happens next?" Martha asked. Konstanze had written about an angel who watches over a young woman, still little more than a child, during the first months of her marriage, protecting her from her husband's domination.

Konstanze shrugged hesitantly. "I won't know until I write it." She looked at Martha uncertainly. "Is that the wrong way to do it?"

Martha shook her head with a smile.

"Maximilian drafts out a plan first." Martha thought about how her husband struggled with the structure of his future work, how before writing the first word he searched for the deepest meaning in what he intended to write. "He doesn't start writing until he knows his story inside out."

"That must be better." Impressed, Konstanze sat down by Martha on the bench. "When I look at a blank page, I hear the story as if someone were telling it to me, and I simply write it down."

Martha was surprised. She had never heard another writer say anything of the sort. Of course, everyone had their unique ways of working, but one thing they all seemed to have in common was discipline and effort. Since she had lived with Maximilian, she was only too well aware of the anguish this could cause. And now this young, heavily pregnant woman was saying the complete opposite.

"So, Martha, do you think I should continue?" Konstanze asked, her eyes shining with hope.

Martha nodded. But before they could say any more about it, Flora came toward them from the house, stopped halfway, and called out, "His Serene Highness is here."

"We're coming!" Konstanze grasped Martha's hands and whispered, "Not a word to Traunstein that I write. It must be our secret, Martha. Do you understand?"

Martha nodded her agreement, and Konstanze gave her an effusive kiss.

By the time the two women arrived at the house, side by side, Georg had already descended from the coach. He kissed his wife's brow and marveled at her girth. "How on earth do you manage, darling?"

He turned cheerfully to Martha.

"Thank you for accepting our invitation, Frau Aderhold." He bowed courteously and kissed her hand. "It's a long way from Berlin."

"Please call me Martha. Frau Aderhold is too formal."

Konstanze linked her arm through her friend's possessively, and they went indoors.

~

Konstanze sat at the table in her sewing room. With everything else pushed to one side, she had a pile of blue writing paper in front of her and began writing the continuation of her story about the guardian angel. When Georg came to fetch his wife for dinner, he found the door to the room locked.

A little later, they were sitting together at the large dining table. Konstanze led the table talk, eating only a little. "Traunstein hates his obligations in Vienna and Ischl. I'd have nothing against a change of scene every now and then. But . . ." She placed her hands emphatically on her stomach with a dramatic expression.

Georg didn't like her talking about his intentions. "I hate to leave, because I'm fully occupied with my land and the estate workers," he said defensively.

"His Serene Highness dreams of an estate with strong links to the land around it," Konstanze continued with a sharp undertone to her voice.

Martha ignored the tension between the couple. "What does that mean?" she asked. "You must forgive me; I'm a city girl."

Georg sensed her genuine interest. "The gulf between the classes should be bridged. I want to establish a way of life in which the best can be brought out of everyone—just as I do now with the soil. We can't always simply sow and reap; we also need to add nutrients," he said passionately.

Martha was impressed by his enthusiasm.

"Traunstein has many modern ideas. Papa even accused him of being a Freemason."

Martha looked at Georg in surprise.

He said nothing. His political ambitions were sacred, not a topic for dinner-table conversation, and he certainly didn't want to expand on them in front of his young wife. Keen to change the subject, he asked Martha about the press and her life in Berlin.

Love was sitting on the window seat. She moved around a lot in summer, never needing to stay anywhere long. Bonds were more easily forged then than in the colder seasons. For this reason, she could take a little time to watch the three of them. She saw the heavily pregnant woman and her husband, with the publisher from Berlin sitting between them. Martha was unaware of her effect on the married pair, but she was glowing and felt freer than she ever did in the presence of her husband. Love thought about him. He was the fourth person.

15

Inspector Lechner—he had been promoted—spent most of the week at his desk, among other inspectors. Whenever he could, he left the office, following up information, inspecting crime scenes, or simply mingling to observe what people were talking and thinking about. He had seen innumerable dead bodies, caught murderers, intervened in fights, and solved burglaries and fraud cases.

And, what was more, Lechner had stuck with the case of Marie Stadler. The girl's body had never been found. The Hotel de l'Opera was by now one of the city's best-known hotels. Half of the court came here, the most famous men of the Habsburg Empire; it was the location of political dealings and negotiations over the future of Europe.

Lechner was driven by a loathing of the aristocracy.

His father, Alois Lechner, was obedient and subservient, and had demanded these same qualities from his son. The boy had despised him for it. Every slap, every thrashing intended to break him had done the opposite. His son had begun to hate first his father and then the nobility. He despised the court with its fossilized rituals. He despised its lackeys who lived off the Emperor. He despised the whole rotten city of Vienna with its Jews, Hungarians, Bohemians, Italians, Serbs, Romanians, Ruthenians, Galicians; the artists, scientists, students, and fortune seekers who came from their backward homelands in the hope of earning a crust in the rapidly developing city.

~

Lechner stood in the entrance to the coal yard, looking across it at the crooked house. Smoke rose from the adjacent washhouse chimney. Together with his sons, Stadler was loading coal onto a cart. As their father vigorously shoveled, the six- and seven-year-old boys gathered pieces of spilled coal into a basket and returned them to the pile. Both were barefoot, their faces black from the work.

Lechner approached. "Hello. I need to speak to your wife."

Stadler recognized the inspector and called over to the washhouse. "Sophie!"

After a while, Sophie Stadler emerged through the door, a two-year-old in her arms.

"Hello." Lechner raised his hat.

"Hello, Inspector." The boy in her arms began to cry.

"There's something I need to talk to you about."

"Have you found a clue?" Sophie asked hopefully.

"You could say that. There's something I'd like to talk to you about, Frau Stadler."

They went into the house, and Stadler watched them go. He didn't like the inspector. What good could he do here?

16

Dice rattled loudly against the leather of the cup and then clattered onto the tabletop.

"Four, five, six," Konstanze counted. She was on top of the world, having won several times in succession and broken the bank. "Next round!" she cried out. "I'm doubling my stake. Will you match me?"

"Of course we will." Georg also spoke for Martha. "May I treat you?"

Martha waved him away with a smile. "No, no!"

Konstanze leapt in immediately. "If you need a loan, Martha, you only need to ask."

Amused, Martha put in her own money.

Her no-nonsense manner impressed Georg. "There's a woman who can take care of herself."

Konstanze noticed the way their eyes met and immediately felt a pang of jealousy. She was jealous not of Martha but of her husband. Georg mustn't be allowed to get close to Martha. Martha was *her* friend, her ally, her soul mate. Konstanze remembered what Flora had said. She wanted to be able to talk to Martha about anything.

Martha rolled a weak set. Georg took the dice cup.

Konstanze suddenly grasped her belly. A sharp pang shot through her body. She turned pale as water ran between her legs to the floor.

Martha was shocked. "Contractions?"

Konstanze looked down at the puddle that had formed between her shoes. Martha followed her gaze.

"Get the midwife, quick!" she urged Georg, who was still cheerfully shaking the dice.

Konstanze's teeth began to chatter. "I'm scared."

Georg jumped up and moved to support her, but Konstanze waved him away.

"I don't need you right now, Traunstein." She clung to Martha and said in a panicked voice, "Stay with me! Stay with me, Martha!"

Flora arrived, immediately grasped the situation, and helped Konstanze out of the drawing room and upstairs.

"Anton! Have the coachman get the carriage ready," Georg called. "Tell him to go fetch the midwife and the doctor."

The butler ran off, leaving Georg standing, bewildered, in the hall of his mansion.

The brass door knocker on the front door sounded harshly. Anton hurried back and informed Georg that the coachman would be ready to leave in a few minutes, before running to answer the door.

"Is your master at home?" Lechner raised his hat.

"Do you have an appointment?" The butler was practiced in deflecting unwanted visitors. "Please, can you leave your card? Now is a very inconvenient time."

"What is it?" Georg approached.

"I'm trying to explain to the gentleman that he has called at a rather inopportune time." The butler stepped aside from the door.

His hat in his hands, Lechner bowed to Georg. "Greetings, Your Serene Highness. My name is Lechner, inspector of the Vienna Police. I beg Your Serene Highness that I may speak to you on a most urgent matter."

Flustered by the ongoing emergency, Georg failed to note that the inspector's visit was unannounced and therefore disrespectful. His butler would happily have resolved the issue for him, but it was too late.

"Please show the man to my study," Georg said, then followed the two of them.

Martha, who was on her way upstairs from the kitchen, helping the maid carry a supply of hot water, saw Georg cross the hall with the stranger.

Georg dismissed his butler outside the study door.

"Please inform me when my wife needs me."

The servant left.

"I'm listening," Georg said to Lechner.

The inspector turned his hat around in his hands. His gaze roved from the globe to the plans for the new village on the easel and the picture of the naked man on the wall behind the desk. Then he bowed submissively once again.

"Your Grace, please regard me as the loyal servant of His Imperial Majesty and Your Serene Highness." Lechner was enjoying the situation. "It is my unpleasant duty, Your Serene Highness . . . It's a matter of a . . . an affair . . . that affects the princely family." Lechner's hesitations were calculated.

Georg could not imagine what it was about. Maybe his links with the Masonic lodge? But this inspector was too insignificant to be making accusations in that regard.

"Go on," he said calmly.

Lechner bowed again. "Very well." He cleared his throat. "There was a maid in the household of your honorable father, Prince von Traunstein. Sophie."

Georg remained silent. Of course he remembered Sophie. His first love affair.

"She got into difficulties."

Georg's blood sank to his boots.

"She was married off, and brought a little girl into the world. Marie. Marie Stadler." Lechner paused to allow his words to take effect. "And now the girl has vanished without a trace."

Georg could do nothing but allow Lechner to talk on.

"Frau Stadler wanted to keep it to herself at first. She's married, after all, and her husband, Marie's stepfather, has adopted her as his own child. But now she's so worried about Marie that she's confided in me."

Lechner looked Georg in the eye and saw he was having the desired effect. Georg was trapped.

"Yes? Confided what?" He knew immediately he should have said nothing.

Lechner took his time in replying. "That you're the natural father."

"Who's giving your instructions in this case?" Georg asked, struggling to keep his composure.

"I came driven by my conscience and my loyalty to Your Serene Highness," Lechner declared obsequiously.

"Is the girl still alive?"

"She hasn't yet been found among the children's bodies that turn up every day in the city." Lechner was enjoying the extent to which his presence disturbed the prince. "But to think of such a young girl in those establishments . . . Sometimes they reappear, years later, gone to rack and ruin." Lechner took the offensive. "A little bird tells me you're concerned for public welfare, that you're not indifferent to simple people. And in this case, it's a question of your own flesh and blood."

Georg stared at the man.

"It would be better for me to find the girl than for us to abandon the case, don't you think?" Lechner kept up the tension. "If you took a special interest in solving this case, it would be a real incentive to me."

The butler appeared and announced, "The doctor has come to see your wife, Your Serene Highness."

Georg nodded and dismissed Anton with a wave of his hand. He stood and went over to the bureau.

"Make sure you use the money to search for the child."

Lechner would never have thought it would be this easy.

Georg wrote out a check.

"I'll consider it my duty to keep you informed." Lechner tucked the check into his pocket.

A cry from Konstanze rang out through the house.

"The heir comes into the world . . . I won't disturb you a moment longer." Bowing repeatedly, Lechner left the room and was met by the butler outside. Lechner sighed with satisfaction as he put on his hat and left.

～

Konstanze fought with all her strength. Martha sat on the bed, held her by the shoulders, and shared her struggle. Both women were soaked with sweat.

"Push, push hard. You're nearly there," Martha encouraged. An overwhelming pain surged through Konstanze. She groaned with the pain, panted, pushed, found strength from somewhere, and gave it her all.

The midwife caught the newborn. "A girl . . . It's a girl."

Konstanze fell back in Martha's arms.

Martha wiped her friend's face. "You've done it," she said with emotion.

The newborn cried. The midwife washed and wrapped the baby, then handed her to Martha. Maybe she wanted the new mother to conserve her energy; maybe she thought her friend was more mature and ready to receive a child. So Martha held the screaming infant, watching her grow calm in her arms. Konstanze looked at her newborn daughter and then at Martha. Why couldn't this moment last forever—her friend by her side with the baby in her arms?

Georg entered the room. His eyes flitted from Konstanze to Martha, who was cradling his daughter. Martha stood and handed him the baby. He gazed down at his newborn daughter. Her little hands were balled into fists, her fine hair was plastered to her head, and her mouth was searching for her mother.

"What shall we call her?"

Konstanze looked at Martha. Georg followed his wife's eyes. Martha answered without thinking.

"Rosa, perhaps? She has such lovely rosy skin."

"Yes, she shall be our little Rosa," Konstanze agreed.

Georg also liked the name. "There's never been a Rosa in our family."

"You will stay for a few more days, won't you, Martha?" Konstanze asked hopefully. Martha nodded before leaving the happy couple to their new arrival.

~

Cassiopeia—the *W* in the heavens—and then the three stars of Orion's belt. Martha looked through the telescope that stood in the drawing room window. Her father used to show her the stars and tell her the legends behind the constellations.

She heard footsteps and moved away from the window. Anton brought a bottle of champagne and glasses. Georg followed a few moments later and reported that Konstanze needed to rest for a while. He was in a state of agitation and told his butler he would fill the glasses himself. Anton left them alone.

"Congratulations!" Martha was euphoric. In contrast to her usual reserved manner, she said effusively, "What a divine moment. You have a daughter now."

Georg handed Martha a glass, went over to the fire, and placed a log on the flames.

"I . . . forgive me," he stammered. "I've just heard . . . it's been alleged that I already have a child." He turned back to Martha. "Another girl. She must be eleven, or maybe ten . . ."

Martha recalled the stranger she had seen briefly as she made her way upstairs.

"I loved a girl when I was fifteen. She was a few years older than I was. Sophie. She was employed in our house." Georg had abandoned any attempt at restraint. "One day she disappeared. I was told that she'd gone to look after her sick mother. I didn't think any more about her." He was unable to look Martha in the eye. "I was fond of her. The passion of youth. But nothing more." They were both silent. "I must acknowledge the child . . ."

Martha was unable to reply; anything she said would have sounded trite.

Georg looked at her helplessly. "Don't you think so?"

~

Würtner had brought Marie first the patent leather shoes and then the white dress, both chosen from the ballet's costume wardrobe. Both were too big for Marie. Yet they made her feel wonderful, special, just like Würtner always insisted she was.

She had been preparing for the evening of the premiere for days. That afternoon he had gone out somewhere again and returned having bought the hair ribbon she used to gaze longingly at from the shop near the hotel.

Marie had been wondering for a long time whether she should ask Würtner for it. Her desire had finally got the better of her. He spoke not a word of protest—on the contrary, Marie sensed the joy with which he granted her wish.

When the performance had begun, and the stagehands and lighting crew had taken their places, Würtner had taken her hand. They had walked down a maze of corridors, climbed stairs, and finally ascended a wooden ladder to the catwalk above the stage. Marie kept looking down at her patent leather shoes and reveled in the way her white dress swung at every step.

By the time they were finally kneeling in their places, the overture was coming to an end. Würtner scanned the rows of the auditorium with his opera glasses and whispered, "Here they are, all gathered together, the fine ladies and gentlemen." He handed the glasses to Marie and indicated where she should look, explaining, "There, on the right, that's the Count von Kinsky's box. Three boxes further on is where the Kuefstein family sit. On the left, look, is the Traunsteins' box. Only the old prince is there tonight."

Würtner watched Marie scanning the seats with the opera glasses. She came to rest at the Traunsteins' box, observing the prince's sharp profile. Suddenly, as though he felt her eyes on him, he turned his face in their direction. Marie shrank back involuntarily, a shudder running through her.

"I've heard that his daughter-in-law, Princess von Traunstein, has just given birth to a little daughter," Würtner murmured. "After the show, they're all going over to the hotel to dine. Just think, my little bird, you no longer have to clean up after them."

Würtner guided the opera glasses with his index finger. Suddenly, the Empress, in her side box, came into view. Her face half-concealed behind a fan, she was looking down at the stage.

"Her Majesty," Marie whispered, enchanted. "Why does she look so sad?"

She lowered the opera glasses.

Würtner frowned at the earnest tone of her question. He took the opera glasses and saw nothing untoward. "She looks like an empress has to look."

Marie took the glasses again. *Perhaps she wants to die,* the girl thought.

~

Eleven-year-old Annie was standing in the hotel foyer, crying loudly. Anna hurried over to her daughter, took her hand, and led her into the office.

She gave the girl a shake. "Anna-Maria, you know perfectly well this isn't acceptable. What will our guests think?"

Annie let out a heartrending sob and gasped for air.

"Annie! What on earth is the matter?" Anna crouched before the girl, who was unable to stop crying. "Annie, darling?"

". . . I . . . can't . . . ," her daughter stammered through her tears. She was fighting a huge pain.

"Are you crying for your Papa?"

Annie cried harder.

"Papa has left us all alone."

Anna stood and handed her daughter a handkerchief. Annie blew her nose.

"You're looking at me as if I could do something about it." Anna Sacher sat on the guest chair in front of her desk, exhausted. "Papa has gone to another place, and I'm sure he's happier there." She drew Annie to her and put her arms around her daughter. "This morning, I was granted the licenses I need so we can stay here and I can keep the hotel going. And I will do it, sweetheart. I'm going to create a hotel that's the talk of the town. Hotel de l'Opera? That's far too ordinary. I'm going to call it the Hotel Sacher." Her voice full of emotion, Anna repeated, "Hotel Sacher—the finest hotel in Austria!"

Annie looked at her mother doubtfully, but Anna continued in her enthusiasm. "And once we've made our name, you'll get yourself a fine husband and marry into a good family."

Annie threw her arms around her mother's neck. "I want to stay with you forever." The girl was filled with horror at the thought that one day she might be a grown woman like her mother.

"Nonsense, Annie. Of course you'll want a husband and children one day."

Anna gently removed her daughter's arms from her neck. "Now you're going to come with me, and Wagner will serve you a slice of torte."

Annie momentarily forgot all her woes. "With cream and a hot chocolate!"

They walked together to the foyer. After Anna had sat her daughter down on a chair and given Wagner instructions, she saw Georg von Traunstein hurrying into the hotel. As he passed, he handed Johann a letter and told him Flora sent her love. "You're welcome to visit us at Traunstein House anytime, Johann."

The bellhop thanked him and tucked the letter into his breast pocket. He looked forward to reading it in peace later.

Anna Sacher moved to meet her guest. "Congratulations on the birth of your daughter, Your Serene Highness. I hope your wife is well?"

"Yes, thank you, madam." Georg kissed her hand. "I need to speak to my father."

"He's dining with the other gentlemen. I'll show you the way."

They headed for the private dining rooms.

"I hear you've been granted your licenses?" Georg could tell from her smile that the rumors were true. "Congratulations."

"And what's more, from now on you'll be staying and dining at the Hotel Sacher," Anna said proudly.

"It will be my pleasure," Georg replied politely.

They entered one of the larger private rooms, where the elder von Traunstein was dining with his friends. They were already on their dessert.

Prince von Erdmannsdorf had a young ballet dancer on his knee. Two of her fellow dancers were sitting to either side, flirting with the other gentlemen.

Count von Kuefen, an old friend of old Traunstein, stroked a young ballerina's cheek. "What's this I've been hearing about a ghost in the opera house?"

"Oh, there must be one!" she replied coquettishly, starting to list the phenomena and feigning a fearful expression. "It's taken my dress."

"And Tamara's shoes have disappeared," one of her friends added, taking up the story. "You can hear it singing sometimes."

"Like a fairy voice."

"They should catch it and exorcise it."

The three girls shuddered exaggeratedly.

Josef von Traunstein's eyes were on his son. Annoyed at having his evening disturbed, he stood brusquely. "What's the matter?"

Anna Sacher opened the door to a side room. "You can talk undisturbed here."

She left the two men alone.

Father and son had not seen one another for several weeks, since the older man preferred to stay in Vienna during Martha's visit to Traunstein House. "I heard it's a girl. Stanzerl all right?"

"Your granddaughter is called Rosa," Georg replied coolly.

"Stanzerl's young and fertile. She'll give you sons in good time," the old man said, without great interest, before asking, "So what brings you here so urgently?"

"Sophie! Sophie Stadler!"

The old prince looked at his son with incomprehension.

"She didn't leave of her own accord. You sent her away."

Traunstein grasped what his son was saying. His voice turned sharp. "You can be pleased that I buried the matter without causing trouble."

"I intend to accept responsibility," Georg countered.

"For a bastard? One that might not even be alive?" The old man's face was red with anger. What was his son thinking, bringing this up now? He turned to go.

Georg barred his way. "Do you know anything about Marie?"

The prince let out a cold laugh. "Why should a worthless guttersnipe mean anything to me?"

"Because she's my daughter!"

"Don't exaggerate your own importance! About a bastard, too!"

"What do you know about the girl?" Georg was finding it hard to suppress his rage.

His father turned away from him and returned to his friends. The door closed behind him.

Georg was seething with shame and anger. He hated his father's smugness, and his mannerisms that radiated smug infallibility. In truth, everything about the old man reeked; he was rotten to the core. Only his name and title gave him any power.

A few days later, a carriage drew up outside the Stadlers' coal yard. Anton, the von Traunsteins' butler, knocked at the door of the house. After a long delay, Sophie Stadler answered. Her three sons crowded into the doorway to catch a glimpse of the distinguished visitor.

Anton handed Sophie an envelope. "I'm instructed to come every month with one of these."

She had grown thin, but he still recognized her as the maid from Traunstein House.

Sophie didn't look him in the eye. Her time there was hidden away behind a wall of pain. At some point she had given up even thinking about it.

Anton returned to the carriage and climbed in. Sophie's fate had touched him. At the same time, he was glad for himself, his position secure, his old age taken care of. The horses set off, and the carriage rolled off toward the better part of the city.

The boys urged their mother to open the envelope. Sophie drew out a sum of money the likes of which she had never seen. But no money could ever compensate her for the loss of Marie, she thought in dismay. It was her fault. She should never have given in to the prince's son. The penalty she felt she was now paying for the feelings she had succumbed to back then seemed more than justified. But why should Marie suffer? She was innocent. Lost in thought, Sophie shook her head. She felt her heart beating wildly and felt faint.

The boys looked at their mother in alarm. The smallest child began to cry.

Stadler came over to her. He had finished work for the day, and his face was black with coal dust.

"Papa, look what a gentleman's just given Mama," his sons yelled in excitement.

Stadler took the money from his bewildered wife's hand. The boys gave him a breathless account of the visit, as overawed by the prince's lackey as they would have been by His Serene Highness himself.

"It's for Marie," Sophie said in a daze.

Stadler nodded. He stowed the money in his wallet, which he tucked into an inside pocket.

Sophie took the soup from the stove and handed out the bread.

17

It was a big day for everyone when Franz Sacher finally departed. Tired of pretending he wasn't getting any older, he had decided to go home.

However much she liked her father-in-law, the moment couldn't have come soon enough for Anna. During his stay, they had spent a few evenings in the kitchen, cooking together, trying out various spices and creating new flavor combinations, always with a bottle of good wine, sometimes two. They had fun together, more than Anna had ever had with Eduard. Franz was charming and let her know how much he appreciated her. One time he hinted that the children had talked of a possible union between them. Anna was shocked, and from that time on made it clear that she saw him only as a fatherly adviser and a grandfather to the children. Even though it would have made it easier for her to deal with the Viennese authorities, Anna had no intention of continuing with Franz the married life that had ended with Eduard. She was enjoying her independence too much.

In any case, there was Julius Schuster, Baron von Rothschild's administrator. The man worshipped the ground she walked on and was willing to grant her every wish. Anna was intoxicated by the cautious meetings they were careful to conceal from public eyes. He was surrounded by the aura of money. And he was already married.

Schuster considered it a pleasure to make a part of his private wealth available to Anna Sacher for her business. If he had learned one thing from his employer, it was that money had to work—in this case, to support the vision of a strong woman.

They had met a few years earlier at a party at the Rothschilds' residence, for which Anna and Eduard had made the catering arrangements. Their brief encounter had made an impression on them both. When Julius Schuster came to dine at their restaurant a few days later, Anna knew it was no coincidence. She served him in person. They talked about trivialities, but between their words lay curiosity and an erotic undercurrent. They had kept in regular touch ever since.

The staff had gathered in the foyer to say their farewells to Franz Sacher. Anna was waiting for her father-in-law by the door, which she herself opened for him. The cab that was to take him to the station was waiting, ready, out on the street. Franz hugged Anna to him as they said goodbye, feeling the softness of her body.

"Send for me any time you need me, won't you?" he said, attempting to deny his age one last time.

She hoped he would simply get in the carriage and go.

He, on the other hand, hoped that at the last moment he would finally drum up the courage to tell her what he desired. But he merely blurted out, "You're a fine woman, Anna."

"Thank you for everything; thank you . . . Father." She used the form of address deliberately to make sure he knew where he stood. Yet she felt sorry for him.

Franz placed his hat on his head and let go of any possibility that Anna would open her heart to him, that they could live and work together.

Anna waved as the cab rolled away, then walked past the line of staff back into the hotel. She walked slowly along the corridor to her private rooms, closed the door behind her, and leaned against it. She smiled. Slowly, she moved away from the door and began to wave her arms and legs, dancing around like a madwoman.

Anna's dream had come true. As a girl she had regularly woken at dawn to the sounds of slaughter in the courtyard outside. She heard the men calling to one another and the terrified cries of the animals. The stink of the bones and entrails being boiled on the open fire penetrated her bedroom despite the firmly closed window. She would lie there dreaming of a life of glitter and beauty.

A little later, Anna was standing in the reception area as Mayr told her about all the guests who were due to check in and out. Miklos Szemere from Budapest—billionaire, playboy, horse fancier, and gambler—had made a booking and, together with his entourage, would soon be occupying his suite on the first floor above the main entrance.

Anna Sacher paused to look around the foyer. Wagner served the "Sacher boys," young men from good families who were sitting at their regular tables in the rear of the room, smoking and discussing a recent play by the young playwright Arthur Schnitzler. Anna had given instructions that special attention was to be paid to "her boys." After all, they were tomorrow's customers, and it was desirable to secure their loyalty to the hotel at an early age.

Anna noticed a student sitting near the Sacher boys, surrounded by books and writing, with deep concentration.

Anna went over to him. Vincent Zacharias quickly got to his feet, embarrassed by the proprietor's interest. He had no aristocratic title, nor had he been raised in an upper-class villa on the Ringstrasse. He was a Jew from Prague.

"Herr Zacharias! I see you're hard at work again. You must have almost finished your doctoral thesis?"

"I'll be done by the autumn, my dear Frau Sacher," he said with a Bohemian accent.

Anna waved Wagner over. "Please bring our future lawyer here whatever he wants to hold body and soul together."

Vincent Zacharias began to protest, but Anna waved away his concerns.

"You're allowed as much credit as all my boys," she said, brooking no refusal.

At that moment, Julius Schuster arrived with his wife and son. He was there to celebrate Anna's independence. Here, in public! It thrilled her to think about it.

Anna went to meet him and gave his wife, Anna Schuster, an ingratiating smile. It was a twist of fate that they had the same first name.

"Welcome to the Hotel Sacher!"

Anna Schuster returned her greeting with an artificial smile. She was well aware of her husband's admiration for this widow who was now running her own business. And although he asserted that it was strictly a business relationship, her unerring feminine instinct told her that this was only half the story.

Julius Schuster Jr., in his uniform of a second lieutenant, bowed neatly.

"My wife and I would like to sample the delights of the kitchen under your esteemed supervision," Schuster Sr. said, taking Anna's hand in his own for a split second longer than necessary.

"The pleasure's all mine." Anna Sacher waved Wagner over. "Please show Baron von Rothschild's administrator and his wife and son to our best table."

A commotion erupted at the reception desk. One of the guests clearly had a problem and was demanding to see the manager.

Anna heard the disturbance and went over to see what she could do. "I'm Frau Sacher. How can I help you?"

"I'm sorry, but I demand to see the manager," the man insisted.

"Yes, sir. What can I do for you?"

"I mean the manager, not his wife."

"This is my hotel, and I'm the master of the house," Anna snapped. And as she said it, she became one with her position. She was indeed the master of the house.

BOOK 2
LIFE

18

Martha handed a book to the critic, a man credited with shaping public opinion on literature in Berlin. *The Woman Behind the Veil*, the second novel by a young author who wrote under the name of Lina Stein, was hot off the press.

The critic opened the book. "I hope it's going to be as successful as Frau Stein's first novel."

"*Guardian Angel* has been praised by the Empress of Austria herself." Martha knew how to create an aura of success around her author.

Their premises were now equipped with all the paraphernalia of a functioning press. Piles of books covered the floor around the two desks, and proofs were stacked on the wooden shelves in the print room. Menning oversaw two journeymen, who were occupied with the typesetting.

Kurt Menning was the life and soul of the publishing house. When things were tough for the business during the early years, he had persuaded the Aderholds to cover their running costs by printing advertising flyers. Now they were into their fifth year, and their accounts were in the black. They had brought their vision to life and had publishing contracts with numerous literary figures, including many from Berlin and Vienna.

The critic seemed gripped by the story even before reaching the end of the first page.

"Of course, our readers will want to know who's hiding behind the name Lina Stein," he said with a nasal twang as he leafed through the pages.

"Frau Stein wishes to write her books out of the glare of publicity," Martha said calmly.

The critic ostentatiously whipped out a notebook and asked, as if to provoke Martha, "Don't you think it's time that Frau Stein revealed herself to her readers and allowed them to get a little closer to her?"

Martha was ready for him. "But people are always fascinated by anonymity."

Maximilian had to smile at her reply. He was sitting at his desk in the side room, his sleeves rolled up, a cigarette in the corner of his mouth, editing a manuscript they had received. Martha knew what she was doing, he thought—witty and sharp, she was never offensive, and she brought a measure of humor to the mix.

Maximilian's childhood and youth had been dry. It was achievement that counted; humor was superfluous. A quick wit was considered rude.

His father was a devout Protestant. The image of him quoting from Luther's Bible, holding the book dramatically in front of his chest, had been burned into Maximilian's brain. He envied Martha her family background.

On their first walk together through the Tiergarten and during the subsequent early weeks of their relationship, Maximilian had been preoccupied with Martha's Jewishness. Martha's family had been assimilated for two generations, and she didn't attach much significance to her religion, but Maximilian had read texts from the Talmud, wanting to appear interesting to Martha and to prove the depth of his feelings. As he learned more about the mystical associations surrounding the ancient texts, he felt even more drawn to her. He began to adore Martha, as much as a representative of this time-honored race as for herself. But the more he concealed his inner conflict and longing behind an intellectual construct, the greater the distance that grew between them.

In the room next door, the critic was now talking to Martha about more of their recent publications. He praised the collection of short stories by a Viennese author and criticized the debut by a young writer from Prague about a schoolboy's fear of failure.

Maximilian despised critics. Their arrogant pronouncements could make or break an artistic career, sucking the lifeblood of a creative person. He had received no critical acclaim for his first novel, *The Prayers of a Useless Man*.

In it, he described a young lawyer in the Ministry of Justice. As an antidote to the mindless nature of his work in the archive, the lawyer had developed a passion for combing the files of the most outrageous criminals in search of the psychological causes of their horrific crimes. The protagonist had long since given up any hope of love when he met a prostitute. Over a number of weeks, the business relationship was transformed into a spiritual union, but the closer they came to one another, the more hopeless the protagonist became, despising himself for feeling such a thing as love. It seemed to him that the only way out of this spiritual dilemma was death, but he lacked the courage to take his own life. It was the woman who finally achieved what he longed for when, while they were traveling together on the coast, she fell from a cliff. The finale of the novel saw the protagonist in his old age, returning to his old life, which he saw as a respite from "too much useless emotion."

Martha was shocked when she read the manuscript. Her first impulse had been to destroy it, just as people always want to destroy something that threatens them. She wanted to protect Maximilian from this raw revelation of his inner heart, but in the end, she limited herself to stylistic advice, and he implemented only a little of that. He sensed she wasn't telling him the truth, and it only made him cling more resolutely to his original text.

Martha was ashamed of her feelings and even more so of her cowardice. She came to terms with the conflict by deciding to view Maximilian, her companion and husband, and the author of *The Prayers of a Useless Man* as two separate people.

Both the critics and the reading public deemed the novel a failure. Maximilian's raw revelation of his spiritual depths simply didn't sell.

He felt he was misunderstood. "*The Prayers of a Useless Man* really have turned out to be hopeless prayers," he scoffed sarcastically, and soon began his next book. But after a few weeks of tireless work, the text lay abandoned and half finished.

Martha didn't ask about its progress, and Maximilian never mentioned it. It was at that time that *Guardian Angel* was published to great acclaim. The author called herself Lina Stein, but nothing was known about her. *Guardian Angel* was her first novel, and she had entrusted it to Martha.

Maximilian refused to take seriously a story about a young woman who was protected from her husband by an angel. Martha's insistence on publishing it triggered an argument between them, and Maximilian mocked the author's simple writing style. But the book sold well despite his predictions.

And now the second novel, *The Woman Behind the Veil*, was out. It told of a woman who, however much she tried, could see the world only as if through a veil. A series of doctors examined her thoroughly but could find nothing wrong with her apparently healthy eyes. But her world and the people in it remained a shadowy blur to her. In place of the real world, she saw strange imaginary scenes.

The language was once again simple, the main characters lively, and the story gripping.

Maximilian was fascinated on first reading it. He tried to conceal that from Martha and always used an ironic tone when they spoke of Frau Stein. The anonymous woman clearly found writing far more effortless than Maximilian did; the text seemed to have flowed out of her. He found himself wrestling with his emotions—envy, amazement, self-doubt.

Martha said goodbye to the critic in the next room and came into the office to join Maximilian. Pretending to be busy, he hardly glanced at her. "How long are you and Frau Stein going to keep your secret, then?"

Martha sat at her desk, smiling to herself. It was not the first time Maximilian had broached the subject.

"Let's just be glad we've contracted her to publish with us," she said, and bent to her work.

Maximilian persisted. "What do you mean, 'we'? I don't know her." With a surly expression, he lit a cigarette. "After all's said and done, I'm her publisher, too. I'd just like to know who this woman is who blithely produces one success after another."

Martha looked up in surprise, and Maximilian backpedaled.

"If you think I'm upset that the same critic who's praising Frau Stein to the high heavens was the one who ripped my novel to shreds . . ." He trailed off and waved a hand dismissively. "I'm simply curious."

He lit another cigarette.

Martha couldn't bear to see him suffer. "Max, you're a brilliant publisher. You find the diamonds among the manuscripts people submit to us. You can see the potential of texts that mean nothing to me. Surely you can allow me my little secret."

Martha had felt exhausted for days. She stood to fetch a glass of water, but as soon as she drank, she felt light-headed and dashed to the bathroom.

Maximilian followed her, concerned, and stood outside listening to her retching. When he heard the flush, he knocked on the door. She opened it, making light of her condition, and dried her face in front of the mirror.

Her pallor worried Maximilian. "You should go and see Dr. Kraft for a thorough examination."

Martha left the small bathroom. "We have to prepare for the book fair. We need to send out the critics' copies. I have to go to Vienna. I can't afford to be ill right now. And I'm not, in any case!"

But no sooner had she spoken than she felt dizzy and had to sit down.

19

"Irma, Rosa, we're going out into the garden with your little sister," the nanny called, cradling little Mathilde in one arm.

Konstanze emerged from her room in traveling clothes and descended the stairs with Flora. A servant followed with the luggage.

"Go outside with Nanny," Konstanze called to her daughters. "Mama will be with you in a moment."

The butler handed the princess her mail.

"You don't need to forward anything to me over the next few days, Anton. There's nothing that can't wait until I'm home."

The butler bowed and left. The delivery included a parcel from the Aderhold Press. Konstanze hurried into the drawing room, picked up a letter opener, and began to unwrap the parcel.

Next door, in the study, Georg was sitting with Vincent Zacharias. Anna Sacher had entrusted the young Bohemian to his care. After Zacharias had achieved his doctorate, Georg had secured him a placement in the Hofburg, and the young man, almost his contemporary, had proved extremely loyal and reliable.

"I have obligations here on the Traunstein estate, so I'd be delighted to know there was someone like you involved in the affairs of the court, someone who could advocate for our shared vision and contribute to establishing a liberal Austria." Georg poured coffee for them both. "How would a move to the Foreign Ministry appeal to you, Dr. Zacharias?"

"As a Bohemian, I like the idea," Zacharias replied carefully. "But as you know, I'm of Jewish origin . . . Of course, I could convert," he added uncertainly. He had thought hard recently about how much the Jewish faith actually meant to him, reaching the decision that his political work was more important. The realization had come as a relief.

Georg nodded happily. "I'll do all I can for you."

The butler interrupted them. "Her Serene Highness wishes to take her leave."

"Please excuse me." Georg rose and went into the drawing room.

Konstanze was leafing through *The Woman Behind the Veil*. The paper was new, the pages still giving off the smell of fresh printer's ink. She looked up as her husband approached.

"A delivery from the Aderholds," she said casually, handing Georg the new publication.

He looked at the book, its dark blue cover adorned with water lilies. The title, in gold letters, stood out proudly: *The Woman Behind the Veil*. Georg nodded without interest. He mainly read nonfiction, with only the occasional novel by a well-known author. The name of this one meant nothing to him.

"When will you be back?" he asked.

He handed her the book and she took it. Even though she would not have wanted it any other way, Konstanze nevertheless felt disappointed at her husband's lack of enthusiasm.

"The dressmaker wants at least two fittings. The Hofburg is going to pieces; the Empress is in Geneva, and there's been no word about when she'll be back in Vienna."

Georg looked satisfied. Why should he spoil his wife's fun? After all, he had the company of Zacharias, and his circle of liberal friends looked set to expand in the days to come.

"Enjoy yourself with the dressmaker. And give Frau Sacher my regards." He kissed his wife on both cheeks and returned to his study.

Georg had always maintained a cold distance because he saw it as the only way of behaving with Konstanze. His wife was in every respect a stranger to him, and this distance had become an unspoken agreement between them. Konstanze, too, had immersed herself in her own life, allowing her husband no part of it.

The nanny was waiting outside with her daughters. Konstanze hugged them.

"If you're good, Mama will bring you something nice back," she promised.

Irma and Rosa clapped their hands in delight and accompanied their mother to the carriage. Mathilde reached her chubby arms out to Konstanze and began to cry. Konstanze kissed her little hands and a few moments later leaned back in relief against the cushions in the carriage.

~

Martha tried to control the shaking that overcame her on hearing the diagnosis. The doctor admitted Maximilian into the consulting room.

While waiting outside, he had feared the worst. The thought that Martha might be incurably ill, that she might die, had paralyzed him, yet . . . had also given him a glimpse of freedom. But he had refused to admit to it, allowing the notion to pass unacknowledged.

"Herr Aderhold, your wife is pregnant at last."

Maximilian took a moment to grasp that it was good news.

"I advise you to take it easy over the coming months. Short walks. Be careful with your diet. No alcohol. No coffee." Dr. Kraft spoke with authority. Maximilian nodded at each of these instructions, while Martha remained in a dazed silence. As he showed them to the door, the doctor softened his tone. "It was one of Mother Nature's whims to make you wait a while."

He saw them off with a warm smile.

Standing in the semidarkness of the stairwell, Maximilian was the first to collect his thoughts.

"I'm going to be a father." He took Martha's face in his hands and kissed her again and again. Then he took her hand. "I hope you're going to be a good girl and do what Dr. Kraft says."

They strolled down Fasanenstrasse to the Tiergarten. The multitude of roles and possibilities vied with one another in Martha's thoughts. Should she leave the business to Maximilian and start preparing for motherhood straight away? The thought was an alien one.

"It's not showing yet, apart from the bouts of nausea. You handle the critics, and I'll go to Vienna. After that, I'll do anything you want," she said, eager to ward off excessive fuss.

"No, darling, it's out of the question. I'll find the books that need to be read through and bring them back home to you. I'll take care of everything else myself."

Maximilian suddenly felt free. Martha was to be a mother—the pregnancy and the baby would take up most of her attention. She would have less time for the publishing business, leaving him to make his own decisions without having to discuss everything with her. He would go to Vienna. Yes, he would go to Vienna.

"You want to go to Vienna?" Martha's heart tightened; she had been looking forward so eagerly to those days away.

"Why not?" Maximilian sounded as though it were a trifle and he didn't attach much importance to the trip. But the opposite was in fact true: he wanted to get to the bottom of his wife's secret.

Martha tried again. "But you've never liked it there."

Maximilian bought two toffee apples from a street vendor.

"I can come to terms with that. Besides, you'll finally have to arrange an introduction to Frau Stein for me," he said, unable to keep the triumph from his voice. With a charming smile, he handed her a shiny toffee apple.

Martha sighed. "I'll let her know. It's up to her to decide whether she wants to reveal her identity to you."

"Even if things are going well for a change, you women will do your best to create a problem." Maximilian bit into his apple with a crunch, and splinters of toffee cracked away. "Or is this Lina Stein a man, perhaps, with whom you're having an affair?"

He laughed, the sugar on his teeth giving him a rakish look that suggested a hint of the boy he once was. Martha smiled and thought that maybe she would soon have a son. The idea filled her with optimism.

20

The Sacher was a hive of activity. Mayr had his hands full looking after departing guests and welcoming newcomers while overseeing the porters and bellhops. He was in his element.

A group of French bulldogs were romping around the foyer, an indication that Anna Sacher was not far away. She strode into the foyer, a puppy on her arm, and handed the little bully to a bellhop.

"Give my Lumpi some apricot jam. The poor little thing's having one of his melancholy days."

Anna noticed her son, Eduard, now fifteen, coming through the main entrance, his school bag over his shoulder. She hurried over to him and said in a low voice, "You should use the tradesmen's entrance, Eduard."

The dogs crowded round him and began to bark; sensing the tension between mother and son, they immediately took their mistress's side.

"I'm hungry and I'm in a hurry," Eduard said angrily, aiming a kick at a particularly excited dog.

"Then go to the kitchen and have them make something for you," Anna said.

"But they can use this door! And them!" Eduard pointed first at the dogs and then at the Sacher boys, who were sitting in the foyer, drinking port and holding earnest conversations wreathed in the smoke from their cigarettes.

"They're my future clientele," Anna hissed.

But Eduard continued his whining. "Is that why you subsidize them?"

"I don't subsidize them. I give them credit." Anna found it an effort not to slap her son.

He continued to ratchet up the tension. "Your darling, Herr Zacharias, seems to have cleared off with your credit."

This time, the slap rang out. "Enough now."

Eduard bit down on a cry of pain, glared at his mother with hate-filled eyes, and left.

Anna saw with surprise that Maximilian Aderhold had arrived. She hadn't seen the publisher since the couple's honeymoon, and she had been expecting his wife. Martha Aderhold had been a frequent visitor with Princess von Traunstein. This time, too, Her Serene Highness was already there.

Mayr gave Aderhold a letter. "Her Serene Highness Princess von Traunstein has left an opera ticket for your wife, Herr Aderhold."

The little princess again, Maximilian thought as he took the envelope and opened it eagerly.

Anna Sacher came over to wish him a pleasant stay. Something told her that things were not quite right, although it was hard to imagine where a threat might lie. Without dwelling on it, she went on her way, walking past Love, who was leaning on the bar.

~

Konstanze sat in her box, peering curiously through her opera glasses to see who was arriving. Someone cleared his throat behind her. She turned and, after a moment's confusion, recognized Maximilian Aderhold.

"Is something the matter with Martha?" she asked in shock.

Maximilian greeted Konstanze with a bow. "My wife's expecting, so we decided that I should come in her place."

"Is she well?" Konstanze asked, genuinely worried.

"A little nausea." Maximilian smiled. "Martha didn't tell me she'd arranged to meet you."

Konstanze relaxed. Martha had told him nothing. She indicated a free chair. "Please have a seat. And here I was, thinking Martha had forgotten my invitation to the opera."

He sat down.

So, she's expecting, Konstanze thought. She was suddenly struck by a pang of jealousy. It had happened at last. The two friends had often wondered why Martha was unable to get pregnant when she wanted a child so much.

Maximilian was surprised to find himself at the opera, sitting next to the "little princess." He would much rather have visited some of the renowned coffeehouses and mingled with the Bohemian crowd in an attempt to discover who was writing for his press under the name of Lina Stein.

Konstanze wondered why Martha hadn't told her she would not be coming. Maybe the letter was waiting for her back at Traunstein House. She could feel Maximilian's eyes on her. Over the years, she and Martha had talked about their husbands, their marriages, their needs and desires. Konstanze knew Maximilian from what Martha had told her, but she didn't know him as a person. How should she behave? How should she react to him?

The lights in the auditorium finally dimmed, and the first bars of the overture to *The Marriage of Figaro* rang out.

21

Her daughter's constant reports of her unhappy life got on Anna's nerves. Since Annie's marriage to Schuster's son, she had come to the Sacher once a week. She was driven by carriage from Vienna's Fourth District, where she lived in an apartment not far from the Rothschilds' palace, to visit her mother in the First District. Anna always welcomed her daughter dutifully, but she skillfully arranged the visits to ensure that their time together was limited.

They usually had little to say to one another, and so it was that day. Anna was fixing a particularly beautiful diamanté collar around a puppy's neck.

Her daughter jiggled a ten-month-old baby on her thigh. He began to wail, and Annie lifted him up and shifted him to her other leg.

"Julius is out all day, and when he comes home in the evenings, he hasn't got much to say."

"That's men for you," Anna replied brusquely, then added a little more gently, "You were the one who was determined to marry the son of Baron von Rothschild's administrator. You have to make the best of it."

Very quietly, almost inaudibly, her daughter gave the reply that had become a long-standing ritual between the two of them. "I didn't want to at all. You wanted it."

Ignoring her daughter's reproach as she always did, Anna changed the subject. "How are your in-laws?"

"All right, as far as I know," Annie said. The baby began to cry again and was returned to the first leg.

As fate would have it, the members of these intertwined families, now three of them, had remarkably similar names. The women were all called Anna, and the two Schuster men, Julius. Anna Sacher and Julius Schuster Sr. had, after careful consideration, arranged the marriage between their children, so that their status as in-laws enabled them to see one another without fear of public censure.

All that Annie had feared as a little girl had come to pass; she had to grow up and leave home far too soon.

And Anna was pleased that she had to bear her daughter's reproachful glares for only a brief hour once a week.

With a loving touch, Anna straightened the bow around the puppy's neck.

"Well, my sweetheart," she said, "go with Annie now and be a good little dog for her. It's Annie's birthday today."

Anna ceremoniously held the puppy out to her daughter. Annie's expression softened. She handed the baby to her mother and took the little bulldog.

"Oh, look at him," she said gently.

"Keep her company, now."

Anna was proud of her gift, while her grandchild left her unmoved. Annie rocked the puppy. Sensing that he was no competition for the dog, the baby reached out and grabbed his grandmother's mouth.

Katharina Schratt came bustling in and immediately dominated the room.

"Schlenther *has* to have his own way," she said, referring to the new artistic director. "The Court Theater productions should be more naturalistic, it seems. I ask you! Either I act or I'm naturalistic."

Only then did the actress notice Annie.

"Annie!" she cried in amazement. "How you've grown."

She stroked the young woman's cheek, then took the puppy and rocked it like a baby, continuing her chatter without pausing for breath. "And Franz isn't prepared to talk some reason into Schlenther. It's his theater, after all." She was referring to Emperor Franz Josef, who didn't interfere with the work of the artistic director, never set foot in the Imperial Court Theater, and left it to the Empress to attend the productions and pronounce her opinion on them.

Anna gave the baby back to her daughter. The infant immediately demanded his mother's attention with loud screams. That was enough for Anna; she stood and indicated unequivocally that she wanted to return to her own stage, the hotel foyer.

Katharina Schratt kept her composure and continued to pet the puppy. "Your little dogs are creating a real stir in court, Anna. They all want one of the creatures." She turned to Annie. "So this one's yours?"

"It's Annie's sixteenth birthday today," Anna Sacher replied for her daughter.

"Good lord, how time flies!" Katharina Schratt was genuinely astonished. "So you've been married for almost a year now." She set the little bulldog down on Anna's desk. "Well, happy birthday, Annie darling!"

The puppy piddled on the desk. Kathi Schratt kissed Annie on both cheeks. "I have to go now, get some decent food inside me."

While Anna wiped away the dog's little accident, something she was practiced at, she called for her head waiter. "Wagner, show our esteemed actress to her favorite table."

The baby hadn't stopped bawling. Katharina Schratt waggled two fingers in front of him in a cute farewell, then did the same to Annie before hurrying away. The baby's cries rose a level.

"He's hungry. I have to go home," Annie said guiltily.

"I'll have Mayr call the carriage for you. It's a real shame; you never have time." Anna Sacher felt her reproach was justified, having suppressed for the moment how pleased she was that her daughter was leaving. She reached for the telephone to call Mayr.

When the doorman arrived, she handed the dog to him and kissed her daughter on both cheeks.

"Bye-bye, darling!"

The opera would be finishing soon, and her customers arriving. Anna Sacher wanted to give them her full attention.

~

In the maid's bedroom adjacent to the Traunsteins' suite, Flora was sitting under a lamp, writing on a sheet of paper littered with notes and deletions. Hearing a knock at the door, she quickly shoved the pages beneath a pile of towels. She opened the door, and Johann took her in his arms.

"Why have you locked yourself in?"

Without waiting for her reply, he drew her to the narrow bed, kissing her again and again.

"My mistress is at the opera."

Flora glanced over her shoulder at the table, where she had left her pen and ink out. Johann had eyes only for her, so he didn't notice.

"The opera finishes at ten. I'm keeping an eye on the time," he promised. She relaxed under his caresses and helped him out of his jacket.

They had effectively been living as a married couple for a long time, and Flora thought how lovely it would be if they could have rooms at Traunstein House, finally move in there and start a family.

"Please, come out to join us. I'm sure they'll find you a good position."

Johann paused. "Join *us*?"

"It's much more peaceful than in Vienna."

"I daresay. And I need the hustle and bustle."

He unbuttoned her blouse. She slipped out of her skirt.

Flora thought of the expansive park around the mansion where they could play with their children in their time off. She didn't understand why he found it so difficult to consider following her.

It didn't take them long to regain their intimacy, however, and they abandoned themselves to their pleasure.

"Make sure you don't overstay your welcome." An aunt who worked as a midwife had advised Flora on how to avoid getting into trouble; coitus interruptus had kept her free from pregnancy over the years.

Johann paused. "Why's it always up to me?"

They looked into each other's eyes. Flora moved to kiss him, but he held her at arm's length, which only aroused them both more.

"You're always the first to notice when it's time." Flora strained to catch his lips.

"How about I give you a clue? When I start rolling my eyes, tongue hanging out . . ." His eyes gleaming in fun, he laughed and ran his hand over her neck and breasts. Flora wrapped a leg around his hips and drew him closer.

"Then I'll slip away from you," she promised.

The clock struck half past nine. The opera would be finishing in half an hour. Johann squeezed Flora tight, smiling. A seemingly endless succession of evenings and nights lay ahead, before the princess was due to leave.

He had been the one who first talked of marriage, not long after Flora had come to work as a chambermaid. Perhaps it would all have worked out differently if his aunt had given him a share of his inheritance back then. But she still sat on her money and made the most of his independence. Once a month, on his day off, he visited her to take her for a walk as she made sure the neighbors saw her on the arm of this fine young man. In the evening, she would invite him to the inn. She was really making him work for his inheritance.

As it was, Johann did not have the means to start a family, but that wasn't the only obstacle. After all, he could have followed Flora to Traunstein House, where the two of them could probably live comfortably for the rest of their days. Anyone else in his position would have jumped at the opportunity. But Johann couldn't bring himself to take that step; it would have made him feel he was shutting a door with finality on a part of his life. The Hotel Sacher was an exciting place where he saw people from all over the empire, and from many countries beyond. He learned their languages and heard the stories they had to tell. He loved Flora and wanted no one else, but he also wanted the world of the Sacher.

At first, they had merely intended to wait out the two years that Frau Sacher had agreed to for Flora. But by the end of that period, Flora had not wanted to leave Traunstein House. Something seemed to be holding her there, something she didn't tell him about. And now it was up to him to come to a decision. He kept putting it off until the next time they met.

"Why do you insist on staying with her? I thought we belonged together?"

Johann wanted to win her over to his idea of a shared life in Vienna. With Frau Sacher's help, they could just as easily find themselves a little apartment near the Naschmarkt or in one of the narrow streets in the vicinity of the Sacher. When their children came along, his employer would surely promote him to a better position. And the time would come when he received his inheritance. When that happened, they could rethink their future.

Flora drew away from his embrace. "I don't know anywhere around here beyond a few narrow streets and the chamber pots in the Sacher."

How could he consider having their children grow up in the dirty streets of the city when they could have a much better life at Traunstein House? She stood up and buttoned her blouse, straightened her skirt. She was more than a maid to Her Serene Highness.

"You don't understand how things have changed."

"Then tell me. Make me understand why we can't be together." Johann's voice grew more insistent.

Flora swallowed. "Because my work with her is important."

"Laying out her clothes, brushing her hair. What's so important about that?"

Now Johann had stood, too. He fastened his shirt and reached to take his jacket from the chair.

"But that's not what it's like at all."

Flora moved to stand in front of the table where the pile of towels lay. She couldn't and wouldn't talk to him about the special position of trust she enjoyed with the princess.

Johann was fully dressed. He looked his beloved in the eye, silently begging her to say more. But Flora remained silent.

He sighed and gave her a kiss. As he did so, he caught sight over her shoulder of the pen and ink lying by the towels. Ink near white linen? But he left without giving it a second thought.

As his footsteps died away, Flora drew out the paper and continued her writing.

22

Maximilian and Konstanze were among the last audience members to leave the opera house. Konstanze sent the carriage back to the Sacher; she wanted to walk the short distance to the hotel. It was what she had always done with Martha. In her friend's presence, all etiquette was put aside for as long as they were together, and she had abandoned her tight-laced bodice in favor of the comfortable modern-style dresses she had acquired especially for her time in Vienna. In the course of her life as Princess von Traunstein, she kept her distance from everything, and during those periods she felt as though she were sleepwalking. But now she was wide awake.

Maximilian extended his arm to Konstanze. He had a feeling of déjà vu—the situation was completely strange yet completely familiar.

"Now I know why my wife's always so keen to come to Vienna." Maximilian laughed. "The opera is excellent."

Konstanze took his arm hesitantly, deliberately keeping her distance. Her curiosity about her friend's husband felt devious. So this was the man with whom Martha shared her days, to whom she gave herself, by whom she became pregnant. Konstanze walked by Maximilian's side, and with every step they crossed another threshold.

Love watched these two people who were linked by an invisible bond. The universe was full of such bonds—an invisible network that drew together scattered men and women from every conceivable direction.

Konstanze thought of what Martha had said—that Maximilian was an outstanding publisher who could discover new talent and make wise decisions. She also said they had founded the press, at least in part, as a vehicle for his own talent.

Konstanze had read *The Prayers of a Useless Man*. She didn't really know what to make of it, considering it more of a man's book. The language was good, though, down-to-earth and clear.

"Martha sent me your novel."

Maximilian pricked up his ears. "She never told me."

"I read it, too." Konstanze looked at him playfully with the little-girl eyes that enabled her to wrap men around her little finger, even though she herself was never aware of the moment she began to turn on the innocent charm. "I discovered how insecure a man can be in his emotions and how much it hurts him to be misunderstood."

Maximilian was charmed by the mixture of sensuality and intellect that Konstanze radiated.

"The critics tore the novel to shreds, accusing me of weaknesses in plot and structure."

He enjoyed playing the victim, a trick he often used with female admirers and young women seeking a publisher for their first literary endeavors. It drew them in and was a balm to him. Martha was immune to it, however; she always pushed him to his limits, never allowing him to wallow in self-pity.

Konstanze immediately rose to the role of comforter of the wronged artist. "People want everything to be scientific these days. Yet we have to find ways of describing things that don't conform to the natural laws."

Maximilian couldn't help noticing her use of *we*.

"You can't have happiness on demand," Konstanze continued enthusiastically. "And when the pain is too much . . ." She broke off midsentence. "How long to go now?"

"What?" Maximilian had failed to keep up with her rapid train of thought.

"The baby. When's it due?" Konstanze asked, her thoughts drifting back to her friend, who from now on would hardly ever be there for her. She knew a baby would demand and receive Martha's love.

Maximilian wasn't sure when the baby was due. It was something he had neglected to speak to Dr. Kraft about.

"In the spring," he replied vaguely.

"It will mean Martha won't have much time for the new books." Konstanze sighed. A catch in her voice suggested she was thinking mainly of herself.

What an egotistical little devil, Maximilian thought. An idea suddenly occurred to him. Could this woman really be so gifted? He leapt in with both feet. "We'll be bringing out another title by Lina Stein soon."

Konstanze flushed. "Oh, really?"

Maximilian kept pushing. "Martha must have sent you Stein's novels?"

"Yes, of course she has," Konstanze said, and changed the subject. "You must continue your protagonist's story. I'd like to read a sequel." Her laugh was bell-like. She was relieved to see they had finally reached the hotel. Maximilian accompanied her to the door of her suite.

"Has Martha ever introduced you to Frau Stein?" he asked, persisting.

Konstanze said nothing, but knocked on the door and waited for Flora.

"Do you know Lina Stein?"

"No!" It sounded false.

At last Flora opened the door.

"I'm sorry. That was impolite of me," Maximilian said, finally dropping the subject. "I wish you good night."

He kissed her hand, noting how cool it was. As the scent of her perfume washed over him, he felt the thrill of the chase.

Konstanze hurried in, and the door closed behind her. Flora helped her out of her coat.

"I've finished all your pages from last week, Your Serene Highness."

The copied sections of the new novel lay on the table.

"You've done well. You can go to bed now."

"Good night!" Flora curtsied and left the room.

"Yes. Good night." Konstanze's thoughts were still on her conversation with Maximilian.

Two floors up, in a plainer hotel bedroom, Maximilian was standing by the window, smoking and thinking. On impulse, he went to his bag and took out a brand-new copy of *The Woman Behind the Veil*. Leafing through, he didn't take long to locate the quote. "You can't have happiness on demand, and when the pain is too much . . ." Maximilian paused for breath. Perhaps she had simply read it and remembered it, but he was not really convinced of that. He gave in to his feelings and enjoyed reading the words that followed: "we look for something to comfort us."

~

Martha was sitting in the print room, editing manuscripts to be published in the new year, when she saw her father arrive. He gave Menning a friendly clap on the shoulder.

"Hello, Menning. How are your wife and children?"

"They're all very well, thank you, Herr Grünstein. This business is flourishing, and I'm glad to report that the same can be said for things at home."

Martha went over to greet her father with an embrace.

"I had to go to Potsdam, so I thought I'd surprise you."

"Max is in Vienna," she said.

"Then I'll enjoy having you to myself."

Martha smiled. She knew he preferred it that way. Maximilian and her father had not grown any closer over the years. The rift had worsened after the publication of *The Prayers of a Useless Man*. Martha had known at the time that it would have been better to keep the book from her father, but how could she have done so? Maximilian was proud of his work. Her father was curious. Confrontation was inevitable.

Grünstein's eyes fell on the pile of copies of *The Woman Behind the Veil* that lay ready for dispatch. Martha handed him a book. "How long can you stay?"

Grünstein put his glasses on his nose. "At least overnight, if you'll have me."

"You'd be welcome for two or three." Martha knew her father would spend most of the time reading their recent publications.

Grünstein weighed *The Woman Behind the Veil* in his hand. "A good one to have on your books, this Frau Stein."

Martha had to smile at this typically businesslike comment. She moved a chair to the window for him. "I hope you won't mind if I continue working for a while?"

"Be my guest." Grünstein sat down and opened the book. "Don't let me get in your way," he murmured, already lost in his reading.

Her upbringing and personality gave Martha the ability to put up with the conflict between her husband and father. She loved them both and knew the reasons behind the thoughts and feelings of each of them. Her greatest strength lay in the way she could empathize with other people, but it still hurt that she couldn't convince her father to approve of her choice to live with Maximilian. His criticism was like a thorn in the side of their marriage.

And now she was pregnant. Without thinking, she laid a hand on her belly, which was still flat. She would tell her father over supper that evening. Perhaps the child would soften his outlook and bring him closer to Maximilian.

Love thought about the couple's near future and how she had her hands full, especially given that the emotions that summoned her presence often led to confusion and sorrow. Her light was accepted for only brief moments before people allowed themselves to be flooded with an expansive, barely describable feeling of happiness, an intoxication that, often enough, lasted for only a few heartbeats. People would do anything to feel it again and again. They sang of Love, they wrote about her, they searched for their one true partner. They slept together, gently or more fiercely. They hurt one another in the name of Love. Killed one another, even. They renounced Love so they would no longer be hurt—and then reached for the next-best feeling that promised a similar intoxication.

It had all begun when a man—wanting to see himself in someone else, to create a counterpart—cut out a part of himself. Wasn't that how the story of God forming Eve from Adam's rib should be understood?

Now, feeling something lacking, man searched for his missing part. He rarely found what he was looking for. And even more rarely was he able to satisfy his longing for his own completeness in someone else.

23

The sun shone down on Vienna that day, September 10, 1898. An Indian summer had settled over the city like wisps of gossamer.

Maximilian and Konstanze sat in the hotel foyer drinking whisky, after spending most of the day in the Egyptian section of the Museum of Fine Arts.

They had both slept badly the previous night, for different reasons.

Maximilian, who believed he had finally discovered the identity of Lina Stein, found it hard to come to terms with the idea that this little woman was more successful than he was. Where did she get her authorial confidence? What could she have experienced that enabled her to write as she did? And why was he denied such ease and success?

Konstanze had tossed and turned, stung by pangs of conscience. She should have gone straight back to the hotel after the opera. She had decided not to meet Martha's husband again. That morning, a bellhop had brought her an invitation from him to visit the museum. Konstanze had dithered. Now, in the clear light of day, she felt surer of her resolve. Apart from the opera and the theater, she had never been in such a public place alone. The idea of strolling through the recently opened museum with him appealed to her.

They met at ten in the foyer and got into the Traunsteins' carriage. Maximilian thought it absurd to be driven such a short distance, one they could easily have covered on foot. Their conversation was difficult, with neither knowing where to begin.

The museum's seemingly endless exhibition rooms flowed seamlessly into one another. Enchanted by ceremonial burial objects and archaeological finds from past millennia, Konstanze let her guard down.

"I'd give anything to be part of an expedition like that. I feel a kind of connection with the Nile. All those temples. It's like a memory, but I don't know where from."

Konstanze used the word *memory* without thinking, but with an enthusiasm that delighted Maximilian. She was particularly struck by the sarcophagi and innumerable grave goods.

"As though the dead continued to live in the realm of the shades," she said in wonder.

Maximilian told her the legend of the night voyage, when the deity Anubis weighed the soul of a dead person against the weight of a feather. "If the soul is as light as a feather, it means that person lived a good life and is entitled to go to Osiris, the lord of the afterlife. But if it's too heavy, or even too light, that life has been lived wrongly, and the soul will have to start over again in a new life, learning and making good."

"A soul weighs the same as a feather?" She shook her head thoughtfully. "How heavy will my soul be when I die?"

"There's still plenty of time before then, and we should enjoy our lives in the meantime," Maximilian said.

"But enjoyment is precisely what leads us astray." No, Konstanze was sure her soul would not pass the test, and she quickly changed the subject. "I can't believe how much you know!" she said, her enthusiasm returning. "Please, tell me more."

Maximilian reveled in her admiration. He had always been able to absorb knowledge and impart it, apparently effortlessly. Skipping boldly over any gaps in his learning, he knew how to play on the other person's lack of knowledge and improvise where needed.

The hours flew by. When they had seen enough of ancient relics and legends, they returned to the Sacher for a late lunch. Afterward, they sat together in the foyer over a glass of whisky. Any caution on the part of Konstanze and reserve on the part of Maximilian gave way to the intoxication of seduction as they circled one another.

"I like my own company far too much. As soon as anyone comes near me, I'm unable to get a word down on paper," he said, playfully provoking her. "What does being alone mean to you?"

"It's not easy to get a moment's peace with three children in the house." She turned the glass in her hand pensively, raising it up to the light. "It's like liquid amber, don't you think?"

Maximilian turned his gaze from Konstanze to the glass.

"It is. Beautiful. Very beautiful." He looked at her again—her profile, her figure. "How do you manage to get time to yourself, Konstanze?"

"I lock myself in my sewing room. It's wonderfully quiet and melancholy there."

"And is that where you write your wonderful novels?"

Konstanze flinched in shock. Maximilian pressed his point.

"Will you tell me your secret, Lina?" The question seemed reckless and at the same time obvious to his own ears. He should have realized it the moment Martha refused to tell him the author's identity. How had she put it? *People are always fascinated by anonymity.* He noticed that Konstanze had turned pale.

"Martha didn't say anything. I sensed it."

He took her hands. Konstanze was unable to reply. She was Lina Stein only to Martha, not to anyone else.

Maximilian persisted stubbornly. "You don't need to hide from me any longer."

"Even my husband doesn't know," Konstanze said, close to tears as the thought hit home.

They were interrupted by Anna Sacher, who brought with her a sense of foreboding as she entered the room. Konstanze withdrew her hands from Maximilian's.

"Please, could I have your attention for a moment, my good people?" There was a tremor in Anna Sacher's voice. The air was still. "It's my sad duty to inform you that Her Majesty, our beloved Empress . . . she's . . . there's been an assassination . . . our Empress is dead."

There was a collective groan. Konstanze's gloved hands flew to her mouth.

A murmur arose, whispered words growing to shocked mutterings. The stunned guests rose to their feet, and men removed their hats. People began talking over one another. No one knew what to do.

There was nothing they could do. But at that moment, no one wanted to acknowledge what had happened.

Konstanze took advantage of the general unrest and bewilderment and hurried up the stairs. Maximilian followed, but lost her in the tumult. Mayr stepped into his path.

"The Empress is dead, Herr Aderhold! Murdered! What a tragedy . . . for Austria!" Mayr was deliberately trying to prevent him from doing something rash, but Maximilian simply shoved him aside and ran, two steps at a time, up the stairs.

Mayr considered whether to follow him, but the phone was ringing remorselessly at the reception desk and his employer was surrounded by harried guests. He decided to stick by her, on the bridge of her ship.

24

It would have been impossible for Love to prevent Death from yielding to the Empress's longing.

Elisabeth had worn black ever since the suicide of her son, Crown Prince Rudolf, nine years earlier. Moving restlessly from place to place, she knew that her life now would never be fulfilled.

She felt that something new lay ahead, something that defied description, something imbued with fear. It seemed to be hidden by a curtain of fog. If one allowed oneself to feel through and let it come, there was a word. Babel. And with it a reminder of the magnitude of the idea, and how from this magnitude hubris was formed, because people no longer knew moderation, particularly with one another. The whole matter of God, the fact that He was annoyed with them because they wanted to build their way up to heaven, was spread by those who needed a god to keep people small. The collapse of their structure, the way it fell into a confusion of languages, the way they drove each other out to the four corners of the earth—a god would never have thought up such a thing for them. It was their own work. For everything always flows from the starting point that people fear themselves, their own magnitude and responsibility. And they justify their fear with this God, who directs them, who punishes, and who loves only when He feels like it. Yet everything people do comes from themselves.

Now was the opportunity for them to recall their big project and continue, although they were not yet ready for it. Never-ending time and the invisible net called them all back together. They only had to listen, to be ready and to fine-tune their senses, in order to hear the message.

The Empress, too, felt this tremendous step they were all challenged to take, and she wanted to be a part of it, but in a different form. And so she had called on Death to fetch her from this life, a life she could no longer bear, because it seemed pointless to her. In the next life, maybe, who knew . . .

Konstanze leaned against the closed door, her breath coming quickly. Today of all days, she had given Flora the day off. There was a knock behind her back, timid at first but becoming more urgent. She heard Maximilian's voice.

"Konstanze?" And, more softly, "Lina?"

She felt that events were outrunning her.

"I have to talk to you. Please."

She didn't want to open the door. But she did.

Maximilian pushed through into the room.

"Maximilian, please. You're ruining everything."

Konstanze's voice was already devoid of resistance. He took her in his arms and kissed her on the cheek, the brow, the lips. Again and again. And as he did so, he felt as though he had found himself. Time was disjointed.

Konstanze again managed to release herself from him. "Max. No. We shouldn't—"

But he was unstoppable and took hold of her again. His kisses roamed down to her neck, her cleavage, her breasts. His desire swept Konstanze along with it. Their actions grew stormier; they sought the bed, fell on it, and collapsed into a passionate embrace. The kind of embrace they had both held back from, throughout their respective marriages.

Love laid a veil over what followed, while Death left his mark. The Empress was dead. She left a written legacy, which came to public light only sixty years later, in which she wrote to the *souls of the future*, foretelling that no *happiness*, no *peace*, no *freedom* would be *at home on our little star. On another, maybe?* Who knew . . .

25

Marie loved the pictures of the Empress she had cut out from newspapers and magazines that Würtner brought her from the outside world.

From the moment she first saw her, the Empress had been a large figure in Marie's life. The girl had long inner monologues in front of her pictures. About loneliness. About Würtner, whose care caused her suffering, yet made her feel safe. The Empress gave Marie the strength to stay.

Sometimes they met before a performance. Just as Marie hid up on the catwalk, above the stage, so did the Empress hide from the eyes of the public, behind her black fan, in a royal box. Everything about her was black—her lace, her pearls, her veil. That made an impression on Marie. Every now and then the Empress looked up toward her, confirming their secret bond.

The years had passed.

Marie was now seventeen, delicately built, with pale skin and deep rings beneath her eyes. She had not seen the light of day for six years. A ventilation shaft below the ceiling of the room gave her a little air and allowed some of the sounds of the outside world to penetrate.

A pot of soup was simmering on a gas ring. Marie set the table. It was originally intended as a place to deposit music scores, although since she had come to live with Würtner it had become a dining table.

"Once more you silently fill wood and vale / with your hazy gleam / and at last . . ." She went over to a music stand and searched the score for the next line. It was Goethe's poem "To the Moon," set to music by Schubert.

Marie had learned innumerable poems and lieder over the years. She lived in their lyrical images, her window to the world outside the confinement of the crypt.

Würtner had taught her to view the outside world as evil. But there was something he had overlooked: that the growing girl would also see him as belonging to the outside world. And so Marie also protected herself from him. She kept him at a distance and used whatever she could get from him. He wanted her to have an education, so Marie read newspapers and books he brought her. She listened as he explained music scores and taught her to sing. Some nights, when they were sure that the opera house was empty, he allowed her to play the piano. She could sit there for hours and allow the notes to resonate around her.

As day dawned, shortly before the first staff members arrived, he came to bring her back to their hiding place. By now, the veil of innocent childhood concealed a cunning spirit. Würtner was proud. He had cut this diamond.

"And at last / set my soul quite free / You cast your soothing gaze / over my fields . . ."

As Marie continued reciting the text, she became aware of noises from the street, reaching her through the air shaft. People talking animatedly. Shouts. Whistles. Even the coaches and cabs seemed to pass at greater speed. She pushed a stool under the shaft and climbed up onto it, but she was unable to glimpse a thing.

The door opened and Würtner entered, his briefcase tucked tightly under his arm.

Marie jumped down from the stool. The soup on the ring boiled over, but she didn't care. "What's happening?"

Würtner leaned against the closed door, breathing heavily from running, and from agitation at the monstrous turn of events.

"Tell me. What's going on up there?" Marie asked urgently.

"Her Majesty . . ."

He broke off, since he knew that nothing would ever be the same once she knew what had happened in the outside world. It even pleased him—now she would finally understand just what it was he was protecting her from.

Marie looked at Würtner, suddenly suspecting the dreadful thing that had happened. "Is she dead?"

"Murdered!" His reply was satisfying.

Marie took a step back, searching his face for a sign he was lying.

"It was someone unknown. Someone sick in the head." Würtner was nodding rapidly to emphasize his words.

Marie felt a pain deep in her heart. Würtner came closer, as though to comfort her. She ducked away from him.

"Leave me in peace."

Marie went between the shelves to her chamber and locked the door behind her. He followed her and banged on the door with his hand.

"Marie!"

She stood in her chamber and looked at her pictures of the Empress. She would never see her again. Marie wiped a hand over her face. Tears. She never cried.

Outside, Würtner continued to call her name and beat his hand against the wood.

"Just leave me in peace!" she yelled back.

"You're being ungrateful, Marie, very ungrateful." Würtner's voice grew louder. "Where would you be today if I hadn't saved you?"

All his pleading, his warnings, his advice, his thoughts—Marie could bear none of it any longer. She took one of her favorite pictures from the wall, the Empress on horseback.

"You'd be dead. Or back at the coal yard . . . ," Würtner called from the other side of the locked door.

A rail held the dresses he had stolen for her from the opera's wardrobes. Beneath them were the shoes he had also filched over the years. Marie picked out a black dress and red shoes.

". . . you'd be at the coal yard, with your stepfather," he continued even more loudly.

In the middle of changing her clothes, Marie stopped short. "Why did you call him my stepfather?"

Würtner bit his lip. He should have kept it to himself. "Because people say your mother brought you with her when she left the von Traunsteins' service."

It was a huge risk, but that was how they were with each other. He couldn't lie to her. He couldn't refuse her anything.

Marie finally opened the door.

There she was, his little bird. "This old world's full of lies and deceit. Only the two of us are true to each other."

Würtner looked at Marie obsequiously. Nothing should ever happen to her. Ever. She should know that only he was there for her and that she would never find a better protector.

"What do you mean, brought me with her?" Marie would not let it go.

"Like I've always told you, men don't behave nicely to women." Marie tried to get her bearings.

Suddenly she heard the Empress's voice telling her to get the whole story. To find out what it was all about! Marie thought for a moment. "Von Traunstein," she said. "The box on the left. Second row."

Würtner nodded proudly. He'd taught her well about the gentry.

Marie recalled how, when she was up in her perch above the stage, she had looked at this box again and again. The old prince always looked like a vulture circling over dying animals. Her own mental image surprised her. How did she know that bird and the way it circled? Had Würtner told her about it? Certainly not. Perhaps she had read about it in the newspaper?

"Who is it, then? The young prince or the old one?"

She was stubborn in her persistence, and the Empress was proud of her.

Würtner didn't like her line of questioning, and liked even less the way he was being sucked into answering. "The son, so people say."

So, the son of the old vulture; Marie remembered him, too. "Tell me where I can find him."

"What do you want from von Traunstein?"

Marie's voice grew sharper. "Tell me!"

"He stays at the Hotel Sacher." Würtner knew immediately it had been a mistake to give in. Her face pinched and determined, she turned and went back into her room. The door closed behind her, and the key turned in the lock.

He stood there, arms hanging by his sides. "My little bird!"

He wondered whether to knock but knew there was no point. When she locked herself in her room, it could be hours before she made her peace with him. He went to his table, removed his coat, and settled down to work.

But he couldn't concentrate. If only he hadn't gone to the coal yard that time, driven by a guilty conscience. He had gone so far as to order a sack of coal, to see the place for himself and confirm that Marie was better off with him, much better off. And then he had heard the rumor in the bar opposite the coal yard. The landlady was telling the story to a customer, who had asked whether Marie had reappeared. The landlady bent over and whispered in the customer's ear—loudly enough for all to hear—that Marie's mother had given birth to her no more than three months after getting married. "She came from Traunstein House, didn't she? It doesn't take much imagination to work out what happened." The landlady looked around triumphantly. Noticing Würtner's interest, she had come to sit at his table and recounted the whole story again, with all the lurid details she knew.

Würtner finally managed to get a grip on his thoughts and turn back to his work. Copying out the notes calmed him, and he slipped into the world of the music.

26

Martha slept badly that night. She had spent a long time talking to her father. The news that he was to become a grandfather delighted him, but Martha had gone to bed saddened all the same. Their conversation reminded her of her fierce determination six years ago. How much of her dream had she fulfilled?

The baby would sweep away false dreams and plans, she told herself bravely. It would give them the stability they needed to progress in life.

Martha grew very cold during the night. She dreamt she was swimming through a pond, growing colder with every stroke. Cramps awoke her as the first light of dawn was creeping through the curtains, and she became aware that her nightdress and sheets were damp, her hands shaking. Forcing her eyes open, she saw the blood and immediately knew what had happened.

On the way to the bathroom, she met Hedwig.

"I need Dr. Kraft." Martha's voice was calm. The cramps had subsided.

Her father emerged from the guest room, rubbing his eyes, as Hedwig ran off.

Grünstein saw what had happened and the black shadows that had stolen his daughter's glow. Martha quickly slipped into the bathroom, leaving her father standing helplessly on the landing. When she had told him over dinner that she was pregnant, her joy had appeared mixed with something else. Things had not seemed quite right to him, although he himself couldn't think of anything nicer than welcoming a baby into the family.

A little later, Martha was lying in the freshly remade bed. The doctor had recommended rest for her over the days to come. She was missing her mother, or at least a good friend. She thought of her days with Konstanze and how they had brought the princess's first child into the world together. Now she felt just as she had after Rosa's birth, suspended between dream and reality. Konstanze had loved to see Martha holding the newborn in her arms, as though she wanted to delegate her own motherhood, or at least delay it for a while. Georg, too, had spent time with the women and his little daughter.

It had been an exceptional time for all of them, and Martha had found it hard to leave. The days at Traunstein House had changed her. She had wanted to share the experience with Maximilian, but when she arrived home she found her husband overtired and stressed. Sunk in his writing, living his story, he had hardly registered her descriptions of her trip. It had taken them weeks to find one another again.

Martha fumbled for her mother's chain, which lay on the bedside table, and fastened it around her neck. It was good to feel the stone against her skin.

Her father came in, sat by his daughter, and took her hand. It pained him to see Martha like this. "This is all too much for you, Martha. If you won't talk to your husband about it, I will."

Martha objected. "No, Father. If our lives won't include a child, then I simply have to accept it."

Grünstein looked at his daughter. He would support her, even if she had acted too rashly in the past. He would help her get her breath back.

But Martha was clearly feeling guilty. "I'm not like Mother. She was kindhearted and gentle," she said. "More than anything, I want the publishing business . . . I want us to succeed. And then I'll be ready to try again for a child."

Arthur Grünstein shook his head. "Ella Blumenthal was a resolute young woman. And you're just like her. When we met, I was an assistant in my great-uncle's office. But your mother insisted I become a partner and lead the business to success before we married." He looked at the lapis lazuli at his daughter's neck. Martha noticed, and laid her hand on it. "You brought us great happiness, Martha. The months when your mother was expecting, your birth, watching you grow up. You really bound your mother and me together."

Grünstein wanted to make it clear to his daughter that it was perfectly possible for her to change the course of her life if she would only free herself from her husband, who obviously wasn't doing her any good.

"Max and I have been bound together from the start."

Arthur Grünstein was too tactful to say any more.

~

"What a dreadful way to die." Konstanze slipped from Maximilian's arms. He tried to hold her fast.

"Lina Stein," he said, full of desire.

But she didn't react, fixated as she was on the fate of the Empress, as though she had to keep it separate from the night they had just spent together.

"It will break the heart of my beloved Hungary. I hope it doesn't mean they'll take our rights away again."

Maximilian sat up and reached for his jacket, to take out a cigarette.

"Please don't!" Konstanze held him back. "My husband will notice it."

Maximilian put the cigarette back in its case. They looked at one another. He drew her to him, and her long hair flowed over their faces. As they kissed, it felt as though they were in a sweet-smelling tent.

"The court will summon everyone to the funeral, and my husband will come to Vienna. You should go now."

Maximilian held her tight, seeking her mouth again. Konstanze responded to his kiss. She had never kissed like this.

"I must get dressed . . . Max . . . please!" She tried to release herself from him. But as his hands loosened their grip, she chose to ignore it. They made love again.

~

"Austrian empress murdered in Geneva."

Grünstein was reading the newspaper at the breakfast table as Martha packed her things in the next-door room. He looked up from his reading.

"Why are you so determined to go to Vienna? You can tell him when he's back," he called out, his voice full of concern. When Martha didn't reply, he stood and went over to her. "You've got to think of your health."

But Martha had decided she was going. She snapped the lid of her suitcase shut. "It was our baby."

Something was drawing her to Vienna. She was sure Maximilian would be staying in the same room they had occupied on their honeymoon. She would keep the promise they had made then and use the experience of the intervening years to begin again.

27

Marie blew the ink dry and inserted the letter into a green envelope before casting a final glance around the little room where she had lived for six years. She had put her pictures of the empress in a cardboard box—her only item of luggage, since she was leaving the dresses and shoes behind.

When Würtner saw her coming, her demeanor so determined, he jumped up from his chair and barred her way.

"I made up that von Traunstein business," he spluttered.

But Marie did not believe him. She knew Würtner was unable to lie.

"There's nothing for you among the gentry."

Clutching at straws, Würtner whisked the blue pouch of money—the one he had found on the dead man six years ago—from its hiding place behind a stack of yellowing manuscript paper. He had not touched the money in it.

"I found this on the corpse. A so-called gentleman paid to have something done to you."

Marie took the blue velvet pouch from him, weighing it thoughtfully in her hand. He backed toward the door. Marie moved to get past him, but he stopped her from reaching the handle. They fought with one another. Quietly. Wordlessly. Their breathing the only sound. Marie at last found the strength to shove him out of the way. The money pouch fell to the floor.

"This is what you raised me for, Würtner! You raised me to expect something better, and you always told me I'm something special, something very special."

Marie picked up the velvet pouch and left.

Würtner stayed where he was, his arms and legs trembling forlornly like the limbs of a marionette. Suddenly, he began to sing. "Bye-bye, little Marie . . . in the forest . . . sweet little girl . . ." Tears and snot ran down his face.

Marie heard his singing as she ran down the corridor. It would follow her from that moment on, insinuating its way into her dreams.

For the first time in six years, she saw the light of day. It hurt, as did the noise on the street.

Standing in a doorway, Death watched her cross the street toward the Hotel Sacher, then hurried toward the music library.

The Hotel Sacher was a hive of activity with the arrival of mourners from all over Austria. No one noticed the girl in the black opera costume and red shoes except one of Anna's dogs, which ran to Marie and began to prance around her suspiciously, keeping a safe distance. Marie handed the letter to Mayr, who raised his eyebrows when he saw the name of the recipient. Anna Sacher noticed the strange apparition and called her dog to heel. The eyes of the two women met before Marie left the hotel.

Among the dresses Würtner had stolen over the years from the stores and wardrobes of the dancers and chorus singers—the dresses with which he had briefly made Marie's eyes shine as she fluttered like a little bird through the music library in her new costumes—he hanged himself, kicking away the chair beneath him.

His soul flew directly into the lap of Death. Perhaps it would have liked to fly around the world like a bird, but Würtner's soul was not allowed that freedom yet. For now, it withdrew into the realm of nothingness, to be healed.

~

Half an hour's walk from the opera house, Marie knocked on the door to the gatehouse of the Daughters of Divine Charity. She had walked past the convent numerous times as a child, and now thought it the only possible sanctuary. Würtner was right about that, at least: she had been away from home for too long and would be unable to explain anything, either about what motivated her or about what she planned to do. A sister opened the door and let her in.

28

Konstanze was preoccupied. Her body felt new, lighter, and more perfect. Flora was helping her dress, her expression giving nothing away.

Konstanze could rely on her maid, but she was nevertheless worried about whether the affair could remain concealed from Georg. The possibility of discovery sent her into a panic. When she thought of Martha, Konstanze shifted the blame to her friend. She should have kept in touch. She could at the very least have sent a telegram to warn Konstanze that she would be meeting Maximilian. There was a knock at the door.

"A letter for you, Your Serene Highness."

She recognized Johann's voice through the wooden door. Flora answered.

"What is it?" Konstanze asked, quickly taking the letter from his tray. She feared it might be a denunciation of her indiscretion, but at first glance she knew the letter, addressed in its calm, even hand, could not possibly have come from a noble household.

Konstanze slit open the envelope, read the few lines intended for her husband, skimmed it a second time, and said tremulously, "Johann, I need my carriage! Quickly!"

A short time later she was being driven along the Kärntner Ring, past the Karlskirche, in the direction of the Belvedere palace. She stopped outside the convent of the Daughters of Divine Charity, a stone's throw from the castle in which the heir to the throne, Franz Ferdinand, resided.

Konstanze waited nervously in the visitors' room. Her surroundings made her think of her mother, who lived in a convent near Linz. Since her marriage, Konstanze had had no contact with her apart from a card or letter on birthdays and anniversaries. Agneta Nagy-Károly did not know her granddaughters. Konstanze had sent her a family photo after Mathilde's birth, as though they were going to stop at the three children, as though something had been completed and captured for posterity with this photo. She suddenly had a dreadful thought: What if her night with Maximilian had not been without consequences? How would she explain a pregnancy to Georg, whose advances she had rebuffed for months? Konstanze went hot all over. She could only hope for the best.

The door opened, and a creature with pale skin and tousled hair entered. Konstanze stared at the apparition in a black opera costume and red shoes. So this was her . . . the little cleaning girl from the Sacher. Marie Stadler.

It was the first time Marie had seen Princess von Traunstein close up. Now that the princess was standing before her, she looked much younger than she had through the opera glasses from up above the stage. The princess seemed agitated, which Marie found surprising.

Würtner had told her so much about the gentry that they had become marble statues in Marie's imagination, removed from all human emotions.

The woman before her had light skin, heavy dark hair, small hands, and short nails. She was a real person. Marie felt like reaching out, touching her and smelling her. In the crypt, she had become accustomed to smelling everything that Würtner brought her from the outside world. Most things smelled strange and unpleasant.

"What do you want from my husband?"

The princess held out the letter Marie had written while still in her old life. The crypt and Würtner were already a long way in the past. Something new was growing inside Marie.

"I'll tell no one but him."

She refused to forge a connection with this woman. Marie had to take every step alone, as she had learned to do when living with Würtner. She could trust no one.

Konstanze concealed her confusion.

"We were all very concerned about your fate when you disappeared."

She thought of the image she had seen fleetingly on her way to the opera, of the girl with the soup pot. She had never been able to forget it.

The door opened suddenly, and the abbess showed a man in a threadbare suit into the room.

"Inspector Lechner." As he introduced himself, he gave Konstanze an impudent grin, his smile revealing nicotine-stained teeth. "Your humble servant, Highness." He turned to the girl. "So you're Marie?" he asked, apparently impressed. "Marie Stadler!" he repeated with a shake of his head.

Marie looked at the abbess. She had asked her not to tell anyone where she was until Prince von Traunstein had been told. Lechner followed her gaze.

"The abbess considered it her duty to inform the police," he said. "Do you know Würtner, the music librarian at the opera house?"

Marie nodded.

Konstanze watched the scene, spellbound. Years of her life had passed in tedious monotony, and now she was hardly able to keep up with events.

"He was found dead." Lechner had his eyes fixed on Marie.

"I'm sorry to hear it," the girl said in bewilderment.

Lechner regarded her. "I'll have to take you with me."

Marie did not move. Lechner hesitated, then went over to her and grasped her arm. Marie wriggled beneath his grip.

"I didn't do anything to Würtner."

Lechner held her fast. "We'll see about that."

Marie looked at Konstanze, to see whether she was on her side. Konstanze saw, and reacted immediately. "The girl is under my protection!"

Lechner paused and looked at Konstanze, his eyes narrowing in amusement.

"Please give your husband my greetings, Your Serene Highness. He'll be welcome to come and fetch the girl from the police station once she's been proved innocent."

29

Anna's dogs were suitably attired with black bands or bejeweled black coats. The Hotel Sacher was like a stage on which a play, *Death of the*

Empress, was being enacted. The final act would take place in the hearts of those left behind. Or was this not the final act at all? Would more be needed before the finale?

Mayr glanced at the entrance, where two carriages were coming to a halt. Georg descended from the coach bearing the von Traunstein coat of arms, while Martha Aderhold got out of a cab. Mayr waved a young bellhop over and told him to accompany him outside, and then sent another to Anna Sacher to announce the guests' arrival.

It took Martha and Georg a moment to recognize one another. During the years following her visit to Traunstein House, Martha had never found the time for a second trip.

"What a pleasure!" Georg kissed Martha's hand. "When she left, Konstanze didn't mention that you'd be in Vienna. How are you?"

"It's lovely to see you again, Georg." Although she didn't reply directly to his question, Martha was genuinely pleased.

Their way into the hotel was barred. Mayr was standing right in front of the entrance, giving complicated instructions to the young bellhop, peppered with plenty of expansive arm waving.

"A suitcase must be treated like a guest, Niklas, because it's an extension of the guest. You should handle it with just the same care and attention."

The young bellhop, who had been at the hotel for only a couple of weeks, nodded enthusiastically and played along with a glow of importance.

The news of the publisher's infidelity with Her Serene Highness Princess von Traunstein had spread among the staff, and they were keen to avoid a scene. Mayr was playing for time, to ensure that the room the couple had stayed in during their honeymoon was perfectly clean and tidy. He had dealt with plenty of similar situations in his time.

"Beginnings are always strenuous, just like carrying the suitcases of the ladies and gentlemen who honor us by staying here," Mayr declared theatrically.

His ploy was working—Martha and Georg were watching the performance with amusement.

"You must excuse us, Your Serene Highness, ma'am. Honestly, the young people of today . . ." Mayr made a show of trying to find the words, but nothing suitable came.

Georg put in cheerfully, "The children now love luxury; they show disrespect for elders and love chatter in place of exercise."

Mayr paused, the wind taken from his sails; it was rare that a guest stole his thunder. "Excellently put, Your Serene Highness."

Georg, who had known the doorman since his childhood and loved trading words with him, reassured him, "I was quoting Socrates."

Warming to the subject once again, Mayr turned back to the bellhop. "Socrates. A philosopher in ancient Greece. You got that, Niklas? You'll remember it?"

The bellhop nodded eagerly.

"So that's how it was in ancient times. No wonder they didn't last!" With that, Mayr finally showed them into the hotel.

Anna Sacher met them in the foyer. After exchanging a glance with his boss, Johann took charge of their cases.

Georg greeted him. "I hope you're well?"

"Very well, thank you, Your Serene Highness."

"We haven't seen you at Traunstein House for a long while. Remember you're welcome any time."

Johann bowed before carrying the luggage upstairs.

"Sad circumstances for a reunion. At first I intended to close the hotel for a day." Anna Sacher gestured around the reception area. "But look at all this! I can't disappoint my guests. Our empress, dead! I can't bear to think about it. First the crown prince, and now his mother. What next, I ask you?"

Georg wished he could have a few moments undisturbed with Martha. As if Anna Sacher had read his mind, she brought her eulogy to an end.

"Her Serene Highness went out in the carriage about an hour ago," she said matter-of-factly, then turned to Martha. "And your husband, ma'am, is usually out at this time. May I welcome you with a drink, perhaps?"

Georg looked at Martha, who nodded, looking pleased. They went over to one of the tables, and Anna gestured to Wagner to serve her guests. After wishing them a pleasant stay, she turned to a group of officers who were enshrouded in an air of awkward mourning and a cloud of cigar smoke.

Maximilian descended the hotel stairs, unnoticed by anyone. When he saw Martha and Georg, he had the presence of mind to hurry a few steps back up so that a wall hid him from the activity in the foyer. He stood there, completely at a loss. Why was Martha in Vienna? Had she sensed his deceit? He had always been amazed at her perception; at the same time, he hated it. Maximilian's thoughts raced all over the place. His encounter with Konstanze had him in a turmoil. It was a cruel twist of fate that now, of all times, just when his marriage with Martha was to be blessed with a child, he had found a soul mate. For a moment, Maximilian felt the weight of the prison that had surrounded him since his early childhood. If only he could escape. He groaned with inner pain, but reminded himself that he was used to coping with defeat. He managed to locate a fire exit and slipped out of the hotel.

As though they were old friends, Martha told Georg about her miscarriage.

"I'd have liked a child. But now I've lost all hope."

"Don't talk like that, Martha. I think you'd make a wonderful mother." Georg remembered the days they had spent together, when Martha carried and cuddled his newborn. He would never forget the images.

Martha gave a tired smile. They looked at one another, and closeness grew between them. Martha realized that Georg had now heard about their misfortune before Maximilian, a fact she felt did not bode well for their marriage. She distanced herself quickly. "Having your own company is also a bit like being a parent," she said matter-of-factly before changing the subject. "But enough of me, how are you? Have you been able to implement any of your plans for Traunstein House?"

"Yes, we've got a school now, a doctor's clinic, and a midwife, and we're paying our workers more," Georg said proudly. "But people still aren't satisfied," he added with genial irony.

"Why not?" Martha was unable to conceal her surprise.

"Because they're not given enough responsibility, perhaps? Or because they prefer to see themselves as victims of circumstance?" Georg spoke out loud what he'd been thinking for a long time. They were problems for which he had no answers, let alone solutions. "The school opened at the beginning of the year, but only a few people send their children to classes regularly. All hands are needed in the fields and the farmyard."

Just as he had years before when she visited Traunstein House, Georg enjoyed Martha's attention. But their time together was limited, and so much of what they really wanted to hear from one another remained unsaid and unasked.

Martha would have liked to know whether there had been any news of his illegitimate daughter in the intervening period, but she dared not ask. Georg, on the other hand, couldn't think of any topic of conversation that would satisfy the longing he had always felt every time he spoke to Martha, or that might bring out more of what they had in common.

Once they had finished their drinks, convention dictated that they should part. At the last minute, Georg suggested that the four of them have dinner together, and of course Martha was glad to accept the invitation. And so they would be apart only briefly, until eight that evening, when the two couples were to meet in the foyer.

Love looked at the two empty glasses, on one of which Martha's lips had left a faint trace. How she would have liked to keep her distance from what was to follow.

Konstanze entered the hotel and saw her husband taking his leave of Martha. Bewildered, she came to a halt. Why had Martha come to Vienna? Had she found something out? Konstanze thought feverishly and at first pretended not to have seen them. Instead, she went to the reception counter and asked with deliberate nonchalance, "Is there any mail for me?"

Mayr played along. "No, Your Serene Highness, but your husband's over there." He pointed across the foyer, where the elevator doors were just closing behind Martha.

"Oh, really?" Feigning surprise, Konstanze went over to Georg. He saw his wife approach and moved to meet her. She dismissed his greeting coolly and, deeming attack to be the best form of defense, took the letter from her little fabric purse. "A letter came for you from one Marie Stadler. She claims you're her natural father. Is this true, Traunstein?"

Georg took the letter and looked in dismay at the envelope with his name on it.

∼

Martha removed her coat. Maximilian wasn't in the room, and she was relieved to have a few minutes to herself. The conversation with Georg echoed pleasantly in her head as she thought about what she was going to wear that evening. She had packed only plain blouses; after all, her trip to Vienna was for a tragic occasion. But now she had her life back, and she wanted to make it as nice as possible.

Konstanze would be surprised that they were to dine together that evening. Of course, they would have to be reserved with one another to conceal the real nature of their relationship from their husbands. Martha wondered whether Maximilian had uncovered the secret of Lina Stein, but she had to smile, as she would have wagered anything that Konstanze had not revealed her identity to him. It suddenly occurred to her that she had written to Konstanze at Traunstein House to inform her she would not be coming. Maybe that had been a mistake and she should have sent the letter directly to the Sacher. But before she could think any more about it, there was a brief knock and Maximilian entered.

He looked surprised.

"Martha? You're here?"

Despite walking aimlessly through the city streets for the last hour, oblivious to his surroundings, he still had no idea what he was going to say to her. After passing the Sacher countless times, he had given up and decided to simply face her.

He kissed her briefly. Instead of waiting to hear what she had to say, he immediately leapt to his own defense. "I don't understand why the two of you made such a mystery of it. What difference does it make to Konstanze's talent if I'm now in on the secret?"

Martha frowned as he spoke. He couldn't look at her, but busied himself removing his jacket and shoes. The relief she had felt a few minutes ago had turned to unease.

Maximilian gave a forced laugh and continued as if his life depended on it. "Great idea, by the way, to publish her under a pseudonym. As you always said, people are fascinated by anonymity."

Martha tried to understand why he sounded so formal and patronizing. She suddenly felt guilty. She had failed; her body had been unable to hold its fruit.

"Of course, we've been spending time together; after all, I'm her publisher." Maximilian moved around restlessly. "I think I'm going to take a bath."

"Maximilian!"

Martha wanted him to settle down, but he kept talking.

"You never told me you'd sent her my book. When two authors talk about their work . . ."

He gave another forced laugh, then stopped.

Silence descended like lead between them.

Martha understood what had happened.

"You were right," she said. "I shouldn't have come here."

Maximilian looked at her, and he, too, understood what had happened. Stunned, he went to her.

"Martha?" He took her hands. She remained motionless. "You lost it," he murmured in dismay.

Love tried to flow around them, but neither of them wanted her near. She was a burden to them. Now it was time for the emotions that accompanied the shock they felt. Injured emotions. Emotions of self-pity, blame, and mutual antagonism.

Martha drew away and went to sit at the desk.

Maximilian stood helplessly in the middle of the room. "It's my fault."

He went to her and knelt in front of her. Cold and motionless, she allowed him to take her hands again. Yes, it was his fault. Martha was shocked to realize that she was exulting inside. Now it was no longer a matter of her failure as a woman, but of his betrayal of trust.

30

Lechner pushed his metal lunch box across the table to Marie and poured her a glass of water. She was sitting in the very same place where her mother, plagued with worries, had sat almost six years earlier.

"I saw your room in the opera house library. It didn't look as though Würtner forced you to be there."

Marie shrugged but didn't reply.

"Did you think it was better than the coal yard, at least?"

Marie remained silent.

Lechner circled her, studying her carefully. "Why did you choose to leave now?"

Marie kept her eyes lowered. "You have to leave sometime," she said quietly.

Lechner nodded in surprise. "You seem like a girl who can look after herself, Marie." He drew up his chair and sat across from her. "But it will look better for you if the police found you helpless and in need of rescuing. People are moved by that kind of thing." His tone was calmly emphatic. "The police freed you because we were onto what Würtner was doing, and that's why he took his life."

Marie thought of the melody that Würtner had sung for her. She swallowed, sorry for what had happened to him.

"Or would you prefer it if people said you murdered Würtner?" Lechner tutted.

"I don't need to murder anyone."

"You know that. I know that. But do the people know it?"

Lechner liked the way she sat there, stubbornly unruffled. He pushed the report across the table to her, just as he had once done with her mother. "Sign it. Then you can go."

Marie hesitated, wondering whether it could be a trap. But everything written there was clear, and it revealed only what Lechner had said it would. That the police had found her beneath the opera house and released her. That the music librarian had hanged himself shortly before the police operation ended.

Lechner watched her sign the report. Her handwriting was even and regular, in sharp contrast to her disheveled appearance. He picked up the paper.

"What will you do now, Marie? Will you go to your mother, or to your father?"

She looked at him in surprise.

"You've got me to thank for the possibility of living a grand life, Marie," he said, his voice almost gentle.

She thought, here was another man who wanted her gratitude. She picked up her cardboard box, stood, and left. Lechner watched her go.

At the door, she met the central inspector. He looked at her in surprise for a moment, and then his eyes moved to Lechner, who stood and bowed to him from across the room.

"Well, Lechner, you were proved right in the end. But don't expect any medals for it. I should say not!"

Lechner smiled ambiguously. The central inspector noticed; he would have to keep an eye on this one. "Well, you've certainly shown persistence and a lot of patience. I should say so!"

Lechner bowed a second time, deeply.

Once his boss had left the room, Lechner sat at his desk, opened a drawer, and took out a paprika sausage, a knife, and a bottle of schnapps. He poured himself a measure and meticulously cut slices from the sausage. He had every reason to be pleased with himself, he thought, as he took a nip of schnapps and chewed a sliver of sausage.

~

"You've been giving her mother money without my knowing? All these years?" Konstanze was shaken. She would never have believed it possible.

"It's my duty." Georg hid behind moral principles.

"Without so much as a word to me!" Konstanze's voice was full of reproach, but she was secretly thanking her guardian angel for giving her this scene and, with it, the strength to launch herself back into life with Traunstein.

Georg stood decisively. "I'll ask a lawyer to take charge of Marie's future."

"No!" Konstanze was determined to retain control. "We'll have the girl come live with us."

He looked at her in astonishment. "But that would confirm all the rumors."

"We'd be doing some good for a poor girl who was held captive for years." She trembled with determination. "We'll do our humanitarian duty. That's how you like things, isn't it, Traunstein?"

Konstanze sat down, relieved now that she had the situation back under control. Georg took her hand and regarded her thoughtfully. His wife never ceased to surprise him. Closeness was beginning to grow between them, but Konstanze could bear it for only a moment before drawing away from him.

31

Death sat on a sofa in the foyer. A pall of mourning lay over the Sacher, over Vienna, over the whole empire. Death knew the Empress's soul was safe and sound.

For an immeasurable moment, it had encountered that of Würtner.

Würtner, who had waited all those years in the crypt until his little bird flew. A forlorn little bird that he had tended and cared for until, big and strong, it had flown the nest and found freedom. It had been his life's work, Death thought respectfully.

He noticed Maximilian and Martha coming down the stairs. Death would have liked to ask for a cigarette, to brush against Maximilian and feel the relief of the dejected man. But Death held back, as on no account did he want to get too close to Martha. She had made his acquaintance only a few days ago.

Mayr gave the publisher his bill. Maximilian was hoping for a smile, a tacit sign of understanding, man to man. But Mayr gave him no such look. His sympathies were always with the women; he could see their spiritual wealth, and he knew the destructive power of the male. That was why he devoted himself so completely to his service in the Sacher and gave his unreserved loyalty to his employer.

"Is something wrong, Mayr?" Maximilian asked, drawing the door-man out of his reverie.

Mayr's reply was prompt and betrayed no hint of emotion. "It's completely unimportant whether there's anything wrong with me, Herr Aderhold."

Maximilian pulled out his wallet and counted out the bills nervously. He found the situation he was in hard to bear. Martha had stopped a few paces behind him, concealing her despondency beneath a veneer of cool self-control.

Konstanze came out of the elevator. The doors had closed behind her before she had time to grasp the situation. There was no going back. At that very moment, Martha turned. Konstanze seized the bull by the horns.

"Martha—"

She was about to launch into a wordy explanation when she was cut short by the sadness in Martha's eyes and the instinctive realization that her friend had just lost her baby, and that was what mattered most.

"Martha!" Konstanze repeated, this time deeply moved, and threw her arms around her.

Martha remained distant. Konstanze drew Martha aside until they were alone. She struck an innocent pose.

"You should have sent me a telegram, Martha, telling me you weren't coming." Even in a situation like this, Konstanze knew how to imbue her voice with a hint of reproach. "He knew right away that I'm Lina Stein. I was caught out before I had a moment to think. And then there was the death of the Empress and all this commotion," she murmured dramatically.

Martha was unable to speak. She suddenly remembered her first meeting with Konstanze in the hotel café. Back then the little princess had come across to her as superficial and almost absurd. If only she had trusted her first instincts, they would never have grown so close. But then they would not have had Lina Stein.

"I didn't mean it, Martha," Konstanze said, her tone pleading. "It was nothing. Please forgive me."

By now, Maximilian had settled the bill and was coming toward them. He heard what Konstanze said and was struck by her words.

Konstanze turned. Their eyes met, filled with the enormity of what they knew.

At that moment, Miklos Szemere entered the hotel. Despite the ambience of mourning for the Empress, the Hungarian bon vivant's clothes were as flamboyant as ever. He was wearing a white slouch hat and a red flannel jacket along with his family's coat of arms engraved on a metal heart.

"Constanze Nagy-Károly, what a pleasure to brighten up all this sadness," Szemere called out, delighted to see the daughter of his former favorite business partner. His vivacity drew the three of them from their unspeakable situation. "There's great excitement in Budapest, everyone wondering whether the death of our queen will affect court politics," he complained, referring to Hungary's special role in the Habsburg Empire. The Hungarians' independence had been largely due to the influence of Elisabeth, who had loved Hungary and had, in return, been popular and revered there.

Konstanze had never been interested in politics, but said, from an innate patriotism, "It's so sad. But I'm optimistic. We Hungarians are a strong people."

From the corner of her eye, she saw Maximilian giving Martha his arm as the two of them left the hotel. She kept her composure and allowed Szemere to kiss her.

"I have to leave now for an urgent appointment with my dressmaker. I'm having a ball gown made. I mustn't delay!"

She sighed theatrically and left the hotel. Charmed, Szemere watched her go.

"Ach, there's only so much mourning the world can do; the ladies keep thinking of their finery, and it sweetens our bitterest hours." He caught the eye of the doorman. "Considering the dramatic worsening of the situation in which the empire, our Austria-Hungary, finds itself, do you think more subdued attire would be appropriate?"

"A man of the world is not influenced by fashion, but fashion by the man of the world," Mayr replied diplomatically.

"I raise my hat to you, Mayr!"

Flattered, Mayr bowed.

"Call me a couturier immediately! I'm going to transform my appearance." Proud of his patriotic decision, Szemere headed for the elevator.

32

The coal yard had prospered over recent years. Stadler now owned it and was even in a position to employ two journeymen.

Hugging her cardboard box containing her photos of the Empress, Marie stopped some distance away. She hadn't wanted sympathy, and she was even less able to bear her mother's tears.

She had accepted her natural father's invitation to live at Traunstein House. Now, having said goodbye to her family, she went out to the street, where the prince's carriage was waiting for her. She turned one last time, nodded briefly without smiling, then climbed in. She would never come back here.

Sophie watched the young woman in the black dress and red shoes leave. The child she remembered had been warmhearted and timid. She cried softly. The tension of the years lost in worry about Marie dissolved; it had been the corset holding her body and soul together.

Georg tapped on the outside of the carriage to signal the driver to leave. He felt dreadful that he had not contacted Sophie personally since Lechner had told him the situation. But now his eldest daughter was sitting here with him, and pride flooded through him, together with the thought that he was gaining a link to a world he had tried to understand since his earliest childhood.

33

Konstanze looked down into the garden through her sewing-room window. It was a warm autumn day, the golden-brown leaves floating down from the trees. Georg was sitting in the garden over a picnic with Vincent Zacharias. Marie was playing croquet on the lawn with her half sisters Rosa and Irma. They had long since abandoned the rules and were now chasing the ball any which way. Whooping for joy, Irma tried to trip Marie, who picked up the little girl and whirled her through the air. Now Rosa wanted the same. Marie had enough strength for them both and romped over the grass with a sister under each arm. Konstanze wondered where the girl got so much energy She had been kept prisoner in a cellar for years, in cramped conditions with no daylight. Only a short time ago she had been a bowed creature, unable to look anyone in the eye. Perhaps these children from the lower classes were more resilient in every respect. Perhaps that was what made them so dangerous.

As if she could feel her gaze from behind the curtain, Marie looked up toward her. Discovered, Konstanze took a step back.

"Marie has settled in quickly here," she said to Flora, who was sitting at the table, copying out a section of her new novel, *Woman on a Journey*. Konstanze hoped that a new book would help rekindle her connection with Martha.

"It must have been dreadful," Flora said, picking up on Konstanze's train of thought. "And she won't tell us a thing about what he did to her."

"He taught her a lot—how to read music, for one thing. I daresay she knew how to wind him around her little finger." Konstanze noticed that last remark seemed to unsettle Flora. "You like Marie, don't you?"

Skirting the issue, Flora replied, "People think it's very honorable of you and the master to take the girl in, almost as though she were your own child."

There was no mistaking the tension between Her Serene Highness and Marie.

"What else are the servants prattling about?"

The conjecture was not the kind of thing that Flora wanted to pass on. No good ever came of getting mixed up in their master's and mistress's lives. She hesitated before answering. "That her mother worked here twenty years ago."

Konstanze nodded, her expression betraying nothing.

Flora added hastily, "But the only one still here from those days is the butler, and he doesn't say much." She turned her attention back to her copying.

Konstanze sat down at her bureau and looked through the newspaper cuttings she had collected about Würtner's death and Marie Stadler's rescue. "Maybe one day we'll find out more about what she lived through, and I can bring it all together into a story."

Vincent Zacharias poured himself a glass of wine from a carafe. Despite the beautiful weather, the air around the table had grown heavy and gray.

"The Bohemians must be given their rights, as the Hungarians have enjoyed for some time now," he said animatedly to Georg. "The political independence of the Slavic peoples—nothing else will do anymore."

They had had this discussion, or something similar, many times, yet they never tired of airing their conflicting views.

"Separate national interests are damaging for us, Zacharias. We should view ourselves as a strong united country, whether we're Bohemians, Hungarians, Germans, or Ruthenians," Georg argued. Try as he might, he was unable to understand his friend's nationalism.

"We Bohemians want our own state," Vincent insisted.

"But the western lands you have your eye on haven't been discrete national states for a long time. Economics, trade, and business can't be contained within the borders of individual countries." Georg was convinced of the rightness of his ideas, which in his opinion formed the only sensible political solution. "People living together with equal opportunities in the crown lands beneath the protection of a central power, Zacharias—the United States of Greater Austria."

The children's ball rolled across the grass. Vincent stood to send it back to them as Marie approached. He threw her the ball. She caught it and threw it back. He ran a few paces after her and threw it to her again. Their eyes met—at first curious, then full of respect and, ultimately, mutual liking. He returned to his place.

The butler came and bowed to Georg. "His Excellency has just arrived and wishes to speak to you immediately."

Georg excused himself and crossed the lawn to the house.

The old prince was waiting for his son in the library. He began without so much as a greeting. "Getting a girl pregnant is one thing, but taking the brat into your own household is truly beyond the pale."

Georg had a vision of the old man as a vulture, tearing off lumps of his flesh and sending them flying through the air.

"Perhaps my daughter's fate would have been different if I'd been allowed to take responsibility for her from the start. I intend to try and make good, at least partially."

"Make good?" the old man echoed, fuming. "How naïve are you?"

Georg remained calm, although his heart thumped harshly against his chest. The old man's eyes bored into his son. "No, you're not naïve. You're vain, raising yourself above everyone and everything. You can go to hell!"

Georg went to reply, but his father wouldn't let him get a word in.

"Your sort, you want to destroy everything. But you don't think of the consequences." Anger raised his voice to a shout.

"I don't want to destroy anything, Father. I want to prove myself worthy of my privilege." Georg, too, had become loud and forceful by now.

"By telling the rabble what they want to hear?"

"At least I don't treat them with despotism and violence."

The old man snorted. "You and your kind! I consider it my personal business to make sure that you see reason."

The old man left his son standing there in the straitjacket that had constricted his breathing since he'd been able to think. The old held the land in their clutches, and there was no prospect of change.

~

A shot rang out, and another, as Marie strolled through the autumn park. The shots disturbed the peace and her connection with nature, but she assumed it was a huntsman going about his business and respected it. Her experience of this aristocratic hobby extended only to the hunting trophies that hung in the castle dining room. She still hadn't grasped that the nobility sought to affirm their inner power by constantly killing wild animals, or that the same bloodlust found its outward expression in blindly holding on to political power. Even the Emperor did it, spending the early hours of almost every day out shooting.

The sights of the gun now followed Marie, aiming first at her brow, then her heart.

Marie brushed her hand over the soft tips of the tall grass. Another shot cracked out. She jumped. The shot must have been really close.

A pheasant fell to the ground, and the hounds rushed toward it. A little later, they returned, one carrying the colorful bird, which it dropped at the feet of its master.

Vincent Zacharias was out on a morning ride, a privilege he enjoyed only rarely in Vienna, as he did not own a horse and was therefore always at the mercy of friends. Although he no longer agreed with Georg on every political issue, he nevertheless felt easy in his company.

When Vincent saw Marie in the waist-high grass, he slowed from a gallop to a trot. Hearing the hoofbeats, she turned. He jumped cheerfully down to join her.

"Hello."

"Good morning."

"May I accompany you for a while?"

"I don't mind." Marie noticed the way he approached. This was how people behaved in the outside world; they gave each other room to decide.

The gun's sights centered once again on Marie, roamed over to Zacharias, then moved back to the girl.

Vincent glanced sidelong at Marie. "You look happy."

"Do I?" Marie was surprised that anyone would notice how she was feeling.

Vincent dared not ask about her time at the opera house, and searched for something to say. They walked on in silence for a while before Marie spoke.

"Is he a relative of yours?"

"Who?" he asked in surprise.

"His Serene Highness."

"No. Frau Sacher was kind enough to put in a good word for me."

"Put in a good word for you," Marie repeated thoughtfully.

"She likes to forge connections between people, and she's very unselfish about it," Vincent explained.

Marie recalled how, as a child, all she'd known of Frau Sacher was a glimpse from where she knelt wiping the floor. She had seemed big and overpowering, but on that day when Marie left the crypt and found the courage to hand the letter to the doorman, they had been the same height.

The finger on the trigger of the hunting rifle squeezed. Another bird was hit and fell to the ground.

"You're not from Vienna, are you?" Marie asked. She liked his accent.

"From Prague," he confirmed, adding, "A day's journey from here in a carriage."

She had read about Prague in the newspaper—the capital of the crown land of Bohemia. It was amazing how many different languages were spoken in the empire. Why wasn't there a single language, Marie wondered. But it probably didn't matter. Maybe there was another language, one that went much deeper and brought out the essential. Würtner had either remained silent or prattled on; she had disliked both. She thought of those times of darkness and loneliness and suddenly felt a bond with Zacharias. "Are you homesick?"

The question came as a surprise. He simply didn't allow himself such thoughts.

"My father fell in the Battle of Königgrätz. I was born in the same year. My older brother now runs the family business. It's nothing much—a tailor's shop in the Castle District of the city. My mother died last year."

Marie nodded. From the way he spoke, he didn't seem particularly happy; maybe he saw himself too much as a victim of circumstance. She patted the stallion's sleek neck. "I've never ridden a horse."

He reached out a hand and helped her mount. She felt clumsy at first, but gradually found she could sit more securely. He led her by the bridle across the meadow and along the lane to the stables.

Josef von Traunstein pulled the trigger one last time. Another pheasant was hit and fell to the ground, and the dogs once again set off after it.

In the house, Georg and Konstanze were sitting at breakfast with their daughters. "Afterward, you'll go to the stables with Nanny and take care of your ponies. Your riding teacher's waiting for you, Rosa," Konstanze told her eldest daughter.

"I want to ride, too!" Irma cried out.

"You're still too small, Irma."

Konstanze always arranged the children's day strictly; after all, she had to make sure her writing wasn't disturbed. Georg never criticized her methods, and he left all the decisions regarding the children to her. He still remembered well how his mother had always wanted the best for him and had known cleverly how to assert herself against his father. She had died far too early, as had Konstanze's father. The experience of loss was one thing the couple had in common, and both silently hoped it was something their children would never have to go through.

Vincent and Marie entered exuberantly after their ride. Irma clapped her hands and stretched her arms out to Marie. Konstanze looked on with envy.

"We've been searching the house for you, Marie," she said, her voice betraying her displeasure.

Georg affected a determined good humor. "No wonder you didn't find her. She was out enjoying the fresh air."

Marie kissed her sisters' hair and stood to one side, a look of amusement on her face.

"More than anything else," Konstanze said, feeling challenged, "she needs to learn how to behave like a young lady."

Vincent moved to Marie's side. The change in atmosphere had unsettled him. "It's my fault. I took up Marie's time."

"I'm a free person, and no one takes up my time if I don't want them to," Marie said firmly.

Georg had to suppress a smile as Vincent realized with some surprise that Marie was not the helpless creature he had thought her to be. Rosa and Irma sensed that a new force had entered the household with Marie, and they looked at her in awe.

"Well, my dear child, as a guest in our house, you'll have to do what you're told," Konstanze said.

Her attitude seemed out of place—she was only six years older than Marie, after all.

"Darling, please," Georg murmured, clearly embarrassed.

Josef von Traunstein appeared in his hunting clothes. Marie watched the butler help him out of his coat. As he did so, a blue velvet pouch fell from a pocket. The butler picked it up and gave it to the prince, who put it back in his jacket pocket. Marie stared. The old man returned her gaze coldly, then sat down. A servant poured him a coffee. Another left to fetch the prince's breakfast. The old man flapped open a napkin, hungry after a morning of ceaseless killing.

"This looks like a harmonious gathering," he said acidly.

Georg turned to Vincent. "After breakfast, I'd like to introduce you to the village schoolteacher."

"I'd love to come with you," Marie said quickly. "With your permission, Your Serene Highness," she added, looking at Konstanze.

Before his wife could disagree, Georg said affectionately, "You don't mind, do you?"

Konstanze went along with the day's arrangements to save herself from losing face. "I've arranged for the dressmaker to come and see Marie after lunch, and her French teacher will be here at six."

Marie appeared to relent, though she knew she had the upper hand. "I'll be home at midday as you wish, Your Serene Highness."

The servant brought the prince salted venison and a carafe of heavy red wine. Traunstein began to eat.

"Tender," he said. "A clean shot. Good death. It's essential," he continued, without looking at anyone.

The nanny came to fetch Rosa and Irma.

"I want Marie to play with me," Irma demanded.

Rosa always wanted to have the same as her sister and complained loudly. "Thief!"

Marie nodded conspiratorially to them both. "Later."

The girls left cheerfully. Vincent, Georg, and Marie followed not long afterward.

Konstanze was alone with her father-in-law. She broke the silence.

"It could all have turned out a lot worse."

"It's bad enough already, Stanzerl, very bad." He shoveled his breakfast into his mouth and washed it down with red wine. She was about to say something, but he interrupted her fiercely. "Keep your thoughts on the subject to yourself in the future."

She swallowed. The reprimand had been harsh. Why did everyone in this house think they could treat her like a stupid girl? She was Princess von Traunstein, in charge of the household. And they all lived off the money she had brought to the marriage.

Konstanze thought wistfully of Vienna. She could move around freely there and be herself. She thought about Martha and how they had laughed together. Shame and pain sank over her as she thought of her dalliance with Maximilian and how she had probably destroyed the best thing in her life.

34

"It's just not working. I need to get my hands on a couple of parts." Menning slid out from beneath the printing press. He could no longer bear the tension that had plagued the Aderholds since their return from Vienna.

Martha and Maximilian were both at their desks, editing manuscripts.

"OK, Menning. You might as well leave early," Martha called from her desk.

Absorbed in his work, Maximilian merely muttered, "Have a good evening."

Menning picked up his bag. "Same to you!"

From the corner of his eye he saw them each concentrating tensely on their work. Martha turned a page, made a note, turned back.

Without taking his eyes from his manuscript, Maximilian reached for a cigarette. Menning shook his head, put on his jacket and cap, and left.

Martha continued with her work as the scratching of Maximilian's pencil pervaded the silence. He stared at the cracked wood of the desktop. He'd had enough. "I hate this." With a sweep of his hand, he brushed the pile of manuscripts to the floor. "Why don't you just have it out with me?"

It was a cry of despair. Martha looked up and saw him start to gather the papers, some of which had torn. His fevered shuffling was damaging the pages even further. She stood to help him, and they brought order to the chaos without speaking. Noticing that the paper was damp with tears, Martha paused.

"I always have to ruin everything," he said. His despair moved her, and on impulse she reached out to touch his face. He took her hand and kissed it, first the back, then the palm, now moist with his tears. Desire flamed up inside him, and he drew her to him. She allowed herself to be swept up; his stormy embrace was doing her good. He lifted her onto the workbench, and they made love passionately next to the cases of lead type. When they opened their eyes, they saw the letters used to form words, to write sentences, to transfer stories onto paper for posterity.

The alcohol was having an effect. Maximilian, shirt open, feet bare, waved the bottle of cheap liquor he had taken from Menning's locker.

"Menning! What a good, loyal soul," he said with a thick tongue. "You can always rely on him."

He handed Martha the bottle. Dressed in nothing but Maximilian's jacket, she was sitting in the old leather armchair. She gulped from the bottle, shuddered, and handed it back to him. He drank and shuddered, too.

"Now, let's really start," he said, taking another swig before handing back the bottle.

"Perhaps Father was right. I should work less," she thought aloud, then drank.

"I'll take the weight from your shoulders. I'll only start writing again once we have a child. When our son has come into the world."

Martha laughed cheerfully. "You want to take over from me to give yourself an excuse not to write."

"Precisely! Things are going to be different around here. We'll do everything differently so that nothing like this can happen again." Maximilian grabbed the bottle, drank, and resumed cheerfully, "Martha, I know we're going to have a son."

She took the bottle for herself. The liquor tasted better with every sip. "I wanted to keep Lina Stein for myself," she said, her own words coming thickly now.

Maximilian nodded. "Didn't work, as Menning would say."

"No." Martha sighed, took another swig, and handed him the bottle.

"Yes!" he said, drinking deeply as if to confirm his statement.

"You know what?" She gestured expansively. "I'm going to drop Lina Stein!"

"Why you? No, I'll drop her. But"—Maximilian raised an index finger in a drunken warning—"she shouldn't be dropped from our publishing house. Or . . . ?"

"No! Under no circumstances," Martha said, as clearly as she was able. It seemed a long time ago that she'd been hurt. The wound was healing. With the euphoria of a convalescent on the mend, Martha snuggled into Maximilian's arms. He stroked her hair, lost in thought.

"We made Lina Stein great. She made us great. So that means, in a way, we're even." He hugged Martha to him happily.

Death, who had been present at their reconciliation, took in the sharp smell of printer's ink and turpentine. Oh, how all this stimulated the senses! You could become envious of life. Then he evaporated though the wooden door of the print shop and blew across the courtyard, past the chestnut tree with its branches reaching as far as the third floor.

35

Konstanze was finding it hard to concentrate on her new novel. There was nothing she wanted more than to make rapid progress, but her thoughts kept wandering from Martha to Maximilian, and to the past few years during which she had been involved with the press. Was she still? Did they still want her there? What would be the point of her life if she were no longer able to publish? Of course, she could always find another publisher. But she didn't want another.

Added to this, Marie Stadler's presence was getting on her nerves. In the beginning, Konstanze's magnanimous gesture to adopt Georg's illegitimate child into the family had given their relationship a new glow. Georg was very accommodating toward Konstanze, and she could sense that he saw her with different eyes. But she couldn't pretend for long. The tension between her and Marie grew with every day that passed.

Rosa and Irma followed the older girl around like little dogs. They had no idea that she was related to them, but they seemed to be confirming the received wisdom that blood is thicker than water.

Georg's friends enjoyed sweet-talking the young woman, who had bloomed during her weeks at Traunstein House. Marie was no great beauty; the years lived beneath the opera house had made sure of that. But she was interesting, and her eyes were so intense that she seemed to be looking into a person's very soul. The recipient of Marie's gaze felt either uplifted or repelled, depending on her mood. It was as though she saw everything and understood it all. It frightened Konstanze.

In fact, Marie was trying to understand the meaning behind her fate. At first, she, the daughter of a coal merchant, had been a cleaner at the Hotel Sacher, and then she had languished, neither dead nor alive, in a crypt. And now she was living in a mansion, and her every wish was granted. But none of that meant anything to her. She wanted to understand the connections.

If her forefathers had possessed a power—an inviolable power determined by their bloodline, that raised them above the lives of others—then she also had that power, since their blood flowed in her veins.

Würtner had been right. She was a chosen one. But it applied even more in her case than to her natural father and grandfather and all the previous generations. For Marie had their blood—but she had also survived death.

Konstanze had struggled with her writing for a few hours but had made no worthwhile progress. She wandered through the house in the still of night. The children had been asleep for hours. Her father-in-law and Georg were in Vienna. She saw a light coming from the library that could only be Marie. Konstanze's first instinct was to turn the other way, but curiosity got the better of her. She entered the room and acted as though she were looking for a book.

Marie affected complete indifference toward her. The two women secretly observed one another in the silent room, until Konstanze could hold out no longer. She went over to Marie and looked over her shoulder to see what she was reading.

"It's a volume of records of our family." Marie held up her fingertips, which were covered in dust. "Hasn't been looked at for ages."

"I am a woman of the present," Konstanze said. She glanced at a page adorned with the family coat of arms, then reached for a reference book from the shelf to back up her pretense.

"'Today is a result of yesterday. We have to find out what this person wanted if we want to know that person's intentions,'" Marie said, quoting Heinrich Heine.

"Did he teach you a lot? Würtner?"

"Our Empress adored Heine's writings. It was there for all to read in the newspaper." Marie snapped the book shut. "Did you know her personally?" she asked with interest.

This could have been the moment for the two women to lay down their arms, open up to one another, and guide their relationship in a new direction.

But Konstanze replied dismissively, "The Empress was very self-absorbed. She snubbed the court far too often . . . Did you see her at the opera?"

Konstanze took another random book from the shelf, failing to notice Marie's disappointment, which she concealed with a laugh.

"I won't tell you anything about my time there, Your Serene Highness," she said sharply.

"Really? Why not?" Konstanze opened the book and feigned interest in the table of contents.

Marie rose from her seat and approached Konstanze. "It was dreadful!" she said, her face contorted theatrically. Konstanze took a step back in shock. Marie followed her and continued, dramatically, "Or was it, in fact, fascinating? Würtner was so ugly. But sometimes he could be beautiful." Sobering, Marie concluded, "You should stop trying to think of ways to make me talk, Your Serene Highness."

Konstanze felt caught red-handed and gave a dismissive laugh.

Marie gave her no quarter. "Isn't that the only reason you persuaded your husband to take the poor little girl in?" Marie moved closer.

"My life is defined by sharp edges. Be careful you don't cut yourself, Stepmother."

She left. Konstanze threw the book she had been holding after her.

Outside the room, Marie heard Konstanze swearing in Hungarian. It made her blood run cold. She recalled the blue money pouch she had seen the old man carrying. She recalled her walks with Vincent Zacharias, and she thought about what her next step would be. Ever since the night of her abduction, she had grown used to thinking deeply about things.

On the day Marie left the crypt, the Empress had visited her again. She had reminded Marie that there was a lot to be done if there was ever to be justice. Marie should use all her power to smash the tissue of lies about the power of blood and the cycle of marriages and births in the name of an eternal authority. Marie was her partner, the Empress had said. A partner who could finally secure freedom—a life without the interference of men, men who made women ill and robbed them of their strength by cleaving to their bodies like vampires and giving them children who in turn would cleave to their bodies, first to their breasts and then their hearts and souls. While caught in this cycle, a woman could never be free.

And then the great professors came along and submitted women to psychological analysis. When women could no longer bear the feeling of being locked away in their bodies and the conventions of their lives, and cried or screamed for freedom, they diagnosed hysteria. As long as men had so much power, the Empress had told her, and women allowed them to hold it, even promoting it in their sons, the world would never be healthy. But you, Marie Stadler, you will see clearly and think clearly, and you will take power for yourself.

At the time, Marie had not understood what she was saying. But now she was beginning to seek the way, the key to carrying out her instructions. She recalled "Mary's Child," the fairy tale from her first book. About the girl who was not allowed to use the key. And Marie realized that anyone who holds a key must use it—must find the lock it fits and open it.

36

Anna Sacher was proud of her Sacher boys' development in the same way a mother takes pride in her own sons' progress. Vincent Zacharias was one of her most hardworking and ambitious protégés. She had taken him under her wing when he was still an insignificant doctoral student, a newcomer to Vienna without a steady income. Anna had demonstrated her insight into human nature when she introduced Zacharias to Prince von Traunstein.

This was the first time Zacharias had sought her out of his own accord. He must want something important. So Anna received him, not in a passing exchange of words in the foyer as she usually did, but over a glass of cognac in her office.

Vincent lit her cigar, and she relished the first inhalation of the Virginia tobacco.

"You're not smoking? I hope you're not ill." She regarded him intently. "But I can see you're not. The fresh air at Traunstein House is clearly doing you good."

Vincent nodded. "Country life has made an impression on me." He had given a lot of thought to leaving the ministry again and working as an administrator on the estate, as well as devoting time to teaching the children in the village school and offering adult classes there in the evenings.

Anna couldn't share the young man's enthusiasm. "Country life has its romantic appeal. But without the necessary capital, an aristocrat can soon become a peasant."

Vincent summoned his courage. "I'd like to ask a favor of you, ma'am."

Anna nodded kindly, her curiosity awakened.

"You know Marie Stadler, don't you?" He hesitated briefly, then came straight to the point. "I'd like to ask for her hand in marriage."

Anna recalled the sight of the girl leaving her letter for Prince von Traunstein at the reception desk. She had no idea what it had contained. Of course, there were rumors, but the princess had made sure the public knew the story that they were taking in the poor girl to bring her some justice after those years of imprisonment. But there were still doubts surrounding the Stadler girl; after all, no one knew exactly what she had experienced during her time in the bowels of the opera house. And now Zacharias wanted to abandon his career to marry her. Anna Sacher enshrouded herself in cigar smoke.

Faced with her silence, Vincent continued, "I have a lot to be grateful to His Serene Highness for, and so I don't dare present my request to him personally."

"If you marry the Stadler girl, you won't be able to pursue your career in court," Anna replied calmly.

Vincent nodded with a guilty conscience.

"So what do you intend to live off as a married man?"

"They're looking for legal assistants in the courts." He said nothing about his idea of living and working at Traunstein House; that was something he wanted to discuss with Georg in person.

Anna Sacher sighed. "I suppose my Sacher boys have to grow up sometime."

Vincent looked at her, full of hope. Was that a yes? Would she put in a word for him? She offered him the cigar box again. "You shouldn't forgo everything you enjoy."

Vincent hesitated. He wanted to be free to live life as a simple man, in love and surrounded by the natural world.

Anna Sacher nodded encouragingly. "I'll see to it that things turn out well for you."

Succumbing to temptation, he reached for a cigar. It would be his last.

Anna watched with satisfaction as her protégé enjoyed his first inhalation.

37

Nothing could touch them now. Martha thought about it almost every day, and about the difficult early years of their marriage. They had made mistakes, both of them. One lie breeds another, her mother had always told her. Martha reproached herself for obeying Konstanze's wish and not letting Maximilian in on the mystery. She and Konstanze had loved their secret and the author they had brought into the world, agreeing she should belong to the two of them and only them. And it had ended with Maximilian falling in love with Lina Stein.

The water came to a boil, and she began making the coffee. Hedwig came in from shopping, bringing fresh rolls and the mail.

"Wait until the greengrocer comes, Hedwig, and then you can go," Martha said, still in her dressing gown.

"Thank you, Frau Aderhold."

Martha nodded happily. "You're welcome." She knew Hedwig spent her free time with her sister, who had a big family. A big family! Was that what she wanted, too—a big family? Martha was no longer so sure about that. She enjoyed having Maximilian to herself. She spoiled him. And his love for her was so carefree, just as she had always wanted it. Martha tucked the mail between the coffeepot and the breadbasket. Since their reconciliation, they had often indulged in lazy mornings over breakfast in bed.

Martha took the tray and returned to the bedroom, trilling, *"Oh, Theophil, oh, Theophil, you were my whole world"* from the operetta *Frau Luna*. She danced over to the bed with the tray. Maximilian had the presence of mind to rescue the coffeepot. *"Oh, Theophil, oh, Theophil, why have you left me out in the cold?"* Martha performed an exuberant pirouette before finally setting the tray down, to Maximilian's great relief.

A little later they were sitting in bed, drinking coffee and smothering the bread with preserves. Martha looked through the mail; mostly bills, with the exception of one letter. She opened it with a frown.

Maximilian pointed at the window; it had begun to snow. "We could go for a walk in the Tiergarten after breakfast, build a snowman," he said with his mouth full. When Martha failed to respond, he turned to her in surprise. "What's bothering you?"

"The Traunsteins are inviting us to the Sacher for New Year's Eve." She handed him the letter. It was from Konstanze.

> . . . *I can't stop thinking about our summer at Traunstein House. How you gave me the courage to break down the barriers in my life. You opened my eyes, Martha, and I can't thank you enough for it. Please, let us be friends again. Maybe the start of the new century is the right time to do so.*

38

"1900." Mayr was directing the decoration activities. The restaurant was being transformed into a ballroom for the evening. Four young bellhops were perched on ladders, each holding one of the glittering silver numbers, ready to fix them in place according to his instructions.

"Up a bit with that zero!" Mayr commanded. "No, the other zero!"

The boys did their best, but still it didn't look right. Mayr sighed and tried new variations.

In the corridor outside the private dining rooms, Wagner had the junior waiters lined up in front of him and was checking their hands and nails for cleanliness, looking to see that their hair was neat and their shoes shiny. Anna Sacher arrived and took charge of the team. Wagner could see she was satisfied, which pleased him, too.

A bellhop came to inform his employer of Annie's arrival. "Your daughter is sitting with your son-in-law in the foyer."

Anna nodded. "I'll be right there." She studied the *1900*. "Mayr, the zeroes look like the symbol for the staff toilets."

Mayr blushed. He was easily wounded by criticism of himself or his work.

"Maybe you could hang the zeroes slightly offset from one another," she suggested. "What do you think?"

"Very well, ma'am. Offset upward or downward?" he asked enthusiastically. Maybe that was the solution for the incredibly lackluster image those numbers presented. They lacked dignity. But it had to be done; they had to celebrate the arrival of the twentieth century. Even in the Hotel Sacher, the future could not be welcomed without a compromise or two.

Anna Sacher had no further suggestions for Mayr's problem and merely left with the instruction "Make sure it looks good!"

"Very well!" Mayr bowed, catching Wagner's gloating expression behind his employer's back. Did Wagner think he'd simply give in? Mayr took a few steps back and suddenly—he always came into his own under pressure—he knew what to do. It was not the zeroes that were responsible for the unsatisfactory appearance. "The nine looks like an upside-down six," he called out to the boy holding the number in question. "You, with the upside-down six, come here. Now let's find the six . . . well, the nine."

The apprentice climbed down from the stepladder. There began at once a search of the floor, where numbers for all occasions lay scattered. It was a matter of perfection. That was Mayr's purpose in life, and he would never be diverted from it. Never! Not even in death, he thought.

On the way to meet her daughter and son-in-law, Anna passed through the potpourri of her guests' languages. Russian, Polish, Czech, Serbian, Hungarian, Austrian, Yiddish. Vienna was truly a melting pot. Even those who kept a distrustful distance in Austria's multiracial empire came together in the Hotel Sacher.

Anna dispensed smiles of greeting left and right as she went. Many of the men were officers in uniform, while the ladies glittered in their family jewels. Some were still tight-laced in the previous years' fashions, while others followed the current trend for styles without rigid bodices.

A little dog in a diamanté collar jumped up at Anna, followed by the rest of the pack. Decked out for New Year's Eve with silver and gold ribbons and bow ties, her darlings were delighting the guests by seeking out their favors beneath tables and chairs.

Anna finally reached her daughter and son-in-law. The young lieutenant was now a mature, lean man with spectacles and a mustache.

"Annie, darling," she said warmly, noticing critically that her daughter was pregnant again.

Julius Schuster Jr. rose and kissed his mother-in-law's hand.

"How are your parents?" Anna asked, her casual tone belying her eagerness to hear whether Schuster Sr. had sent his greetings and whether he would be attending the party—without his wife, of course.

"Very well, thank you, ma'am. Father sends his greetings and regrets to inform you that he has to stay at home tonight. He'll be sure to visit soon in the new year," Schuster Jr. said impassively. Annie wouldn't meet her mother's eyes. All three knew the true nature of the relationship.

Anna made light of her disappointment, bending down to caress her dogs. She straightened, once again the master of the house, and turned to her daughter. "So, are you enjoying your little dog?"

Her question momentarily dispelled the tension. They all understood one another. Annie hugged her dog close. "She's an absolute sweetheart. Now that she's stopped piddling in every corner, she's making us very happy."

Anna's son-in-law ruffled the dog's coat tenderly. "You're a sweet girl, aren't you?"

Eduard arrived and gave his mother an exaggerated bow. "Hello, Frau Sacher." He had been drinking already. "My dear sister! Oh, and you've brought the boy along, too!" Eduard tweaked the nose of his brother-in-law, who was in fact several years older than he.

"For goodness' sake, stop it, Eduard," Annie said in the voice of an older sister.

Anna found her children's affectations embarrassing. "You've been drinking!" she snapped at Eduard, and waved at a waiter to bring a mocha.

"The new year's just around the corner, and I intend to start as I mean to go on." Eduard giggled foolishly.

The bulldogs sensed their owner's agitation and made for Eduard's trouser legs. He shook them off.

"Stupid creatures." The waiter came with the mocha. "I need a whisky," Eduard barked at him. "Now!" He almost knocked the tray from the waiter's hands in his drunkenness. Annie grabbed his arm at the last moment.

"Don't make a scene. If you intend to, you can all leave right now," Anna hissed to her children.

"Do you really think I'd do you that favor?" Eduard babbled cheerfully.

Anna walked away. God knew she had better things to be doing this evening than letting her spoiled brats wind her up.

Eduard watched her go in amusement. "Poor Papa died because of her hideous nature."

"You're such a beast." Annie hated it when her mother got angry. She so wanted a happy family.

Eduard grinned shamelessly. "So I am! Like mother, like son." He snatched a glass of champagne from the tray of a waiter who was hurrying past.

The guests kept streaming in. Anna Sacher greeted Konstanze and Georg von Traunstein, who had brought Marie Stadler. "You're most welcome, Your Serene Highnesses." Anna looked at Marie, feigning surprise. "My, how you've grown! Life's treating you well now, I've heard."

Marie simpered, affecting a false girlish smile, at the old *my-how-you've-grown* chestnut. Konstanze noticed and raised her eyebrows, exchanging a knowing look with Anna Sacher.

Vincent Zacharias approached them. He had been waiting for the Traunsteins and Marie to arrive. He saw the unnatural smile, too, and it made him uneasy. He had never seen such an expression on Marie's face. Was it a side of her character he was unaware of? But the joy of seeing her again pushed aside any doubts, and the moment, together with the thoughts it conjured, failed to take root in his consciousness. But he would soon have a decision to make, and this feeling would guide him subconsciously.

This lack of self-awareness, this instinctive behavior of individuals, peoples, nations—this was what the celebrations of the turn of the twentieth century ushered in.

~

"No, ma'am, I'm truly sorry," Mayr told Martha. "If I could, I assure you I'd gladly move heaven and earth to connect you. But I'm afraid that's not in my power."

Disappointed, she hung up the telephone. "All the lines are engaged."

Maximilian was standing in front of the mirror, knotting his tie.

"I'll have to send Father a telegram," Martha decided.

"It was a stupid idea to come to Vienna." Maximilian untied his necktie again, betraying his nerves. "Take a portion of high-society airs and graces, add three good pinches of formal atmosphere, and garnish the whole with a spoonful of silly operetta. But be careful not to overdo it," he added ironically. Martha took the two ends of the tie from his fingers and began to knot them.

As they put the finishing touches on their evening attire, they appeared to be a fine, harmonious couple. Martha was wearing a silver-gray dress that complemented her pale skin.

"We're celebrating tonight! And tomorrow we'll go to the Secession exhibition and the Grillparzer play at the Imperial Court Theater," she said with enthusiasm.

"Lessons begin at a quarter to eight. Just how I'd imagined spending the first day of the new century. My wildest dreams fulfilled, Headmistress."

The tie was now perfectly tied.

When Konstanze's invitation had arrived, they had not spoken of their feelings; everything was now going so well between them. Each of them had silently wrestled with the idea of refusing. But Maximilian had been keen not to give the impression that he wanted to avoid meeting Konstanze, as though he were unable to face it. And Martha had been unwilling to admit, above all to herself, that she had not come to terms with his infidelity. The wound had healed, but the scar still pained her.

"I'm so glad you've come." Konstanze came to meet them, her expression one of delight. Georg excused himself from Vincent and Marie to join them.

"Thank you for the invitation," Martha said formally, aware of how tense she sounded.

Georg kissed her hand. "We've missed you at Traunstein House, Martha." He turned to greet Maximilian. "I'm delighted to meet you at last. I'm sure our wives would like a moment to themselves. May I introduce you to my friends?"

Konstanze immediately linked arms with Martha without giving Maximilian so much as a word of acknowledgment. "Off you go, then," she said without looking at him. "We've got plenty to talk about."

Georg led him over to a group of men. Vincent parted reluctantly from Marie and joined them for the sake of appearances. Maximilian looked back at the women, hoping to get a glance from Konstanze, but her attention was solely on Martha.

"You will read my new book, won't you?" Konstanze asked, hoping Martha would forgive her and they could resume their friendship after the extended silence.

Martha released herself from Konstanze's arm, took a glass of champagne, and gripped it tightly.

"Please!" Konstanze kept up her attempts to win back Martha's heart. "You do want me to keep writing?"

"But you don't write for me," Martha replied, raising the glass to her lips.

Konstanze looked at Martha as though she must know that she wrote only for her. Her look tugged at Martha's heart.

"Martha . . . what happened . . . I'm sorry. Can't we put it behind us?" Konstanze asked hopefully.

The way she was so open about her feelings was what had drawn Martha to her on their first encounter in the Sacher's café, and it had increased her sympathy during her stay at Traunstein House. Konstanze was always searching for happiness. When she liked someone, she showed it. Her stories were like that, too; it was the secret of her success. Martha admired it. She herself had experienced her share of disappointment and hurt, and to protect herself from pain she had created a safe space inside herself. But to Martha, worse than getting hurt herself was to hurt another, to disappoint them or expose them. For that reason, she usually forgave more quickly than was good for her. As now.

Martha steered the conversation carefully to more neutral ground. "You say you'll have it finished in four weeks? You must have been busy."

Konstanze was relieved. "My Flora is a real treasure. She's often up until dawn copying out the manuscript."

"Maybe you could finally invest in a typewriter," Martha suggested.

"But it makes such a horrid rattling noise."

Martha looked over at Georg. He caught her eye and smiled.

"You're a very successful author. Why don't you tell him at last? You never know; your husband might be pleased."

"I don't want Traunstein to read my novels, ever," Konstanze said, horrified. "Then he'd find out what I really think."

Martha shook her head. Konstanze took this as a first sign of reconciliation.

Anna Sacher called the company to dinner. The men moved to offer their arms to their wives. Vincent Zacharias accompanied Marie Stadler.

They entered the private dining room set aside for the Traunsteins and their guests.

~

"Feel free to call on as many agents as you need. I'm giving you free rein, Gruber. Eventually we'll have something we can use against even the highest of the gentry."

Lechner pushed the informant's report into a file. The other man nodded and took the money. As he left, he bowed eagerly, several times. Lechner paid him no further attention, as the next informant was already handing over his notes. Lechner looked up in surprise.

"Is this from a trustworthy source, Pospiszil?"

The informer nodded.

"Make sure you keep an eye on those Peace Society guys! I should say so!" After listening assiduously to his superior's words and accent for so long, Lechner found himself imitating him. "If you need to travel, you'll be given expenses from now on," he said patronizingly.

Like his predecessor, Pospiszil bowed out of the office backward, hat in hand. He almost bumped into the central inspector, who already had his coat on, ready to take leave of his trusty employees both for the day and for the year.

"Don't stay too late, Lechner, my boy! I should say not!"

"Of course not! I just want to clear my desk for the new year," Lechner replied, very pleased with the impression he was giving his boss.

"But you should go out celebrating at least for a little while. I should say so!"

"I'm intending to pop out later for a beer at the Five Crowns."

The Five Crowns was a favorite haunt of the German nationalists, and stopping in there always brightened up Lechner's day. In general, he rarely socialized and was reluctant to spend money in a bar, usually preferring to stay at his desk until it was time to go home to sleep for a few hours.

"Well then, Lechner, I'll wish you a happy New Year."

Lechner clicked his heels and bowed. "Thank you, Central Inspector. The same to you and your good lady."

Lechner was alone at last. He stretched in his office chair and looked around the large room. From his lowly place in the back corner, he had progressed forward to the desk of a senior inspector. Year after year he had earned himself ever-greater respect, and he had been rewarded with promotions.

Lechner took a package from his desk, opened it, and held a calendar for 1900 in his hand. He fixed it to a suitable hook on the facing wall, fetched a bottle and a glass from the filing cabinet, and poured himself a drink. As he toasted himself, he clicked his heels again. Lechner paid tribute to himself and drank to the new century.

～

The silver numbers in the restaurant were now looking good. As Anna Sacher regarded them in satisfaction, Mayr smiled to himself thankfully.

Anna joined Georg, and Wagner served them two glasses of champagne. They clinked glasses and enjoyed a moment alone.

"I hope everything's to your liking."

"It's a wonderful celebration, as it always is, my good woman."

Anna Sacher turned her gaze to Vincent Zacharias, who was deep in earnest conversation with Marie Stadler. "Dr. Zacharias has come on well, thanks to your help, Your Serene Highness."

Georg nodded in agreement. "He's a clever man, and I admire his loyalty." Their friendship outweighed their political differences.

Anna came to the point. "Don't you agree it's time he found a wife?"

Georg frowned. Was Anna suggesting a union between Marie and Vincent? He didn't like the idea. He had noticed the growing closeness between them at Traunstein House, but had been grateful that Vincent had not hinted at any possible plans.

"A marriage that would strengthen the young man's position," Anna said, clarifying her intention somewhat. She could feel Traunstein's tension and boldly completed her thought. "And one that would give him a position of greater responsibility."

Georg wished Marie all the happiness in the world, but it did not suit Georg's plans for Vincent to marry for love, robbing himself of the prospect of a future at court. It was something he could not begin to contemplate. A marriage was a contract that should be character building and form the foundations of a future family. It should create the basis for personal affluence and power in society, a power that should be used for the good of the people.

As if he sensed they were talking about him, Vincent turned toward Anna and Georg. His eyes sparkled with the hope that they both would support his desire. He raised his glass and drank to the future with Marie.

"To everything that lies before us!"

Marie also raised her glass. "Does something lie before us?" she asked impishly. Vincent's expression spoke volumes as their glasses clinked together.

Anna Sacher sighed. "Ah, love! It can also lead to ruin."

"I'll talk to the grand master of the court about an appropriate match." Georg was grateful to Anna Sacher for bringing the matter to his attention, giving him the option of making sure his friend's future was not left to chance.

~

"It's so hot in here, isn't it?" Konstanze went to the faucet and ran cold water over her wrists. She had followed Martha into the powder room.

They had eaten, drunk, laughed, and told stories, but with midnight fast approaching, Konstanze still did not feel that Martha had forgiven her. The two women's eyes met in the mirror.

"A lovely party." Martha smiled. A waltz was being played in the ballroom, the music reaching their ears faintly.

"Tell me what I can do to make things right with you, Martha." Konstanze moved toward her. "Please!"

"Just try and do nothing for once, Konstanze." Martha's voice had its friendly tone of old.

"I can't. I can't," Konstanze said happily. Martha shook her head with a smile. Konstanze was still a child. Relieved, Konstanze put her arms around her friend and swayed in time to the music.

"I love you, Martha," Konstanze said effusively. Her voice became more subdued. "I love you as much as any person can love another." It was meant in all seriousness. She was about to tell Martha more emphatically, when three young women burst in and began to don masks and cloaks. Konstanze took Martha by the hand and led her out.

They ran into Maximilian, who was ready to leave the party and had come to look for Martha. Konstanze linked arms with him happily, and Martha went to Maximilian's other side. The two women were feeling relieved after their heart-to-heart. They pulled him into the ballroom, where the music had hushed to an anticipatory silence for the last few seconds of the old year.

"Ten, nine, eight . . ." The chorus of guests began the countdown to midnight and the start of the new century.

Glasses clinked. New Year's greetings were exchanged in a variety of languages, along with hugs and kisses to the left and right, with the widest variety of intentions: honest, loving, friendly, expected, stolen, forced. A few used the situation to obtain what was usually denied them.

The staff had also come into the restaurant—cooks, waiters, chambermaids, and even the janitor—to celebrate the festive moment.

Mayr and Wagner exchanged a look of appraisal—friendly rivalry— and clinked their glasses together.

Anna Sacher moved through the crowd, at this special moment making no distinction between guests and staff.

Georg kissed Konstanze. Maximilian kissed Martha. The two couples wished each other luck and happiness. Konstanze's expression was open again now, and included Maximilian. The music resumed with Strauss's *Emperor Waltz*. In high spirits, the couples moved onto the dance floor. One of the masked girls beckoned Maximilian to dance, and he cheerfully allowed himself to be led away. One of Georg's friends asked Konstanze to dance. The central inspector and his wife tripped past Vincent and Marie. He didn't recognize the elegant young lady.

For the first time that evening, Martha was alone with Georg.

"So you've taken Marie Stadler in," Martha remarked as she watched the others dance.

"She's not an easy person to deal with. I don't really know what I can do for her."

"Let her have her independence," replied Martha, who had no idea about the closeness that had developed between Marie and Vincent.

Her suggestion bewildered Georg.

"Perhaps she wants to learn a profession? Or study? That's something women can do now here in Vienna," Martha continued.

"Yes, we did achieve some things this century." Infected by her energy, Georg found himself swept along on a wave of joy. Maybe his time would now come. Maybe all this battling with the older generation who devoted all their power to holding the young ones back, this battling with the like-minded ones who focused on so many different formulations and lost themselves in a bewildering array of conflicting details, this battling with the workers who didn't understand that they must change, too, because they could grow only if they grew together— maybe it would all bear fruit and make way for the new. Yes, he would give Marie the opportunity to live independently. "I must admit that, surprisingly, I wouldn't find it so easy with my other daughters," Georg said. "But they're still young, thank God." He, too, would continue to grow, he thought cheerfully. And there was no telling what was yet possible.

Couples exchanged partners on the dance floor. Maximilian extended his hand to Konstanze. Martha saw and said boldly to Georg, "Will you dance with me?"

"It will be my pleasure." He led her onto the dance floor.

Maximilian was surprised by the desire he felt again for Konstanze. "Do you still think of us sometimes?"

"Of course. But I'm so glad that Georg never noticed anything and Martha has forgiven us. It could have had such a dreadful ending."

"How do you mean, dreadful? You think we might have been executed, perhaps?" Maximilian would have given anything to leave the room with Konstanze and have an open talk, but the dance now required the couples to separate and move on to new partners. Maximilian glided across to Martha.

Konstanze glided across to Georg, who was still inspired by his conversation with Martha.

"What do you think about renting an apartment for Marie in Vienna?" Georg swung Konstanze energetically in time to the waltz.

"The girl will run wild," she said immediately. "But why not?"

There would once again be peace in the house, and Marie's influence over her three daughters and the servants would come to an end. As they danced past Martha and Maximilian, Konstanze smiled at Martha. Maximilian saw. He wasn't ready for it. It hurt him. He was overcome by the need for creativity, for something that would make him feel less lost in a life he still thought of as false.

"I want to go home, Martha. I want to write, write a lot. I want—"

"Everything." Martha finished his sentence for him. She knew her husband well, maybe better than he knew himself. In their thoughts, the two of them were already on their way back to Berlin.

January 1900 was almost an hour old when Anna at last found the time to toast the future with her children. Wagner followed her with the champagne, but the sight of the young people at the edge of the room shocked them both. Annie had fallen asleep on the sofa. Schuster Jr. was greedily eating a slice of the cream torte that had been brought out at midnight, two bulldogs watching eagerly in anticipation of a morsel falling from the fork. They fell, growling, on the sweet tidbits, snuffling them up from the carpet, trouser leg, or shoe where they fell. Eduard slumped drunkenly across one of the tables, talking to himself, as Anna's favorite, little Lumpi, nibbled at the cuff of his trousers.

Anna stroked her daughter's hair. "Annie, darling, shall I have a bed made up for you?"

But Annie turned away and refused to be woken. Anna looked sheepishly at Wagner, who stood there with the tray of champagne. At that moment, the elder Julius Schuster arrived, a dusting of snowflakes on his coat, and began to greet acquaintances politely, shaking hands and wishing one and all a happy New Year. A bellboy came to take his coat. Anna took two glasses from Wagner's tray as Schuster came to meet her, smiling radiantly.

"You managed to get free?" Anna flirted.

"I stayed long enough to wish the children a happy New Year." They clinked glasses, all thoughts of children dispensed with. They had their own lives, after all.

Death was sitting on a bench by the Danube, looking out across the waves that carried the old year away. The night was still young, and he had time to ponder what was to come. There would be plenty to do. Death saw lost souls moving over ruined landscapes. He would not be able to bring them all home. There would be too many. He was momentarily comforted by the fact that all this lay in the distant future.

In the distant future, Love thought . . . only fourteen more years of peace.

BOOK 3

LOVE

39

Fourteen years had passed.

"The Sachertorte belongs here in my hotel!" Anna declared as she swept into the office, where Schuster Sr. was waiting for her with the family lawyer. She held out her hand for both men to kiss, then sat at her desk. "Without so much as a word to me, Eduard has opened a coffeehouse just a few hundred yards from here, and he's damaging the torte's exclusivity."

"Your son isn't doing anything wrong, Anna," Schuster said, attempting to pacify her.

"Then have it declared wrong. The Sachertorte will be sold here, and only here."

Anna looked challengingly at the lawyer, who cleared his throat.

"Maybe we could first seek a peaceable solution. A way of settling family differences. Of course, I'll do all I can to help with that, ma'am." The lawyer glanced at Schuster, who tried to soften Anna's mood.

"Listen, it would attract a lot of attention if you were to take legal proceedings against your son, Anna." Schuster offered her a light for her cigar. "No one in this city would prefer Eduard's coffeehouse to your Hotel Sacher."

"Fair enough. He won't get any customers." Anna drew on her cigar. "But it's a matter of principle, Julius. Eduard has always stood against me. And now he's trying to get at me with this." She was determined to pursue a case against her son, and nothing they said that afternoon could deter her.

"I'm relying on you," she said, unyielding, as she bid the lawyer farewell. As he left, the lawyer threw Schuster a final glance, pleading with him to make Anna Sacher see reason. The door closed behind him. Anna turned to Schuster.

"My Annie would never have done such a thing. You know what she said once, when she was little? 'Mama, I want to stay with you forever.'"

Moved by the memory, Anna looked at the photo of her daughter she kept on her desk. "And now she's been dead for over twelve years . . . chose death over life . . . like her father." Anna rubbed a fingerprint from the picture frame with her lace handkerchief. "Have you heard anything from our grandchildren in Silesia? Since your wife died, we've hardly heard from your son."

"The eldest has her confirmation this year," Schuster replied.

"Oh, really?" Anna stood, went over to a sideboard, and poured two sherries.

They raised their glasses.

"The grandchildren aren't allowed to come and visit me. Annie said too many bad things about the Sacher, and their new mother doesn't seem too keen, either," Anna complained.

"Do you want to be at the confirmation?"

"You go, Julius. I can't get away, in any case. Especially not now, with Eduard . . ." She trailed off.

"The best thing would be for me to have a serious word with your son," Schuster said. "He should be making himself useful here in the hotel. You're going to need a successor, Anna. He might yet prove up to the job."

"Not Eduard!" Anna was horrified by the idea.

Schuster sighed. He regularly tried to resolve the confrontations between mother and son, and was given the brush-off just as regularly.

Anna stood and smoothed her dress. Schuster rose, too. They had been a couple for over twenty years now, and he knew she was itching to get back to work. He kissed her hands. "Do you remember our special day?"

She smiled. "How could I forget?"

Vincent Zacharias was sitting in the foyer, reading a paper. When he saw Anna Sacher coming, he stood to greet her.

She looked at him, her eyes radiating goodwill. "Baron von Zacharias, how are you? And your wife and children?"

"We can't complain, thank you."

"I'm always pleased to see one of my protégés doing well," she said with satisfaction. Vincent bowed courteously. The distance between them had increased over the years.

He had been married for more than a decade now, and was the father of a son and two daughters. The financial worries of his early years in Vienna were a thing of the past.

Georg von Traunstein approached. Johann, now a man in his early forties with the first signs of gray in his hair, followed with his bag.

Georg extended his hand to Anna Sacher. "I'm pleased to see you, ma'am."

"The pleasure is all mine, Your Serene Highness."

Georg gave Johann a generous tip. "Please have our luggage sent to the station. We'll be catching the late train to Berlin." He turned to Vincent. "I've a family matter to see to. Will you come with me? We can go from there straight to the station."

As the two men took their leave, Anna Sacher wished them a pleasant journey and took Vincent's hand. "Bring your family back here soon for a meal."

Vincent nodded, something about his manner indicating that he would not be accepting her invitation. Anna watched them both leave, her eyes wistful. But she always made every effort to do the best for the people who put their trust in her, to help them and give them every support.

40

The visitors sat informally on scattered armchairs and dining chairs in the unconventional atmosphere of two rooms divided by a sliding door. The assortment of furniture, ornaments, bric-a-brac, pictures, and curtain fabrics was more an indication of a passion for collecting than of good taste. Coffee and punch were served, and those present were smoking self-importantly. The salon was again well attended that afternoon.

Marie Stadler, by now a little over thirty, was at the center of the group. She was wearing a light, loose-fitting dress in the modern style, and the girl next to her was dressed similarly. The outward appearance of the two, as well as the way they moved and spoke, marked them unmistakably as sisters.

The speaker, a woman of around fifty in a high-necked black dress, was unctuously bringing her reading to a close. ". . . the reverberation of that past wisdom for which this country was renowned can still be felt; the endless echo of humans' desire to excel. Maybe our growing consciousness of the common ground and mutual dependence inherent in all forms of our thinking will enable us to find this wisdom again."

She paused for a suspense-filled moment. Then she snapped the Helena Blavatsky book shut.

The audience applauded rapturously. The Russian philosopher's books, and her thoughts on the human spirit, often formed the basis for the discussions in Stadler's salon. The attendees debated emotional sensitivities and believed they were in a time of decline, from the ruins of which a new, glorious world would arise. Echoing the style of the apartment, the theories expressed here came in all shapes and sizes.

Marie enjoyed leading her guests' discussions. She, on the other hand, never committed herself. She held the golden key. Whether and when she used it remained to be seen.

Lechner, dressed as ever in his worn suit, sat to one side and watched the activity with amusement. He wanted to be seen as an outsider at the meeting and deliberately clapped out of time.

A harpist began an improvised rendition of celestial music, and a bare-foot young dancer floated in from the side room. Her nakedness was covered by nothing but a white sheet and her hip-length dark hair. Her shoulder was adorned with a striking tattoo of the Indian sun wheel, which in a few years would become the swastika, the symbol of Fascist aggression.

Lechner leaned over to the girl at Marie's side. "Don't your parents mind you coming here and discussing politics, Fräulein von Traunstein?"

"Leave Irma be, Lechner," Marie said, coming to her sister's aid. "Take no notice of him."

"The inspector's entitled to ask," Irma said. "I don't have to answer."

Lechner cheerfully lit a cigarette.

"Anyway, it's not politics, but theosophy," she added.

"Parents should count themselves lucky if their children concern themselves with important issues, don't you think?" Marie said.

"Provided their children don't outgrow them." Lechner indicated two visitors being shown in by the maid.

Irma stayed stubbornly in her chair.

"Good evening," Georg said brightly to the assembled company.

"God's blessing, Marie," Vincent said, using the traditional Austrian greeting. They hadn't seen each other for a long time, and he was surprised how self-possessed and clever she had become.

"We prefer simply to wish one another a good evening here," Marie replied coolly. She had lost all trace of her dialect, and there was nothing left of the girl from the crypt. "Do take a seat. We're involved in a discussion of whether a war that ultimately leads to a radical disruption of the status quo to produce something better is not only justified, but even necessary," she said, summing up their topic for the afternoon.

"No such war is possible," Georg replied. He and Vincent remained on their feet.

"Do you believe that the origin of the cosmos and the course of evolution were free from violence?" Marie asked provocatively.

"We're not living in the hell of the cosmos, but in paradise, known as the earth. A place where the old should be able to exist alongside the new, and vice versa. But I'm afraid we don't have much time to pursue the conversation further. Irma, are you coming?"

Irma folded her arms. "It's so interesting."

Lechner took a notebook from an inside jacket pocket and leafed through it. "You should go with your father, Princess. He's in a hurry. He probably wants to catch the late train to Berlin."

Georg refused to be provoked, his gaze remaining steadfastly on Irma. She responded stubbornly, "Herr Lechner, as a police agent, you must know that I view the world completely differently from the way my family does. In any case, my father's always in a hurry."

Marie reached out to Irma and pulled her from the armchair. "Be a good girl, now, Irma."

Georg gave Marie a grateful smile. Irma followed her father reluctantly.

Marie and Vincent stood facing one another.

Lechner watched the encounter closely while feigning interest in the contents of his notebook.

"Your salon's the talk of the town," Vincent said with restraint.

Marie laughed. "People are interested in a woman first for her air of mystery and secondly for her mind."

"I'm not people," Vincent said. "And I regret that I'll never get to know either."

He longed for a look, a gesture, to indicate that Marie understood the decision he had made years ago.

Years ago . . . Shortly after that New Year's Eve, Vincent had visited Marie one last time at Traunstein House. She had assumed he had come to ask for her hand in marriage, but instead he had come to say goodbye and to explain that he saw his future above all with the Bohemian people, that their fight was his, that this was his mission and the reason, deep down, he had come from Prague to Vienna. Marie regarded him thoughtfully as he spoke. With every word he felt increasingly embarrassed and traitorous. At the end of his long monologue, Marie stood, went to the piano, and searched the music for a sheet, which she handed him.

"Goodbye, Herr Zacharias," she said matter-of-factly. "I used to like singing this song with lyrics by Goethe. I always felt that there would never be peace in my life, that I was not born to enjoy happiness in the conventional sense. You have a mission, as you say. It gives me the strength to search for my own." Marie looked at him calmly and waited for him to go.

She was no different now, her smile frozen into an impenetrable, detached mask.

Lechner turned to Vincent. "So, you're on your way to Berlin?"

"Good evening, Herr Lechner." Vincent regarded him coolly. Lechner gave him a moment to get his feelings back under control.

"Will you be meeting the liberals there, the ones we have under particular observation?" Lechner, too, had dropped most of the traces of his local dialect.

Marie reprimanded him sternly. "Fritz!"

Lechner yielded. "Very well, ma'am."

Vincent took his leave with a curt bow before following Georg and Irma.

"What good people," Lechner commented. "And to think he chose another before you. Jews, hey?"

Marie hit him with her fan and asked in an amused tone, "Do you want to avenge me, perhaps, Herr Inspector?"

"I certainly do, Marie. After all, I rescued you from Würtner."

Marie did not contradict him. She knew she could rely on him.

~

On the way to Berlin, Georg and Vincent spoke little, each lost in his own thoughts.

Georg had noticed how much his friend was troubled by his encounter with Marie. As he saw it, they both had everything they needed for meaningful and settled lives. He certainly did not share many of his eldest daughter's views. But that wasn't necessary. He was more concerned by the fact that his relationship with Vincent had become increasingly difficult. Their points of view on matters such as how to deal with the current situation in the country, and in Europe, were moving farther and farther apart. It was only seldom now that the old feeling of earnest debate resurfaced.

Vincent was still brooding over his brief encounter with Marie.

It had not been until he was on her doorstep that he had realized he would see her. He should have waited in the carriage. But his curiosity had been greater than any concern that old feelings might erupt to the surface.

41

The old Prince von Traunstein had grown frail. His hand shook as he took a cigar from the wooden case Wagner offered him.

Erdmannsdorf, the central inspector, the chief of police, and Traunstein had met for lunch at the Sacher, and were now enjoying a mocha.

"I hear your son's in Berlin, meeting with members of the German Peace Society," Erdmannsdorf said, moving the conversation on to the reason they were there as he took the first few puffs of his cigar.

"Georg has become infatuated with the European idea," the old prince groaned. He exchanged a look with his friend Erdmannsdorf and struggled to his feet. "Please excuse me, gentlemen."

The old man reached for the stick hanging over the back of his chair and left the room. He would accept no responsibility for anything they went on to talk about—a man should keep his hands clean where family matters were concerned.

"We feel that the young Prince von Traunstein's political ambitions are a cause for concern. Equal rights for all the peoples of the crown lands. A European league of nations. Peace at any cost." Erdmannsdorf did not hesitate to get to the point.

"A policy that's music to the ears of the Socialists," the central inspector blustered.

Erdmannsdorf shook his head pensively. "You do understand that I can't approve direct action against the prince?"

"Of course," the central inspector replied immediately.

An eloquent silence followed.

"You could single out one of the prince's group of cronies." The chief of police took up the thread. "Someone who . . . shall we say . . . isn't explicitly associated with the Emperor . . . but who's conspicuous for his radical political ideas." He spoke in measured tones, as though he were philosophizing on a matter that had no practical relevance.

Erdmannsdorf shrouded himself in cigar smoke, as though he could make himself disappear from the conversation.

"Suspicion of a conspiracy between Jews and Freemasons?" the central inspector suggested, building on his superior's idea.

The chief of police threw him a look of surprise at this level of creativity. The central inspector misinterpreted the look and explained hurriedly, "Don't misunderstand me; I believe the suspicion of such a thing already exists. Some names have been brought to our attention."

The three fell silent, allowing what had just been said to sink in. They all had a mutual interest: to prevent change. To preserve the status quo.

Josef von Traunstein returned.

"Well now, my esteemed prince, I think a father has a part to play in the times that are upon us," the central inspector said loudly and jovially.

"As far as I know, you have only daughters," Traunstein replied caustically as he took his seat.

"Believe me, the females have all gone mad since this Schnitzler's been allowed to get away with murder in his plays."

"And he's a Jew, to cap it all," Erdmannsdorf added scornfully.

"The people are tearing apart the very land that would keep them safe." The aging prince stared bitterly into space, where his old eyes saw the decline of the world.

Wagner arrived with whisky. They drank to the health of the Emperor and the continuation of the empire.

Late that evening, the central inspector found Lechner in his office. Inspector Lechner now had his own room.

The central inspector leafed through the files that Lechner handed him. "Zacharias. A Bohemian nationalist?"

"And spy. I've reported on several occasions that he's been seen meeting suspects." Lechner stiffened his back, suppressing the impulse to bow. "However, the baron's a protégé of the young Traunstein."

The central inspector closed the files and rose to his feet. "That's no longer a problem."

Now Lechner did bow. The hour he had been working tirelessly toward had finally arrived.

42

"I'll negotiate a good price for Father's house, and at the end of the week I'll seek his banker's advice about how we should invest the money." Martha gathered up the manuscripts she had selected to read on the journey, and put them in her bag.

Maximilian helped her into her coat. "I won't touch a penny of your father's inheritance."

"You don't need to worry about a thing, Max. I'm the one who manages the money, and you won't even know which pot we're drawing from." Martha was no longer willing to tolerate Maximilian's childish rejection of anything to do with her father.

The cracks in their fragile relationship had started to show after his affair with Konstanze. In the early years, they had been willing to ignore the notes of discord, but as time went by, the infidelity sounded harshly like a false note struck on the strings of their life together. The harmony of their love no longer rang true.

"I'll wire you when I've finalized everything in Bremen." She kissed him on the cheek, picked up her luggage, and crossed the print shop to the door.

"Bye, Menning," she said to the heart and soul of the press.

"Have a good trip, Frau Aderhold!"

Maximilian took a deep breath as she left. "Please don't disturb me now, Menning. I'm reading Frau Stein's new manuscript."

Menning looked at him in amazement. "It's here? Your wife just asked me about it."

"The mail was handed to me." Maximilian covered his guilty conscience with a smile he hoped would convince Menning. The printer nodded. The couple's relationship had nothing to do with him.

Maximilian closed the door, sat down at his desk, took a thick envelope from his drawer, and opened it carefully. A letter slipped out, followed by the manuscript.

> *Dear Martha and Maximilian,*
> *I hope you're both well. You know you'd always be wel-*
> *come here at Traunstein House. Things are still the same*
> *here; the days go by and I'm just pleased that I have my*
> *work, which I can't truthfully call work.*

"Lucky thing!" Once again, Konstanze had succeeded in something that eluded Maximilian. After so much time had passed, she had recovered the energy to complete the novel *Woman on a Journey*. He settled down on the sofa, lit a cigarette, and began to read.

Konstanze's latest novel was a love story. The female protagonist met an engineer and fell in love. Renouncing her family and her title, she went with him to San Francisco, where he was involved in the construction of a bridge. From her self-imposed exile in a foreign country, she longed for home, but return was impossible for her. There was nowhere left where she would be accepted, no family members who understood her decision. During the building of the bridge, her lover fell to his death. She stayed, poor and lonely, in the foreign city with their daughter.

Night had fallen as he read. Menning and his assistants had long since gone. Maximilian was moved as he read the final paragraph.

> *She looked through the window at the lights illuminating her street. She heard the young men shouting out suggestive comments and the girls giggling. For the first time, she felt it was all a part of life; even pain was life and longing.*

The hero of Konstanze's story had found the death that Maximilian had wished for his own protagonist in *The Prayers of a Useless Man*. He could almost believe that Konstanze had written a sequel to his novel. Maximilian felt as though she understood him, as though her story was a tribute to him. He hugged the manuscript to his chest.

The more time passed, the more he longed for those days with her. He wondered why he hadn't fought harder for his love at the time. He had left, made his peace with Martha, and carried on with the life they had planned together. Why in God's name had he not paused to reflect on himself and his desires?

Things were little different for Martha. She had lost both her husband and her friend. What was more, she no longer experienced that naïve joy in their work together. She forbade herself from thinking about it—after all, their undertaking had turned out well: they now ran a successful publishing house. She traveled frequently, often by herself, sometimes with Maximilian. Authors, readers, and critics alike showed the Aderhold Press respect and loyalty. That meant a lot.

But when Martha looked to the future, it rarely brought her pleasure. What was there to look forward to? More successful books, more profits, recognition; maybe an author of theirs would be awarded a major literary prize one day.

There was one memory that filled Martha with silent joy—the memory of her brief encounter with Georg at the Sacher. They had chatted and drawn close to one another, neither of them yet suspecting that their spouses had already strayed. Georg had invited her and Maximilian to dinner. Martha had stood, taken the elevator up to her floor, and walked along the corridor, every step bringing her closer to disillusionment. Those had been the last moments of her innocence.

Georg was still innocent to this day; he still had no idea of Konstanze's infidelity.

Martha yearned for Georg, as though with him she could regain her own innocence. That, and her happiness.

~

"I forbid you to have anything to do with Marie Stadler." Konstanze had given Irma the same lecture countless times over the recent months. "An impossible woman. She's had every opportunity to make something of her life, but instead she chooses to set up this obscure salon."

Konstanze was merciless when it came to her daughters' upbringing. At no time did it occur to her to grant her daughters the freedoms that she herself enjoyed in her alternative persona as Lina Stein. The girls would continue in the conventions of their position in society.

Preparations were already being made for Rosa's wedding, an arrangement with a family from Georg's circle of friends. Rosa had met the family's son at the Vienna Opera Ball, and care had been taken from that moment on to ensure that the two of them met regularly and grew to like each other—or, even better, grew to appreciate and sympathize with their families' intentions.

Since the preparations for her wedding had been in progress, Rosa had proved very grown up. She took pride in her appearance and now sat in an armchair, reading, as her mother and Irma argued. Rosa, the girl Konstanze and Martha had brought into the world together, was an enthusiastic ambassador for her class, unlike the rebel Irma, who spent every free minute with Marie in Vienna.

The girls had known for a long time that Marie Stadler, "the poor girl who was held captive," was their half sister. Irma had met Marie in secret and brought the news home. She had been in regular contact with her ever since, and had even managed to win her father's support.

"It's just that Marie doesn't want to be dependent on you," Irma said, in defense of her sister.

"With the benefit of our money, she can well afford to be independent," Konstanze said coldly. When Irma went to reply, her mother cut her off with an impatient wave of her hand. "As a Traunstein princess, you have family responsibilities. If it becomes known where you spend your time, no man will be interested in you."

Irma looked from her sister to her mother. "I want to remain free," she said triumphantly, "and earn my own money."

Konstanze gestured irritably.

The telephone began to ring in an adjacent room.

"My life will be wonderful," Irma continued.

Rosa couldn't resist. "You'll end up an old maid, dependent on handouts from your family."

Irma cuffed her older sister's side. "Poor Rosa, about to be married off," she gloated. "Your life won't be your own from now on."

Rosa lost all pretense of decorum, jumped up, and ran at her sister.

"You'll have to do everything he says." Irma pushed a chair between herself and her sister.

"Enough!" Konstanze was on her way into the study, where the butler had already taken the call.

"Enough of what?" Mathilde walked in from the park with the dogs, glowing warm from her walk, her coat and shoes thick with snow. A servant hurried over to take her wet things.

"Rosa's freedom," Irma crowed as the dogs joined in the sisters' fight. Mathilde went to the piano and began to hammer out a polka. She enjoyed these rare moments of unrestrained togetherness with her sisters.

Konstanze entered the study, and the butler handed her the receiver. "Herr Aderhold from Berlin, Your Serene Highness."

Konstanze kept her composure. Had Maximilian gone completely mad, to be calling here? That privilege was reserved for Martha alone. Flora was still the only one at Traunstein House who knew that she wrote and was published by the Aderhold Press.

At first he heard only her breathing, followed by a cool "Yes?"

"I've just read your novel," Maximilian said. He had her to himself, even if it was only on the telephone.

Konstanze glanced around. Her daughters were still romping about in the drawing room, but she nevertheless spoke softly and with self-control. "Martha called me because she thought the mail had gone astray."

"I wanted to be the first to read it."

Konstanze was disappointed. The book belonged to Martha first.

"I was excited to see what you've been working on all this time," Maximilian said. He rarely managed to show his feelings. He could do so with her.

Konstanze smiled, the sound of his voice awakening Lina Stein in her. "So tell me, do you like it?" she gushed, all caution thrown to the wind. "I'm still not sure, especially where her lover is concerned. Did you understand him?" Konstanze didn't wait for an answer. "The woman and the man approach love very differently. He's seen it all; he's weary and has no illusions. And she's innocent, a dreamer . . ."

"You know, a man has never seen it all. He can be just as innocent." Maximilian thought about the brief time they had spent together.

"But you like the novel? Do you? Anyway?"

"I love your stories. You know that." He spoke gently. In fact, he had looked forward to the succession of short stories she had written over the years, and read them all several times.

Silence fell suddenly. They heard one another more clearly when they weren't talking. Konstanze heard Maximilian's desire. And he heard her loneliness.

"Martha's in Bremen."

"So she won't get around to reading it until later?"

"Her father died."

"Oh, I'm sorry." Konstanze was moved.

"Should I put my thoughts about your novel down in writing for you? Or . . ."

"In writing . . . yes . . . ," she said hesitantly.

He had grabbed the telephone on impulse, and had nothing planned. "Or should we meet?"

Konstanze didn't reply.

Maximilian improvised quickly. "I've got to go to Vienna on business anyway."

Konstanze's daughters could still be heard at their silly games in the other room.

"I need to come to town, too . . . to see my dressmaker," Konstanze said, improvising herself. She could justify the trip with the excuse of investigating some items for Rosa's honeymoon wardrobe.

"I'd so love to see you again."

"I can't promise anything," she replied uncertainly.

"Very well. I'll be there tomorrow," Maximilian said boldly.

"Goodbye, Maximilian." Konstanze hung up, having made no decision. She went back into the drawing room, where Rosa and Mathilde were now sitting at the piano, playing a duet. Irma was waltzing lasciviously, like the dancer she had seen in Marie's salon.

Maximilian stood by the telephone, wondering whether to call again to tell her how serious he was.

Konstanze sat down in an armchair, gazing vacantly at her daughters' antics. She had rarely been to Vienna since the death of the Empress. She had begun to write short stories just so that she could keep in contact with Martha. The two women met twice a year at the Sacher, but the warmth of the early years was gone.

"Your messing around doesn't go with our music at all," Mathilde protested.

"Then play in a way that suits my dancing."

Unperturbed, Irma continued in the same vein.

Konstanze couldn't imagine changing her plans on the spur of the moment and going to Vienna. But what plans did she have? She had finished her novel and had nothing else underway.

43

They were already playing the overture to *The Marriage of Figaro* when Anna entered the box, late and a little out of breath. Schuster stood, delighted, and kissed her hand, luxuriating in her warmth. To him, she embodied the energy with which she took charge of her life.

"It was here, twenty years ago, that you sat with me for the first time," he whispered tenderly as he guided her to her seat.

She smiled calmly and recalled her early days as a widow and the support he had given her, especially in financial matters, and at those silent meetings; and how after years their discretion had finally dissolved, first at the opera and then after a weekend in Karlsbad. After their children's wedding, their roles as parents-in-law had enabled them to be seen together in public more often.

On the stage, Figaro was beginning to plan his wedding to the maid Susanna. Schuster reached into his pocket, and a diamond ring sparkled before Anna's eyes. He placed the ring on her finger, took her hand, and kissed it tenderly.

She started to say something, but he shook his head. They would talk about it all later, over dinner.

~

They began again where they left off, as if the intervening sixteen years had never been. Maximilian stroked her neck, kissed her throat, wound his fingers into her long hair. She took his hand and guided it to her breast. Konstanze had never ventured into such passionate waters with Georg. Only once in her life had she known herself as a sensual woman—and that was in Maximilian's arms.

Only once in his life had Maximilian felt physical love and the eternal music of the soul come together in a single place—and that was in Konstanze's arms.

They forbade one another to think of afterward, and simply gave themselves to the moment, the interplay of their bodies, the passion of their senses—and the adventure for which they had both been emboldened.

~

Flora lay in bed, reading a story by Ferdinand von Saar. There was a knock at the door. She quickly pulled on her dressing gown and opened it. Johann slipped into the maid's quarters. She saw right away how tense he was, as though he were carrying a great burden. They hadn't seen each other for almost six months—it was that long since Her Serene Highness had come to Vienna.

"Will you have a drink with me?" he asked. He was carrying a half bottle of wine and two glasses. She nodded, as if there were ever any doubt about it. It had long since become a ritual between them.

Johann filled the glasses. "My aunt died. She's left me eight thousand kronen!" Flora shook her head in disbelief. He nodded. They toasted the news.

Flora drew him onto the bed and took him in her arms. "You're free now."

Johann pulled away, gripping his glass with both hands. "Perhaps I'll invest the money in war bonds."

"War benefits no one, so the Traunsteins say." She looked at him intently. "What's the matter? You don't look happy at all."

It's all this talk of war, she thought. *It spreads a black cloud over everything.*

"I'm not alone anymore, Flora," Johann burst out. "She's younger than we are. She wants children . . . I waited so long for everything to come together." He couldn't look at her, but poured another glass instead.

His announcement pulled the rug out from under her. They had been together for over twenty years. They had grown older together. He had never been alone—or had she underestimated their periods apart? *With a younger woman, Johann can have everything he always longed for with me,* Flora thought.

"But I don't know if I can." He wanted to give her an opening, wanted her to fight for him, to tell him what she really felt.

But Flora didn't want to stand in his way. Unlike her, he still had every chance to start a family. She took his hand, "Don't let me tie you down, Johann."

He saw the encouragement in her smile and was amazed at how lightly she was taking their parting. Because it was a parting. He knew that now. Until this moment, he had suppressed the thought that he would lose Flora when he took up with Margarete.

He had met Margarete Ebner one Sunday afternoon by the Danube. They had walked together and later stopped for refreshments at a dairy. By the time they parted, several hours later, they knew each other's life stories.

Margarete made her living as a telephone operator at the Vienna telegraph center, was independent, and lived in a room in the Grinzing district of the city.

From that time on, they met regularly, whenever Johann was free.

Margarete encouraged him to use his inheritance to follow his dream and start a business, building on all that he had learned at the Hotel Sacher. As soon as a child arrived, she would give up her job and assist him in his restaurant. Margarete was clear and decisive in her opinions, a woman of action. It appealed to him after waiting for so long.

Johann looked at Flora. She was still gentle, delicate, and beautiful. He topped up their glasses one last time.

Death glided through the room. He liked to be around people who were in the process of parting. One of his little quirks. He wanted to provide consolation.

Love shook her head in despair. For people to believe that their love died was pure illusion. Only their vision of love was capable of dying.

She always has to be so precise, Death thought mildly about Love.

~

"What do you think, Julius—should I invest my money in war bonds?" After the opera, they entered Anna's private rooms, where the table was laid for dinner. Julius helped her out of her coat.

"There won't be a war." He kissed the back of her neck and went to the table to fill their glasses.

"But there's a lot of talk of war around my tables." Anna looked at the ring on her finger.

Schuster came over with the glasses. They toasted one another.

"This is a wonderful evening, Julius."

"You go out so rarely. Did you notice how people looked at you? You're an institution, Anna."

She smiled at his words and the way he said them. They sat at the table, and Anna passed him the platter of cold meats. He took what he wanted and added a healthy serving of horseradish. She watched him eat heartily.

Sensing her eyes on him, he looked up. Her hands were clasped, and the ring shone.

"Listen, my business can only be run by someone who's above everyday gossip. I've been working on it for over twenty years." She stood, took the little box from her purse, and drew the ring deliberately from her finger. "I can't be your wife, Julius. To my guests I'm Frau Sacher—an institution, as you said yourself."

He went over to her and pushed the ring back where he believed it belonged. "I know, Anna. But I want it out in the open, so that the time never comes when we look each other in the eye and regret missing something." He kissed her. "Make me happy by wearing the ring anyway."

They continued eating. "I think it would be for the best," she said, "if I gave Eduard a monthly allowance to help him along. If a member of the Sacher family is running a business, it ought to be a successful one. The lawyer would have cost me anyway. At least this way it will remain in the family."

Schuster smiled.

~

"Why didn't you answer any of my letters?" Maximilian blew out smoke from his cigarette and passed it to Konstanze. They were lying naked between the sheets.

"What would have been the point?" Konstanze had never smoked. She inhaled and gave him the cigarette back.

"Have you had any other men?" He turned, keen to look her in the eye.

"No." Her voice was clear; she had her stories to live in. She passed the question back to him. "Have you had any other women?"

"I tried again and again to forget you."

Her laughter tinkled like a bell as she took the cigarette from his hand. "What about Martha?" she asked after a while, her voice full of reproach. The fact that the two of them were lying there was bad enough, but at least they had the excuse that they were already connected. The fact that he was unfaithful to her friend affected her.

"She really is a good person." Maximilian's voice sounded bitter.

"Georg is too." Konstanze sighed.

They thought of the other two.

Maximilian changed the subject. "Do you have any ideas for your next novel?"

"Mr. Publisher needs to make plans," Konstanze replied with amusement.

"I'm asking you as a smitten reader." Maximilian leaned over her. "In any case, I don't want to wait another fourteen years for one of your books."

"I've written so many stories for you."

"Short stories are short"—he kissed her—"much too short."

She stretched. "I don't know. I've been feeling so listless recently."

He looked at her. "What if we left all this behind . . . Portugal. New Zealand. Canada. We could be free." Maximilian fell back onto the bed. How much he wished for that.

"Freedom. My daughter Irma goes on about it at every possible opportunity. She thinks she needs to tell her old-fashioned mama what life's all about." Konstanze laughed sadly.

Maximilian fished for a box in the drawer of his bedside table and handed it to Konstanze. She opened the gift to see a fountain pen lying cradled in blue velvet.

"I know you don't want to use a typewriter."

He had thought for a long time about what to bring her, and then this pen had caught his eye in the Kaufhaus des Westens department store on the Wittenbergplatz. He had decided not to have it engraved, and now he regretted it—this time he wanted to profess his feelings to her. That much was certain.

She thanked him for the gift with a tender kiss, lay back in his arms, and looked dreamily at the pen. "Has it occurred to you that seduction and abduction aren't so different from one another?"

"Interesting," he said. As he thought about the meanings of the words, he remembered another similarity he'd thought a lot about. "Wonder and wound, too."

"Wound . . . ," she repeated in surprise. "A couple of letters different and pain is turned to mystery."

They contemplated in silence these intangible connections.

"I could imagine writing the story of Marie Stadler," Konstanze said, returning to his earlier question.

"You mean as a kind of revenge on your husband?" Maximilian said in bewilderment.

"Oh, go away, Maximilian. I'm interested in Marie and how she saved herself."

"Her abductor was murdered, and her savior died. That's the story," Maximilian said matter-of-factly.

"Not at all. She lost everything and then she reappeared, like the phoenix from the ashes."

"Look out—it's taking you over already." Maximilian sat up straight.

"You think so?"

"Yes! Your eyes are shining and your heart thumping." Her drew her close. "An author has to be mistress of her material, not the other way around."

"How clever you are." She relished his affection.

"You're making fun of me," Maximilian said between kisses.

She laughed, and her hands crept beneath the sheets. "That's what I find fun."

~

Johann lay on his bed and listened to the snoring from the next room.

Flora stood by the window of her maid's bedroom and watched as the moon melted into a cloud before disappearing. She would never again look forward to a trip to Vienna.

Anna lay in Julius's arms. She would not relinquish her freedom for anything in the world. She had arranged her world according to her own rules, and everything fit together like the pieces of the jigsaw puzzles that had recently been obsessing her friend Kathi Schratt, now that she was no longer on the stage. Anna Sacher was the empress of her own empire. And if she really thought about it, she had more power and more opportunities than the Empress Elisabeth ever had. With that thought, Anna fell asleep.

44

The first thing Georg noticed when he entered the courtyard was the chestnut tree whose branches reached up past the third floor as if stretching up to the sky. He was often struck by how trees could survive and even flourish in the most confined spaces.

The office of the publishing house, which now occupied the whole ground floor of the side wing, had a shop window facing out onto the courtyard. Georg's eyes fell on *The Prayers of a Useless Man* among other books in the display. He entered the print shop.

Against the cacophony of the printing machines, Menning approached him and explained apologetically that the owners were away. Georg was disappointed. Reluctant to leave immediately, he asked about Maximilian's book, saying he wanted to buy a copy.

"It's by the publisher himself. A good choice," Menning said as he fetched a copy. It was only now that Georg realized he had hardly thought about Maximilian and the possibility that he would be there, too.

Martha, on the other hand, had not been far from his thoughts over the years. He had followed the press's success story through Konstanze and also knew from her that the Aderholds had remained childless. But the friendship between the two women seemed to have cooled off recently. Georg attributed this to the physical distance, to Martha's workload, and, not least, to his conviction that the differences between the two were far too great for a lasting friendship. None of these thoughts came close to the truth.

"Give it to me, Menning," came a voice from behind Georg. "I'll wrap it for the gentleman."

He turned and there was Martha.

She had seen him through the window as she crossed the courtyard.

"Martha!" he said in delight.

"I've just returned from Bremen. I'd planned to catch the night train, but I finished early and . . ."

. . . and we might have missed each other by a hair's breadth, they both thought.

Menning handed her the book. "Herr Aderhold decided at short notice to go to Vienna. He'll be stopping off in Leipzig on the way home."

Martha nodded, surprised.

"He said he'd be sending you a telegram," Menning added before leaving the two alone.

Her delight at Georg's visit outweighed any feelings she had about Max going to Vienna without telling her. So this was a chance for them to have some time to themselves.

After wrapping Georg's book, she showed him around the premises, telling him about the success they had enjoyed over the years. Georg stopped at a shelf on which the books were arranged in alphabetical order by author, and took out a novel by Lina Stein.

"This has been all the talk among our maids. I've always thought it must be very simple," he said. "But perhaps I've underestimated the author." He put the book back in place. "I can't imagine you'd publish anything without substance, Martha."

She smiled and said nothing. She recalled the next manuscript due from Konstanze and thought fleetingly that she'd have to ask Menning whether it had arrived yet.

Georg stood in the kitchen in his shirtsleeves, a towel around his waist as an apron, peeling potatoes. Martha had invited him to eat with her. Pleased by this chance encounter, they had decided to cook together and were preparing a traditional Berlin potato soup following Martha's mother's recipe.

"We had a fierce debate." Georg was telling her about the Peace Society meeting. "Some of the group have changed their minds and now believe a war could result in reshaping Europe."

Martha was stirring a vanilla sauce while listening intently. Georg was appalled by the ignorance of his political fellows. "No problem has ever been solved by war! And the European states are posturing like beasts of prey facing one another. Dear God in heaven! As if the Congress of Vienna had never taken place." In his agitation, he cut his finger; he rinsed the blood beneath the faucet, talking on all the while. "It's like the worst kind of family get-together. The atmosphere is dreadful. One wrong word could trigger a fight."

Martha passed him a bandage. "We're receiving a lot of manuscripts with descriptions of human life as something full of ferocity and hostility. It seems there's a sense of shattering the old to make way for the new."

"I'm afraid destruction and devastation have always had a seductive appeal," Georg agreed. "But surely the new can grow while acknowledging what already exists, can't it?" He turned back to peeling the potatoes.

Martha melted butter in a pan and said matter-of-factly, "No one seems to be interested in peace during peaceful times."

Georg was nonplussed. That clear, simple thought encapsulated the truth about centuries of human development. Everyone longed for quiet times—to see their children grow up in peace and prosperity, to be able to eat and drink, live and love. But they were unable to sustain calm, to keep the peace, in either their private or their political lives.

Georg watched Martha move gracefully as she prepared the food. After his sobering days with the activists who had until recently been advocating peace, he felt his optimism returning. He mustn't give up; he had to give courage to the others. He had always believed his task lay in reminding people of their most noble qualities and appealing to them.

Martha noticed his smile, and he caught her eye. They were surprised at how good it felt to be here, cooking and putting the world to rights.

Georg cleared his throat awkwardly and changed the subject. "When I was a boy, I loved sitting in the kitchen, watching the staff."

"My mother always cooked herself. No one else could ever have done things right for her." Martha passed Georg a spoonful of vanilla sauce to taste. "One of her recipes—plenty of vanilla beans and a blend of cinnamon and cognac."

He tried it. "Frau Sacher would turn green with envy."

"Don't let her hear you say that." Laughing, Martha moved away from him and returned to the stove.

He followed and watched over her shoulder. "Berlin potato soup. Who would have thought it!"

She felt him at her back and gathered her courage. "Would you like to stay in Berlin for another day? We could have a coffee in the Adlon and go to the cabaret—but I'm sure someone will be expecting you."

Georg had also toyed with the idea. "Nothing I can't put off until later," he replied cheerfully. "But I ought to—"

"Please feel free to use the telephone . . . the typewriter . . . the post office is only two blocks away."

Georg looked at her happily and went to call Zacharias. They had arranged meetings with fellow political campaigners for the coming days, to discuss their position on the armament of the great powers. But at that moment, Martha meant everything to him.

As Martha gathered plates and silverware together, she wondered what Max would think if she offered Georg the guest room. He wasn't a stranger, after all. Yet she felt uneasy about it. She told herself her husband had gone to Vienna without telling her; he could easily have reached her by telephone in Bremen. What was he doing in Vienna, anyway?

Georg returned to the kitchen, his face pale. "Vincent Zacharias . . . you know him . . . He's been arrested. Accused of spying."

Their pleasure at having some time together collapsed like a house of cards. Georg stood, undecided. Martha made the decision for him. "I'll come with you to Vienna. My husband's there, after all."

~

"You remember that night when we were at the opera? Marie and that Würtner were living so close by," Maximilian said, recalling the night they had walked back to the Sacher.

Konstanze shuddered. "What a disturbing thought."

"A life apart, separated from us by little more than a curtain," he continued.

They were lying naked in bed, and had begun to work on Marie Stadler's story. Konstanze had told Maximilian everything she knew, and both their imaginations were working overtime. A man had put his fate into the hands of a girl.

"You must make the girl an equal," Maximilian said. "She mustn't be portrayed as Würtner's victim."

Konstanze nodded. She was already writing the first sentences of the story, using the new pen and Hotel Sacher letterhead paper.

Maximilian watched her from the side as she lay there looking so sensual as she lost herself in her work. Konstanze sensed his gaze on her and realized how much she had been hiding herself away for all those years. She had made herself invisible so she could live out her passion. It did her good to be out in the open.

She's waking up, Love thought. *At last she's waking up!*

This awakening would continue, and by the end, they would all— Georg, Martha, Maximilian, Konstanze—realize they only needed to reach out their hands and, each accompanied by the other's partner, continue the course of their lives.

45

"Don't reproach yourself!" Kathi Schratt sat with Anna in the hotel office, feeding preserves to her friend's favorite dogs.

The Sacher's proprietor was embroidering the autographs of her celebrity guests onto a large tablecloth.

"If I hadn't made young Zacharias my protégé, he'd only be a court clerk by now, but at least he wouldn't be in trouble."

"I've already asked Franz if he'll intervene," Kathi said, trying to reassure her friend. "But as you know, the Emperor will do anything but get involved in politics . . . Sometimes, when he's sitting there . . . You know, if his eyes weren't open, you could believe he was no longer . . ." She broke off. There was nothing more to say.

"Since my Annie died, it feels as if I bring nothing but bad luck to everyone around me," Anna said, sinking further into self-pity.

"Oh, come on, Anna, your Schuster's alive and well. Eduard's coffeehouse will prosper now that you've got him under your wing. And look who's stayed at your hotel." Kathi Schratt indicated the tablecloth. "Everyone who's anyone."

The tablecloth did indeed show the important names of high society: kings, archdukes, barons, princesses, renowned artists, business magnates, and of course ministers and senior civil servants from all over the world. The first signature, made with a joyful flourish, belonged to Otto von Habsburg. The others had followed the archduke's lead, and now Anna had the idea of preserving this sacred relic for posterity.

Mayr appeared and announced, "Ma'am, His Serene Highness Prince von Traunstein and Frau Aderhold have just arrived."

All trace of weepiness fell from Anna in an instant. "Please tell the other lady and gentleman that their spouses have arrived."

Mayr left.

Anna quickly folded up her embroidery, but then paused to collect herself. "The Emperor has never sat down at my table!"

"He's no man about town," Kathi Schratt replied.

Anna pointed to the center of the fabric. "I've left this space free." She pressed the tablecloth into Kathi's hand.

"This isn't an autograph book I can simply shove under Franz Josef's nose," Kathi protested.

But Anna was already hurrying out of her office, leaving Kathi Schratt staring at the tablecloth in her hand, the dogs' pleading eyes, and the jar of preserves.

~

Georg and Martha entered the hotel. They had traveled on the night train, the pleasure of their hours together overshadowed by their worry for Zacharias.

Georg had told Martha the story of their friendship, and how the gulf between them had widened in recent years. At the Peace Society meeting in Berlin, Zacharias had spoken out in favor of taking the radical road, using warlike means if necessary.

When the train pulled into Vienna, she was sorry that their shared journey had come to an end so soon. She could have traveled on forever.

They spent the cab ride in silence, sitting shoulder to shoulder and feeling each other's warmth. They would have liked to hold hands, but did not dare.

~

"God's blessing, Your Serene Highness. Welcome to Vienna, Frau Aderhold," Anna Sacher said warmly. She feared that this time the embarrassing situation could not be kept under wraps. "We've just sent word to your wife, Your Serene Highness."

"My wife is in Vienna?" Georg was astonished.

Martha had suspected as much ever since Menning had passed on Maximilian's greetings and told her where he had gone.

"I'll just go and say hello to Konstanze," she said to Georg. "I'm sure you two have things to talk about," she added, meeting Anna Sacher's eyes. Martha wanted to spare Georg this time, too.

"I'm sure she'll be delighted to see you," Georg said innocently, kissing Martha's hand in farewell. They looked at one another for a brief moment before Martha went to the elevator.

"I'm worried about Baron Zacharias," Anna Sacher said. "Spying! I can't imagine anything of the kind."

"It's probably a misunderstanding." Despite their political differences, Georg was convinced of Vincent's loyalty.

"You'll take up his cause, won't you?" Anna asked, her voice filled with concern.

"Of course." Georg nodded, looking her in the eye. As he did so, he realized something was not right.

Paper covered in writing was scattered all over the floor of the room. A bottle of champagne and two glasses were lying in casual abandon, along with the remains of a late breakfast.

The telephone rang ceaselessly. Maximilian finally reached out for the receiver. "Yes?"

Konstanze heard the agitation in the caller's voice and sat up.

"Your husband and my wife have just arrived," Maximilian said, perplexed, as he hung up.

Konstanze jumped out of the bed and began to gather her things in a panic. She suddenly paused, as though she had just taken in the import of the news. "What's my husband doing in Vienna with Martha?"

Maximilian went over and put his arms around her naked body. "I don't want to carry on acting as though we don't feel as we do about each other."

Konstanze waved him away. "I don't want a scandal, Max. Please!"

She saw Martha standing in the doorway, followed only a few moments later by Georg.

46

Martha sat at the desk, writing.

The hotel room was neat and tidy; no traces of the previous night could be seen. A chambermaid saw to a few final details, then quietly left the room.

Maximilian entered. He had bathed and was freshly shaved. "You could have called and saved us this embarrassment," he said irritably.

Martha didn't look up.

"But you probably didn't want to spare us."

"We've been sparing you long enough, Max."

Her calm struck him. "Who are you writing to?" he snapped.

Martha addressed the envelope and rang for a bellhop. "Since I'm here, I'd like to meet some of our authors."

The bellhop arrived, and Martha stood. "Will you take the mail, please?"

"Certainly!" The bellhop took the letters and left.

Martha put on her coat, unable to bear Maximilian's presence. He barred her way.

"The press, our authors, my books," he said. "Discipline, progress, keeping control. Just show me for once what you're feeling."

She could see his rage. And she was unable to stop herself from slapping the face she had once loved.

Martha had never hit another person and had never been struck herself. The palm of her hand stung. She feared he would hit her back, that he would unleash his hatred on her. But nothing happened. She looked at the glowing red mark of her hand on his face for a moment, then reached for her hat.

"I'm tired. It's tearing me apart. This life, everything about it—it's so meaningless," he fired at her. He wanted to provoke a response.

She turned. "My life isn't meaningless."

She walked out.

Maximilian lowered himself onto a chair and buried his face in his hands.

Martha couldn't get as far as the elevator. Her blood sank to her feet, sweat broke out on her brow, and she leaned on the wall.

Then she felt a pair of hands supporting her, and she was enfolded by the smell of tobacco and strong perfume.

A little later, she found herself back in Anna Sacher's private suite. A glass of water was pressed into her hand, and after a few sips she felt life returning as the nausea receded.

"I'm sorry about what happened." Anna Sacher poured Martha another glass of water. "Can I get you a cognac, perhaps?"

Martha shook her head. She was embarrassed by the whole situation. But she still could not stand.

"Is divorce really the only option, do you think?" Martha finally articulated what she had been thinking for years. "What happens then?"

"Fate." Anna Sacher trimmed a cigar and lit it. "Listen, my good woman, I see it here every day. People in love. People destroying themselves for love. I'm afraid love is a fleeting thing." Anna thought about her marriage with Eduard and about her children. "You have your own business. Make the most of the possibilities you've created for yourself with your own strength and determination, Frau Aderhold. My hotel has always given me strength and consolation. And books last for eternity."

Martha was no longer sure she had the energy or the desire to run the press. She longed so much for peace, for someone else to hold her up.

Anna took Martha's hands. "Now, go downstairs and have a coffee with whipped cream and chocolate liqueur." She guided Martha firmly toward the door. "When people are hurting, they need something sweet. It always helped with my dear Annie."

Love was indignant. There it was—this existential misunderstanding between people and herself. She was no fleeting apparition—on the contrary, she was the most constant thing in the universe. Not loaded down with human emotions, however, but as the free energy of creation. And what was that about? That recommendation to use sweet things as a distraction from pain . . .

~

Flora packed Her Serene Highness's clothes into the suitcase. Her separation from Johann was making her miserable. What did the future hold, apart from war? Perhaps she'd die, Flora thought with some relief.

Georg had changed and now headed for the foyer, where the lawyers acting for Zacharias were waiting for him. As he left the suite, he passed Konstanze, who was adjusting her hat in the mirror. She jumped and tensed, expecting a confrontation with him. But he merely said soberly, "I'm going to stay here for a while," and left without another word.

Konstanze continued to fiddle with her hat. Flora mustn't see her crying.

~

Martha sat over the coffee with cream and chocolate liqueur she had ordered. The sweetness was easing the pain. Her tears dripped onto the tablecloth.

Georg arrived and sat down by her.

"Much too sweet. But it helps a bit," she said. "How are things with your friend?"

"I don't know yet." Georg longed to be able to walk away from his dilemma. To begin again, as far as possible from the rumblings of war, from all the accusations and charges. That was why he had immersed himself in the estate over the years—at least he could find a little peace there. But the conflicts followed him mercilessly.

He took her hand beneath the table as both of them thought about the hours that had just passed.

"Now isn't our time, Martha," he said softly.

"I know."

Waiters bustled around them. Guests placed their orders, coming and going, as Martha and Georg sat in silence, holding each other's hands, in an oasis of calm—like the eye of a hurricane.

47

Marie Stadler waited with Lechner in the visiting room of the police headquarters.

Two uniformed officers finally brought Vincent Zacharias out.

"Take the handcuffs off the man and wait outside," Lechner ordered the officers and bowed to Marie. "Be my guest, ma'am."

Pleased to be doing her a favor, Lechner left.

"Good day, Baron von Zacharias."

"Marie!" His voice was hoarse.

He indicated for her to sit at the visitors' table, but she refused.

"I want to make the best of my advantage while I have you alone." Marie looked at him thoughtfully.

Vincent, too, remained on his feet. "What happened, the decision I made back then, the decision I had to make . . . I really want to explain it to you," he said quickly.

Marie waved him away. "Forget it. It belongs to the past."

That wounded him.

"My life couldn't be better," she continued, looking him in the eye. "You were the first person, the first and only one, with whom I felt like a woman of flesh and blood. Simple and alive." She spoke with warm sincerity. "I'd like to thank you for that."

He couldn't accept it. Not right then. He wanted her to understand; she should give him absolution. Only that could bring him any relief in this situation, make him feel that not everything had been meaningless. "I believed I was doing my duty, following my obligations. I placed them before my feelings," he said, his voice cracking.

"Don't worry about it at all!" Of course she understood his conflict, but she was unmoved by it. "Freedom's what I value above all."

His betrayal had given her the impetus to lead an independent life. The residual emotion she felt for him—her dreams and possibilities— paled in comparison.

She smiled. "I don't like unfinished business between people. It's like an undercurrent, preventing you from ever finding calm. That was why I had to see you one more time."

The door opened, and Georg arrived with the lawyers.

"I was about to go," she said, without greeting them.

"Hello, Marie!" Georg noticed the tension between his daughter and his friend.

Marie offered her hand to Vincent.

"Do you forgive me?" he asked, with a trace of hope in his voice.

"But of course. Adieu. I wish you all the best." She left, her head held high.

Vincent watched her go.

Georg tore his friend back to reality. "These are our lawyers, Herr Fuchs and Herr von Straub."

They shook hands and sat around the table.

"You're accused of high treason. You're said to have conspired with the English?" Georg hoped that it would all turn out to be lies and conspiracy, and that he could rescue his friend as soon as possible from this shameful situation.

"Yes!" Vincent wore a thin, hard smile.

It was not an expression Georg had seen on him before. "I thought we could trust each other," he said, shocked.

"Trust?" Vincent repeated thoughtfully.

"Yes, trust . . . we've worked together for so many years."

"That may be, Georg. But we're from different worlds. And that hasn't been changed by your obtaining a title for me. Or by the fact that I tried to adapt in every way, so I could become your equal."

Georg made to contradict him, but Vincent was unwilling to let him have his say. He had to have it out. A feeling at first, now it was a certainty. "Trust, Georg, means meeting eye to eye. You enjoy your privileges by the grace of God. I'm a Bohemian fighting for self-determination."

Tears flowed down Zacharias's face—it was a pain he had been suppressing all his life. The strain of having to fulfill his mission at any cost.

Georg sat, speechless, in front of his former companion. They were lost to one another.

The lawyers took over. Their business was no less than clearing Vincent Zacharias of high treason and saving him from the death penalty.

48

The early spring sun shone into Konstanze's bedroom. It was late morning, but the tray with her breakfast lay untouched on the bedside table. She clutched her teacup as Flora read her one of the first reviews of *Woman on a Journey* from the newspaper.

Martha had commissioned someone else to edit the novel, and had published it without herself paying any heed to the contents. A business decision, justified by the novel's success.

"Frau Stein expertly describes her characters' longing for fulfillment in life. The heroine breaks away from her old world to find happiness in a new one. But to reach the new means more than a journey from one place to another. Freedom only brings renewal through self-knowledge. A courageous book and an enchanting story. The vivid portrayal of the main character is like a map of the female psyche."

Flora looked up proudly from the paper. "You deserve it. So many sleepless nights."

Flora thought of her own sleepless nights, and how she, too, had lived out the heroine's life with her.

Konstanze suddenly felt sick. She got up and went to the bathroom to vomit. Flora brought her a towel. The women looked at each other in the mirror.

"You despise me, don't you?" Konstanze asked.

"No, not at all," Flora replied.

"We've known each other for so long now, Flora. You can be honest."

"You're a good wife and mother . . . and you write such lovely stories. You can live so many lives." Flora thought that she had lost the rest of her own life along with Johann. "I still have only one—Flora's."

Konstanze saw the tears in her maid's eyes and took her hand. "Surely you're not crying for me?"

Flora shook her head, and that was how Konstanze knew that Johann intended to marry another.

49

A case of high treason was brought against Vincent Zacharias. The judges and expert witnesses did not take long to reach a verdict and sentence him to death. Zacharias's lawyers submitted an appeal. After the sentencing, Georg wanted to visit his friend in jail, but Zacharias let him know through one of the officials that there was nothing more to be said between them.

Georg brought Zacharias's family—his wife and children—to safety on a country estate near St. Pölten. He couldn't come to terms with his friend's decision and considered himself partly to blame. Georg refused to contemplate that renouncing Marie had been at the root of any of

Vincent's actions. The two had been unsuitable for each other, and besides, a union between them would have pushed Vincent onto the social and political sidelines.

But Georg did reproach himself for one thing: he had backed Zacharias's career while keeping himself out of the intrigues and power games of the court. He had handed over his own obligations to his friend.

~

When Georg first arrived home after the tumultuous events, he found the entrance hall decorated with bouquets of daffodils and tulips.

The butler informed Konstanze of her husband's arrival.

She found him in his study, opening the mail.

Georg greeted his wife politely before turning back to the letters. "They intend to sentence Zacharias to death. The lawyers have appealed."

He busied himself with the papers, without looking at her.

"Is he guilty of what they're accusing him of?" Konstanze asked in dismay.

"The continued failure of the Bohemians to achieve independence incited him to take advice from the Britons on the subject of democracy. In the current times, that counts as high treason."

Not a word of what Georg said betrayed his thoughts on his own role in the entanglement.

"Zacharias stepped out from your shadow and went astray," Konstanze said. Maybe she was also thinking about herself.

Georg had no desire to discuss the subject with his wife. He turned the conversation to her dilemma instead. "What are your plans?"

"I don't have any," she said angrily.

"Aderhold has given up everything in Berlin and is now living at the Sacher," he said in an attempt to provoke her.

"You believe I'd do something like that?"

"Is there anything that could still surprise me in this sorry affair?" He turned back to his papers.

Konstanze looked at him. He'd asked for it. "I'm expecting a baby."

Without reacting, Georg took some letters from his briefcase and leafed through them.

Unable to bear it any longer, Konstanze slapped her hand down on the desk in front of him. "Why do you have to act so superior? You're driving me mad." Her voice cracked for the first time in their marriage, possibly in her whole life.

"Shut up. Just shut up!" he roared in reply.

They glared at one another like opponents about to declare war.

Georg made a final attempt. "Please, will you go?"

What he would have given to be free of her. Forever. Konstanze sat down theatrically on the guest chair at his desk. She was so fed up with him.

50

Maximilian sat over a coffee in the foyer of the Sacher, writing down his thoughts about Würtner. He was surprised to find that the ceaseless comings and goings, the swell and fade of conversations in a variety of languages, helped him concentrate. He had to think through the blanket of noise, which shut out the distraction of other thoughts.

He was constantly plagued by his situation and the memory of the few days he spent with Konstanze. He still hoped she would come back, but he would not put pressure on her. He wanted her to return to him of her own free will, like the heroine of her novel, who left everything to follow her beloved across the ocean to a new world.

Maximilian had interpreted that as Konstanze's longing. He could not imagine that she would prefer to live in the seclusion of Traunstein House, with a husband who remained a stranger to her, rather than throw herself headlong into an adventure of love.

Then Maximilian would think of Martha, of her quiet beauty and their work together.

During these weeks, the Sacher seemed the only place where he could bear his own company and his situation.

The work on Würtner gave Maximilian a degree of satisfaction—it kept him close to Konstanze. The conversations they had had during the hours they had spent together echoed, still alive, in his mind.

Maximilian spent time in the library, poring over old newspapers, reading reports of Marie Stadler's disappearance and articles from six years later about the death of the music librarian. He talked to employees at the opera house who had known Würtner.

The new music librarian had three assistants with whom he divided his work. There was no longer the kind of solitude that might drive someone to such strange actions. He was married, a father of four; his employees knew and liked him; and every effort had been made to ensure that nothing like what Würtner had done would ever happen again.

Maximilian drank a schnapps in the small bar opposite the coal yard, where Würtner had heard Marie's story. The landlady was now a matronly woman in her sixties, with wrinkled breasts encased in a tight bodice. Maximilian could smell her sweat as she leaned over him.

"Stadler's taken a younger woman into his house." Maximilian listened with interest as she added, "They locked Sophie up in the asylum. All that business with Marie drove her crazy. But Stadler's happy enough to take the money. The fine gentleman has no idea that Sophie doesn't live here anymore."

He wove the fruits of his research into passages of the story. Perhaps Konstanze would want to tell Würtner's side, too, eventually. He had no idea whether she was still actually writing the story, but he carried on regardless.

Maximilian attended the salon once. Marie did not recognize him, and he introduced himself under a false name.

That afternoon, there was a reading of the new book by Guido von List, *The Ancient Language of the Aryo-Germans and Their Language of Mystery*.

Maximilian studied Marie Stadler with interest. She sat a little to one side, like a spider waiting at the edge of her taut web, making it sway slightly and shimmer seductively in the light.

The salon was an outlet for unemployed Bohemians, poverty-stricken aristocrats, joyless wives, aimless students. Maximilian saw how they all crowded around Marie, how her every word carried weight, and how she directed the group without any of them noticing. He saw her weariness and her appetite. *Würtner has created a homunculus, a being who derives satisfaction from observing the world and projecting her own interpretations into the minds of others,* Maximilian noted in his writings. He forgot about the girl she had once been, who had survived years in a cave where she had learned to see the shadow play outside as hostile. And now she had to control that world so that no one in it could ever harm her again.

51

All was quiet; the only sound was the clink of silverware on plates and the wheezing of the prince as he ate. Only a few days after his meeting in the Hotel Sacher, the old man had suffered a stroke. He was a pitiful sight, the way his hand shook as he raised food to his mouth and struggled to keep it there as he chewed.

Irma pushed her food listlessly around her plate. Only Mathilde made any attempt to behave properly. Rosa was away on a visit to her future parents-in-law. Her fiancé was doing his military service, on a maneuver at the Serbian border.

Of course the girls knew about their parents' quarrel and their mother's pregnancy. Irma had made inquiries and unearthed the scandal. Although Flora had said nothing, there was no preventing the gossip among servants of both the Hotel Sacher and Traunstein House.

Having had enough, the old man wanted to be wheeled from the table. A servant sprang to his assistance, and the old prince left the room without a word.

Konstanze had also finished eating.

"You may go to your rooms," she said to her daughters.

Irma left as abruptly as her grandfather. Mathilde gave a farewell kiss first to her father, then to her mother. Konstanze relished her youngest daughter's tenderness.

The maids were waiting nearby until they could begin clearing the table, but Konstanze dismissed them with an edgy gesture. She needed to be alone with Georg, to clarify the situation.

Their marriage contract meant she would be well provided for financially should they divorce. She could have lived off the royalties from her novels alone. But it was not a matter of money to Konstanze. She wanted security for herself and the baby she was expecting.

Georg felt miserable. "Do you love him?" he asked stiffly. He wanted her to make a decision, to enable him to make his own.

"Since when have you been interested in love?" Konstanze was amazed at this sign of sentimentality from him.

"I've always tried to be a good father and family man, to fulfill your wishes."

"But you don't know the first thing about me, Traunstein."

"And he knows you better?" he asked jealously.

"You only cared about your utopia, and my dowry was useful for that. But you were never interested in me." She said it calmly, without self-pity. "It's just the way you are. I've come to terms with it. But please don't oppress me with your virtue."

They sat in silence.

"I want to stay and have my baby here," Konstanze said after a while.

He did not reply.

She stood and left the room.

Georg drained his glass in one swallow and refilled it. A divorce would have made sense. But how would that look in the public eye? Their daughters' futures would be in ruins. He felt as though his skin were being flayed from his flesh. All sense of self-respect lost, he feared the future.

~

That afternoon, Death had been in the prison courtyard.

Safe in the knowledge that his family was secure, Vincent Zacharias broke away from his supervised circuit of the courtyard and ran calmly to the gate.

The guards called him back. When he refused to obey, they blew their whistles. He continued running, and they unleashed the dogs.

Barking aggressively, the animals surrounded Vincent and bit into his leg. He defended himself, knowing that his kicks and blows served only to increase their bloodlust.

The soldiers called their dogs off. The first shot hit him in the shoulder, the second in the neck. He fell on the cobblestones.

It's not my betrayal of Marie that made me what I was, Vincent thought at the end. *It was my betrayal of myself.*

52

On June 28, 1914, the old world ended.

In Berlin, Martha stared at the photo of the heir to the throne, Archduke Franz Ferdinand, and his wife, Sophie, Duchess of Hohenberg, that took up the front page of the daily paper. Smiling, the couple that represented the Habsburg monarchy were leaving the town hall in Sarajevo. They were dead less than an hour later. The first shot had pierced the side of the vehicle and hit her. The second shot had torn into the carotid artery of the heir to the throne. The shots had been fired by a young Serb who had come to Sarajevo for vocational studies—Gavrilo Princip, eighteen years of age, recruited by the Black Hand, a Serbian terror organization.

Georg feared that the calls for retribution following the terrorist attack would have incalculable consequences. It would be the match needed to light the fuse of the European powder keg, making it explode.

Just a few hours after he left for Vienna, Georg received a telegram announcing the death of Vincent Zacharias. Shot while attempting to escape, it said. Georg went to a nearby park and cried.

∼

Maximilian stood in shock in the foyer of the Sacher. At first he had believed Konstanze would return to him, but then he had seen her at Georg's side. They had walked past him without a word of greeting.

A little later, in their suite, Konstanze rang for a bellhop. "Please, will you take this card to Herr Aderhold?" She turned to Flora, who had finished unpacking the suitcase. "You can have this afternoon off."

"Thank you, Your Serene Highness." Flora curtsied. For the first time, she would spend her free hours in the city without having the evening to look forward to.

Konstanze stayed behind in the silent room. She went to the window and looked out at the back of the opera house, at the cars and cabs swishing past, then turned and moved restlessly around the room. She stopped in front of a mirror and neatened her hair with a few deft movements of her hand. She was exhausted.

There was a knock at the door, and Maximilian entered. Only then did he see that she was pregnant. "Is that my child?"

He wanted to hug her, but she held him back with a gesture.

"I've decided in favor of my family."

Maximilian was at a loss. She'd summoned him, after all. Maybe she was acting a part? Maybe Georg had forced this decision on her?

"I want to give this baby the same opportunities in life as my daughters." Her voice sounded calm and determined.

"You want it to be a Traunstein?"

He still couldn't believe that was what she really wanted.

"I want to give this child the security that you can't offer," she insisted. "They're all talking about war. I want peace."

Her clarity of mind was sobering to Maximilian.

"Peace?" he echoed sarcastically. "The world will be torn apart, Konstanze." His child was to be taken away from him. As long as such a thing was possible, there would be no peace. "And perhaps the world needs to be torn apart precisely to make us feel something at last. *Feel*, Konstanze!"

She looked at him sadly. They seemed to have known one another for an age. "Leave it, Max."

"I'm its father," he said in a last attempt.

"Go now. Please!"

Maximilian stared at her. Was this the same woman he had adored ever since reading her first book?

"Farewell," she said finally.

He nodded and left.

Konstanze stayed there, her thoughts with Martha.

~

"We have to create order by striking first. It's war now" was the first thing Georg heard as he entered the Crown Prince Rudolf Room. The men who had gathered here were standing or sitting on furniture from the room where the crown prince had taken his own life because his father, the Emperor, had denied him any involvement in the shaping of the empire. The bullet holes had been preserved.

Sixteen years earlier, a few days after the death of the Empress, the grand master of the court had determined that the room dedicated to the crown prince's death should be removed from Mayerling, where the event had occurred, to the Hotel Sacher, to be preserved on neutral ground.

Georg looked into the heated faces of the empire's officers and functionaries. He saw the men clutching glasses of whisky or port, clouding their minds with drugs. War was a drug. A deadly drug.

Death was leaning on a windowsill, listening.

They all agreed that the Imperial and Royal Army should be mobilized and the empire should call on her allies. They all believed unequivocally that the Serbian government was behind the assassination.

"It was the act of a terrorist organization," Georg said, trying to appeal to reason. "We should remain calm."

But no one listened.

Death thought that assassinations and murders always seemed to be a guaranteed way of showing those in power where their limits lay, of attracting attention and provoking a reaction. And those in power were all too willing to make use of these provocations, for the crimes of the other party were an excellent way of covering up one's own crimes. Sometimes they even organized such attacks themselves, in order to rearrange and underpin their ruling interests.

Death had known all this since time immemorial. He was amazed at people's unwillingness to see it clearly; they preferred to take a case that could be solved by a police operation and stir it up into military action between nations.

"After a war, we will be able to act freely once again," Erdmannsdorf thundered with enthusiasm.

"How do you intend to wipe the slate clean when your hands are bloody, Erdmannsdorf?" Georg asked calmly.

"Please, Traunstein, this isn't the place for your opinions—you, who've been working for decades alongside a traitor to the fatherland."

Georg shook his head, thinking that the men here in this room were old and had no future of their own. They were unsatisfied with what they had achieved in their lives, squandering their time on pomposity and prattle instead of working for the good of society. They wanted to see some action at least once in their stultified existences, and in so doing unscrupulously risked everyone's future.

53

Five weeks later, the war had arrived. The aged emperor signed the declaration of war at his summer residence in Bad Ischl, supported by the German emperor.

The monarchs in London, Saint Petersburg, and Berlin—cousins who had addressed one another since childhood as Georgie, Nicky, and Willy—nominally held power in their countries, but, even had they wished to object, they would have been powerless against the will of their generals and foreign ministers. Opposition to the war was unpopular, since the masses, the simple people, promised themselves that a war against their neighbors would improve their living conditions. Men marched to the front with determination. Their wives waved them off with white handkerchiefs and colorful bouquets. They all intended to be home by Christmas, with a new world order in place.

~

In the Hotel Sacher, the patrons separated according to their warring nations' alliances. Hardly anyone was aware of how serious it was. On the contrary, the delight that war had finally arrived could not have been greater.

It was with great regret that Mayr wrote out the bills. "I'm sure we'll have the pleasure of your company again soon, Excellency," he said to the British ambassador as he waved the bellhop over to carry his suitcases.

Anna Sacher walked up to the reception counter and looked at the register. Almost all bookings by regular guests from abroad had been crossed out.

"I hope this will all blow over soon like a good, clean family argument," Mayr said.

"It will, Mayr." Anna had invested her money in war bonds. A short, sharp war would be good and a longer one tolerable, provided her financial investments yielded profits afterward.

Anna followed her doorman's gaze to the door.

She saw her son entering for the first time in years. Eduard was wearing a lieutenant's uniform and had clearly come to prove his manhood to his mother as well as to obtain her blessing.

"Did you volunteer?" Anna asked as she went to meet him. "Who's going to look after your coffeehouse while you're gone?" she added pragmatically.

"I won't be gone long."

"Very well . . . Wagner can keep an eye on it. After all, some of my money's invested in it."

"I wanted to say goodbye. That's all," the young man said caustically.

"That's all? I don't understand why you're always so harsh with me."

"I don't understand why I keep setting foot over this threshold." Eduard turned as he spoke and vanished into the throng of officers and departing guests.

Anna walked past the empty private dining rooms and called, "Wagner, we need to stock up. Wine, whisky, cigars, cocoa."

Wagner hurried over to her. "Yes, ma'am. There'll be victories to celebrate."

"It doesn't hurt to keep the stores full at times like these, in any case."

"I'll have a word with the chef and get him to place the orders, ma'am."

He offered a light to his boss. She inhaled her first draft of cigar smoke.

"My son, Eduard, has volunteered for the front, by the way," she said. "We'll be taking care of his coffeehouse."

"Very well, ma'am."

Anna went into her office, closing the door behind her. She looked at the framed photos of her children and picked up the one of her son. "God be with you, Eduard!"

She gave him her blessing.

54

Maximilian returned to Berlin. He had to work despite this war. He had sent a telegram to Martha in advance: *I really hope I can count on your understanding and kindness.* He didn't refer to Konstanze's pregnancy.

Martha sat at the desk, reading euphoric letters from some of her authors at the front, most of whom had volunteered. She looked up from her reading as Maximilian entered.

Maximilian breathed in the familiar smell of printer's ink and coffee. He was home. He set his suitcase down and clapped Menning on the shoulder before going to Martha in the office. After greeting her, he dove in. "Konstanze is expecting a baby."

It took Martha a moment to grasp that this was Maximilian's child. He was to be a father.

Unsure what to do next, Maximilian left his luggage where it was and did what always made him feel secure: he removed his jacket, sat down at his desk, and began to work.

From that moment on they avoided the subject and all the hurt it might inflict. In times like these, it was good to be back together.

55

The war machinery had begun its work, and it was keeping Death on the go. Vast swaths of land were laid waste, people mutilated and blown apart. Abandoned battlefields were strewn with the corpses of horses, their intestines spilling out. Birds of prey circled above the dead.

Maximilian recalled Spielhagen's *Theory and Technique of the Novel* and the question he had not wanted to discuss with Martha two decades ago: whether the poet or the artist "is the inventor, the creator, of something new, something never seen before, that has only come about through him" or whether he finds something that was there to be discovered by anyone. Maximilian thought about cause and effect. In their pictures and texts created long before the outbreak of the war, had artists and writers conjured up a Sodom and Gomorrah? Had they effectively called the apocalypse into being, so that it materialized and was now made physical? Were images of the end of the world possibly sketches of a future in the invisible realm of human existence? And must they all now live out these images of terror?

With these questions came the accompanying consideration of the power of human thinking—and the question of people's responsibility for their thoughts.

~

"Why has God abandoned us?" sighed Love when confronted with the devastation.

Death, who encountered her far more frequently now than in times of peace, replied, "Humans have abandoned themselves. They are their own murderers. I am only Death."

Love and Death worked hand in hand, often on the same people. Hasty weddings and sudden engagements were an everyday occurrence. Men and women wanted to declare their binding attachment to each other at the last moment, fearing that they did not have much time left.

Johann had toyed with the idea of marrying Margarete, too. But he was unable to make the final decision after being independent for so many years. Did he really want to rush headlong into tying himself down?

Johann went to war with the firm intention of returning. He would consider his future then. That was what he wrote to Flora. He hadn't been able to forget her during the months leading up to the outbreak of war, and repeatedly questioned whether his plans with Margarete really could replace what he felt for Flora.

~

"He's stationed in France now." Flora had just opened Johann's letter. Konstanze nodded, absorbed in her work.

"He writes that there's no resolution in sight. Everything seems more and more confused," she said, silently reading the tender words and recollections with which he always concluded his letters.

Konstanze stared pensively into space. She could still hear the words Maximilian had spoken during their last argument. *And perhaps the world needs to be torn apart precisely to make us feel something at last . . .* Feel, *Konstanze!*

But I do feel, she replied in her head, racking her brain to grasp what he could have meant.

She remembered the months before her wedding, and how she had sought out all manner of diversions to prevent her from having to think about the forthcoming marriage. She remembered her first nights with Georg and how afterward she was glad to be alone. She thought of her pregnancies. And she came to the conclusion that she had shut out all feelings so she could bear her life.

Yes! She had created freedom for herself by fleeing into her sewing room and filling blank pages with words.

The baby moved. For the first time in her four pregnancies, Konstanze enjoyed feeling the little being grow inside her. She was curious to know about the person who would see the light of the world through her. She looked forward to the midwife placing the newborn in her arms. This time she wanted to do it all differently. She would devote herself to her child. She would take care of all its needs.

She thought of her daughters, of Rosa, who was now married. They had spoken on the telephone a few times over the months. But did Konstanze really know what her eldest was feeling? At last she intended to make time for her daughters. Filled with optimism, Konstanze continued her work.

It had grown late. She laid the pages she had finished that day to one side, ready for Flora to copy out, and then she went through the darkened house to Georg's study.

The Aderhold Press telephone rang. Martha picked up and heard Konstanze's voice.

"Martha . . . how are you?"

"I assume it's Max you want," Martha said dismissively.

Maximilian overheard and moved closer.

"Is he back in Berlin?" Konstanze had not considered that possibility.

"I'll put him on."

"Wait! It's you I wanted to speak to . . . It's lovely to hear your voice."

Martha said nothing.

"Martha, do you remember when Rosa was born and you were with me?" Konstanze said, recalling one of the best moments of her life.

They both recalled in silence the days they had spent together, a time when they had been carefree in a way they never could be again.

"Do you think this war will last long?" Konstanze would far rather have asked, *Do you think we'll see each other again after the war?*

"We're getting daily reports from the front. No one has any hope of a quick end," Martha replied matter-of-factly. She sensed the unspoken question and Konstanze's longing.

"Farewell, Konstanze!" Martha handed the receiver to Maximilian and went into the side room.

She wished she could start living her own life at last. When the war ended, she would divorce Maximilian. She would take over part of the publishing business and transform it into her own press, drawing a line under the past. Martha also thought of Georg. But she wanted no more entanglements.

"Should I come and see you?" Maximilian asked anxiously.

"No! I think it's going to be a boy. I wanted to ask you about names."

The question drove him to his emotional limits. They might be having a son. His son.

"Andreas . . . ?" he asked, his voice cracking.

"Andrasz . . . I like it."

They fell silent, each listening to the other's breathing.

"For the first time, I understand what Georg has been saying: each one of us has our place in the world—and if we don't occupy it, it leads to bewilderment and pain."

"We also have a place within ourselves. What about that?"

He was struggling. Could she not feel that they belonged together?

"Farewell, Max." Konstanze hung up.

Martha had filled two glasses with schnapps from Menning's bottle and sat down on the bench in the print shop. She handed Maximilian a glass and they drank.

"He'll be a Traunstein. His family tree will be traceable to the fourteenth century." Maximilian gave a bitter laugh and tipped the cheap liquor down in one gulp. "Plenty of indiscretions in those family trees . . ."

Martha poured them another. "We haven't successfully managed to be lovers . . . or to become parents." She said it without reproach.

"Why not? Why couldn't we do it, Martha?"

It occurred to Martha that maybe she did not have a child because the little being had sensed in advance that its parents would be swept away by a catastrophe, and millions of others along with them.

Martha took Maximilian's hand. She wanted nothing more than to hold his hand.

Love reclined on the sofa where Maximilian always read the manuscripts they were sent. She looked around the little room in which so many thoughts swirled—so many visions, plans, doubts, so much fear of failure. She thought about human lives and how complicated people considered them to be—so many imponderables, so much beyond their comprehension—a constant burden they carried.

Maximilian drew Martha into his arms, and they sat, holding one another tight, crying.

56

It was a sunny November day. The nurse had wrapped the old prince in a blanket and positioned him in the sun, the pavilion sheltering him from the wind.

Josef enjoyed the stillness.

A shadow fell on his face. Had so much time passed that the nurse was already there to take him back to the darkness of his suite? Josef opened his eyes.

The face above him was silhouetted against the sun, and he was unable to make it out. He sensed something heavy falling onto his lap.

"Here! Returned with thanks!"

He recognized Marie Stadler's voice. She moved closer so he could now see her face and her smile.

"My life could not have had a better start." There was triumph in her voice. She was in the prime of her life, while he was an old man.

"When the rats start crawling out of the woodwork, it means the end is nigh," he spat, full of hatred. He felt his money pouch in his lap.

"The rats! All your money could do nothing against this plague," she replied with relish.

"I could have prevented your birth, torn the baby from the body of that serving wench."

"But I'm here, and I'm your flesh and blood." She tossed her head playfully. "Marie von Traunstein! No, I really don't like the way it sounds." She pushed the tip of her parasol between his legs. "Your dynasty is at an end, Grandpapa!"

Groaning in pain, he hoisted himself up and moved to scratch her in the face. She was ahead of him and kicked the wheelchair out from under him. It bumped along the path for a few yards before tipping over.

Marie opened her mandarin-colored parasol, which an admirer had brought her from Shanghai, and ran back to the castle. At last she had got rid of that money pouch.

Behind her, the prince called for help. Two gardeners heard and helped him back into his wheelchair.

"Irma!" Despite her advanced pregnancy, Konstanze hurried down the stairs. Her daughter was standing with Georg in the hall. She was in her coat, her luggage ready by the door.

"My mother is carrying someone else's baby, so you'll no longer be able to marry me off as befits our social status. So I don't need to play along with your farce a moment longer," Irma pronounced fiercely.

"What your mother and I do is one thing. But the family is of concern to us all." Georg's voice was as calm and circumspect as ever.

"Family? So why didn't you take care of Marie and her mother back then? They're family, too," Irma replied angrily. Georg was horrified to realize that, at that moment, she looked like the old prince.

Mathilde was standing at the top of the stairs. If Irma carried out her intention, she would be left there alone.

"Why must you go, Irma?" Konstanze tried to pacify her.

"Why, Mother? Because this house is like a tomb."

"But where will you go, my child?" Konstanze asked anxiously.

The front door flew open to reveal Marie on the doorstep. "She's coming to live with me!"

"With my sister," Irma said triumphantly.

Konstanze was pierced by a stabbing pain.

Marie picked up Irma's suitcase and extended her hand to her sister.

Irma made the most of her departure. "I'm sorry for this baby, that it's going to be born into a tomb."

Mathilde winced. Georg moved to stop Irma, but she freed herself from his hands and said sharply, "Do you want to shut me in like Würtner did to Marie?"

Georg took a shocked step back and let her go. Irma and Marie left. The labor pains had begun, forcing Konstanze to sit on the stairs. "Call the midwife!" she gasped.

"Mother!" Mathilde ran down the stairs to her side as Georg hurried to the telephone.

~

Irma stowed the luggage in the trunk, and Marie opened the passenger door of the coupé she had been driving for three weeks now.

Death took a good look at the car. He regretted that he could not go with the two women back to Vienna. It would have been fun.

As the dust from the vanishing car settled, he saw Love. She waved at him. "Couldn't we go halves?" she called from afar.

"But we are two, my Love," Death replied, pleased with the original way he had addressed her.

"I mean, you limit yourself to one soul and leave me the other." As she looked at him imploringly, he regretted replying. The error was, *she* believed that *he* could control the limits of what he was doing. Surely she knew better. Now with her, things were altogether different. She was an energy, an unbounded energy. He was a vehicle that carried souls through the veil of the world.

"So you won't cooperate?" Love asked, disappointed. Death folded his arms and looked intently up at the blue sky. He didn't want to fall out with her . . . *This war,* he thought, *it's driving even us crazy . . .*

Mathilde knelt by her mother. Konstanze reached out and stroked her youngest daughter's hair. "Please go to your room, Mathilde."

Her daughter hesitated, then tore herself away obediently.

The pain was so great that Konstanze was unable to stand. She had to remain where she was on the step. Georg sat by her. Konstanze took his hand. "I'd like this to be our child."

~

Georg had become quieter during the days when he had worried for his friend's life, battling with his own guilt over Vincent's arrest.

He and Vincent had joined the Peace Society together and had been members of the same Masonic lodge. The Traunstein and Zacharias families had met regularly to celebrate festivals and birthdays. Their friendship seemed to be multifaceted; it was serious and cheerful, deep and binding. When Georg saw the blossoming love between Marie and his friend, he had petitioned the Emperor for an aristocratic title for Zacharias so as not to lose his fellow political campaigner, while at the same time seeking the advice of the grand master of the court on a suitable marriage. He would never forget the look on Vincent's face as he produced the list of possible matches. Vincent was ultimately too loyal to Georg to protest; on the contrary, he asked Georg's advice on which family he would favor.

Georg had counseled his friend, guided him through all the social conventions, and stood by Vincent's side as witness to the marriage. By then, Vincent had held the title of Baron von Zacharias.

But Georg had failed to notice how much his friend had suffered. For, in truth, Vincent had felt used by Georg.

Not once during their endless discussions over the political future of the country had Georg tried to understand his friend's arguments.

Worse still, he had verbally attacked Vincent's desire to see an independent Bohemian nation-state, holding himself to be the cleverer of the two.

But now Georg recognized that, where his friend was concerned, he had disregarded his own fundamental principle that all people are equal. *Sheer arrogance,* Georg chided himself. He had failed as a friend. He had failed as a human being.

And so Georg was determined to remain true to Konstanze and their marriage, a gesture that would be his apology for his arrogance. He had sworn to himself that he would love this child like his own daughters, and now he also gave Konstanze his promise.

57

Josef von Traunstein sent the nurse from the room and maneuvered his wheelchair to the cupboard where he kept his hunting rifles. He had bagged almost thirty-five thousand game trophies in sixty years. That was about two a day. The most magnificent skulls and antlers adorned the walls of the corridors and the dining room, where they would remain for posterity.

Power needed blood. And blood always accompanied the seizure of power, Death thought.

The old prince thought about the war, and the fact that nothing good would now come of it. He grasped the gun that he always kept loaded, and removed the safety catch with a shaking hand. It still felt good in his grip. He put the barrel of the gun in his mouth. He tasted metal and burnt powder . . . *How could I have gone so wrong?* he thought. Then he pulled the trigger.

Konstanze heard the shot as she struggled to deliver her baby. This time, the birth was more painful than it had been with her daughters, and fraught with fear.

Death welcomed the old man's soul. It wanted only one thing—to finally be at peace.

Love had taken a seat next to Konstanze's sewing table, hoping that Death's presence would not be required here.

Georg rushed into his father's room below them. Retching, he held a handkerchief to his mouth and called for the servants.

In his study, Georg paced restlessly for hours. He thought about his father's undignified death, about the child that would soon be born, and about Konstanze, tormented in labor.

It was long past midnight when the newborn's cry at last echoed through the house. Georg hurried from his room and ran up the stairs. He met Flora coming toward him.

"It's a boy. But your wife's losing a lot of blood."

He ascended the stairs at a run. As he entered Konstanze's room, he saw a maid moving the bloodied sheets aside. The midwife handed him the baby so she could be free to help the doctor.

Georg gazed at the newborn boy. For a moment he believed he could see Martha's smile. He smiled back.

Konstanze called to him with a weak voice. He moved closer and tried to place her son in her arms, but she had no strength. She merely touched the baby's feet and Georg's hands. Her touch was like the flutter of a butterfly's wing.

"What happened? I heard a shot," she said quietly.

"Father is dead."

Konstanze said nothing. She struggled with her memories and sense of guilt.

Love saw Death enter the room and shook her head. Death came to stand beside her.

"And you'll love him like our own three daughters?"

Georg nodded, handed the baby to the midwife, and sat down on the edge of Konstanze's bed.

Love still hoped that everything would turn out for the best. Death held himself back.

"Do you forgive me, Georg?" For the first time, Konstanze used her husband's first name. "You must forgive me. Please, Georg!" she begged. Her request went beyond the adultery; she was also referring to an old story about which she had never spoken.

He nodded again.

"Say it aloud. Please say it." Her voice sounded as though it were coming through fog.

"I forgive you." Of course he forgave her. If only he could forgive himself.

"Thank you, Georg!" She smiled as she died.

Death looked at Love. They had known it twenty-two years ago, on that November 28. What had changed since?

The women had changed, Love thought. The women had grown braver; they had discovered their needs and begun to stand up for them. And if the women awoke and reminded their men that they could emerge together from the endless games of power and impotence, then the murder on the battlefields could also come to an end. Then they would all remember that they were one people, that there was only one God. And that God was themselves.

Martha lowered the telephone receiver slowly and went into the guest room where Maximilian was sleeping. He woke and understood before she had the chance to break the news.

Georg looked at Andreas. *Lots of girls first,* he had said to Konstanze an age ago. *We've plenty of time for a boy.*

Flora entered, her eyes red from crying. "I'll send for a wet nurse."

Georg looked at the newborn. "Yes . . . we'll need a wet nurse." He handed Andreas to her.

Flora took the baby carefully. "I'll do everything I can to help him come to terms with the loss of his mother."

Georg nodded. It never once occurred to him to consider entrusting Maximilian with the boy's upbringing.

~

According to custom, a large number of mourners attended Josef's funeral. Konstanze's burial took place on the following day, among just a few family members.

Afterward, Georg called Martha on the telephone. She told him that Maximilian had decided he would go to the front as a war correspondent so that he could write about the horrors of war from his own experience.

"He'd like a photo of his son."

Georg promised to send one and told her about Konstanze's death, and how important it had been for her to be reconciled with him.

~

During the night before Maximilian's departure, Martha felt as though Konstanze were visiting her.

They didn't speak; it wasn't necessary.

Konstanze leaned over Martha and kissed her, as she had done on that New Year's Eve. *I love you, Martha; I love you as much as any person can love another.*

58

The trench warfare is raging while going nowhere, like an insatiable monster that swallows everything in its path. Even when the shelling finally quiets and a soldier raises his head in hope, the insidious gas will kill him.

Reports and articles arrived weekly from Maximilian at the front. Martha passed them straight on to Menning for typesetting.

We print everything you send, my dear Max, she wrote to him. *Every one of your words rings true, and your descriptions bring to life the horrors you're living through.*

The war had all of Europe in its grip.

In the Austro-Hungarian Empire, hundreds of thousands fled the crown lands in the face of ethnic attacks, pogroms, and plunder of their property. Refugees also arrived at Traunstein House. Georg housed them in the school. When there was no longer enough room there, he made accommodation available in his farmyard outbuildings. The infirmary was full. The doctor and midwife were kept busy around the clock. Mathilde helped where she was needed.

We have almost a hundred people to house now, people who have been driven from their own regions, Georg wrote to Martha. *Typhus and other fatal diseases are rampant. It's only thanks to my friends and contacts that I can organize sufficient bandages and medicines.*

Berlin is full of mutilated men, marked by the war forever, Martha replied. *I feel as though the light has been extinguished, that we've gone beyond the limits of humanity. This peace we're all waiting for—what will it look like?*

~

Maximilian moved over the battlefields of France in his capacity as war correspondent, looking for the glue that held this war together. He talked to simple soldiers and to their officers.

Men who had been nameless in peacetime were soldiers belonging to a company in wartime, members of a fighting body. They felt elevated, as they now had power over the lives of the men on the other side of the trenches.

They don't know their enemy, but they hate him, because they have been told that these here or those there are their

enemy. Once a war has begun, it is almost impossible
to end it. To go to war and keep it going, the men have
shut down all reason, suppressed all feelings. The officers'
whistles order them into battle. But no man still in pos-
session of his senses would allow himself to be sent to his
death by a whistle.

Maximilian wrote and wrote. Whenever he was in a place of relative safety, he hammered out his thoughts on a typewriter. When he lay alongside the soldiers in the trenches, he wrote by hand in his notebooks. He sent them all home to Martha. He wanted her to later give them to his son so that he would learn from them.

During the Spring Offensive of 1918, during the Fourth Battle of Flanders, Maximilian was torn apart by a shell.

When he and his comrades heard the howling of the missile as it flew toward them—and when they heard how huge the shell must be, and that it was heading right for them—they knew immediately that everything would change, forever.

Parts of Maximilian's body were thrown into the air together with wet earth. Bloody lumps of flesh, impossible to differentiate from those of the soldier next to him, fell back into the crater. They were released.

They were released from their lives and from the battlefield, where the murder continued unabated. A barbaric exodus.

Amid the carnage of so many soldiers, Maximilian's soul was not given the privilege of meeting Death. It ascended from worldly experience to the realm of peace, to rest and recover for a while. Later it would follow the calls of the others, until they were brought together and would all go on to speak the same language.

~

Martha was sent Maximilian's private things in a cardboard box. As well as his typewriter, his notebooks, and his manuscripts, there was also an envelope containing his watch, his wedding ring, and the photo of his son.

It was a Friday.

For the first time in her adult life, Martha lit the Sabbath candles. She broke bread and thought of Maximilian. He had looked for a mythology in everything. "We have to decode the old legends in order to find out who we really are," he had said to her once.

The mailman brought Georg a box full of letters. Most of them were for the refugee families, but there was one for him. He recognized the handwriting and withdrew to the calm of his study to read it.

That was when he learned of Maximilian's death. Martha had been sending him his articles and essays over the years. Georg was familiar with the author, but he knew nothing of Maximilian, the man. Andreas would soon be four. The boy would never know his natural father.

59

The portrait of Emperor Franz Josef had been draped in black crepe since his death in 1916. The war had now ended, and the last emperor had fled abroad with his family after being forced to declare the surrender of the empire. Independent states were formed from the crown lands. Vincent Zacharias's desire for an independent Bohemian nation was fulfilled as citizens there joined with Slovakia to found the independent state of Czechoslovakia, with its capital in Prague. In a few years, this state would be annexed by Hitler's Germany and destroyed by a new war. After the end of that war, Czechoslovakia would pursue a socialist path—which would fail. The Czech Republic and Slovakia would separate again, to find a new unity as two sovereign states in the European Union. But in time, that, too, would be beset by doubt . . .

~

Anna walked down the corridors of her hotel. Most of the rooms were occupied by officers on their way home. Some had lost everything and no longer had homes. They all felt empty and degraded, their bodies or minds—or both—ruined.

Anna had lost almost all her assets in the war. Schuster was no longer alive, either. Although they had never married, she was once again widowed.

Her eyes fell on a mirror in an empty room. She stopped and looked at herself, thinking of her girlhood dreams, how she had imagined and got this hotel.

Yes, it's true that a person shapes their own future, she thought proudly. The world had shown it to her.

But if that's the case, she realized suddenly, *then we must all have thought this damned war into being. Just as the spirit is at the beginning of all creation.* She shuddered.

The homecoming soldiers sat in the foyer, whiling away the time over games of chess, cards, or dice. Some, exhausted, were asleep in their chairs. Some of them had been Sacher boys.

Anna went to sit by Katharina Schratt, who was doing a jigsaw puzzle.

"Franz Josef was always opposed to war, and everything turned out even worse than he imagined. I'm just glad that he didn't have to experience it," the former Imperial Court actress murmured as she fitted a piece into the picture, which, once finished, would show the Prater park in peacetime. Anna's dogs, infirm with age, lolled at her feet.

"Laphroaig . . . Berry Brothers and Rudd . . . bottled . . . 1908." Szemere's cracked voice set a poignant tone for the sorry scene.

Mayr shook his head regretfully.

The Hungarian bon vivant savored the noble spirit on his tongue once more and guessed, "1904?"

"Almost, my dear Count. Laphroaig. Berry Brothers and Rudd. 1903."

"There's nothing wrong with me, Mayr." Szemere waved him away with the maudlin demeanor of an old man.

"But no, my dear Count. It's merely an indisposition, a temporary condition, just as our present circumstances are temporary." Mayr bowed to the group and went to the reception area.

Szemere tried to rise, to go to his suite, but Anna held him back. "Stay and sit with us a while, Szemere."

Anna called Wagner over with the whisky bottle.

Before the Hungarian could protest, Anna said, "Of course I'll give you this on credit. Don't you dare refuse."

It had become a daily ritual between them, one that Anna never considered beneath her. For she couldn't, and wouldn't, simply turn away those who had brought money into the hotel in times of peace.

Anna turned to her loyal head waiter. "Do you remember, Wagner, how my late husband and I saw you in the Varieté and recruited you, back in the early nineties?" she reminisced.

Wagner beamed. "As though it were yesterday, ma'am!"

Anna raised her glass. "Our good health!"

"May your kindhearted hospitality last forever, my dear Frau Sacher."

Momentarily reanimated, Szemere began to flirt with her. "To your immortal beauty and your incomparable charm."

"To be pretty as a young girl is a blessing; to remain likeable as an old woman—that's something you have to earn." Anna raised her glass to each in the group in turn as she spoke.

The door opened, and a cold breeze blew through the foyer.

A returning soldier entered the hotel, emaciated, his eyes feverish. They all turned to look at him.

"Johann!" Anna got to her feet. "Wagner, a whisky for the home-comer—immediately!"

60

Flora came to Georg in his study with a letter she had been pondering over for several days. She had made her decision.

"Flora?" Georg looked up from his work.

"Johann's back from the war. He's in Vienna. Frau Sacher wrote to inform me, and also to say that he didn't tell me himself because he's lost an arm."

"And now you want to go to him?"

Flora nodded. "Frau Sacher has offered me the position of housekeeper, and Johann's now a bellhop."

"Well, I can't compete with the Sacher," Georg said with a smile.

"But what about Andreas?" Flora was heavyhearted at the thought of leaving the boy. If Georg tried to persuade her to stay, her resolve might well be shaken.

"He'll miss you, Flora, but he'll have to make do with his father," Georg said. He meant himself—he was the boy's father, and no one would ever have reason to doubt it. "I wish you luck, Flora."

Now really is the right time to leave, she thought.

"Your wife once asked me to look after this key." Flora handed a dainty key ring to Georg. "It's the key to her desk." She curtsied, as she always had, and left the study. He looked at the key in surprise.

～

Georg had not entered Konstanze's rooms since her death. Everything was just as she had left it. He sat on the chair by her desk. The door to her sewing room was ajar, and the work table there was empty. Only then did he realize that he had not seen a scrap of fabric there in all those years. Konstanze had never been interested in needlework, yet this little room had been her refuge. He was surprised that he had never thought anything of it.

Georg unlocked the desk and folded down the top. He looked at the ink stains on it, and the scratches her bracelets had made. Konstanze's perfume rose up from the wood, as though she were still sitting there.

He saw Lina Stein's books arranged in a compartment. *Woman on a Journey, The Woman Behind the Veil, Guardian Angel.* Next to them was a copy of *The Prayers of a Useless Man.* His curiosity aroused, he looked in a file and found newspaper clippings and reviews of Lina Stein's novels.

At the center of the drawers was a small door, inlaid with tortoise-shell. Behind it, he found a manuscript bound with a cord. He read the title, *A Story of Seduction*, and the name of the author, Lina Stein. Leafing through it, he saw that the comments and notes in the margins were in his wife's handwriting.

He remembered a fleeting image he had glimpsed shortly after Rosa's birth and subsequently forgotten: Martha and Konstanze discussing something passionately as they walked in the park. Konstanze had made notes, which Martha either rejected with a shake of her head or read with approval.

Suddenly, Georg knew what it all meant, and realized that not for one moment of their life together had he had the slightest idea what Konstanze did when she withdrew to her room and shut herself off for hours. Martha had known. The two women had been linked by so much more than he would ever have considered possible. Shame, pride, hurt, and respect flooded through him.

He began to read the manuscript and was soon totally absorbed in the story.

I promised myself to the marriage in the sight of God, with a pure heart, for better, for worse. At least, that's what I thought at the time, for I was barely more than a child, too young to understand the contradictions of life. I heard rumors of something that had long since been common knowledge among the servants, that my future husband had got a maid pregnant. He had fathered a child with a woman of the common people. A daughter! She would grow up and discover who her father was. She would make claims, demand her rights. How could I look to the future with peace of mind? How could I ever feel secure?

❡

Irma opened the door to her father and Andreas. "Father!"

"Hello, Irma!"

She allowed him to take her in his arms.

"Hello, little Andreas." Irma reached out her hand to her brother, and Georg saw the similarity between them. He had to smile at how life had a way of forming internal connections between things and people.

Andreas pressed against his father's leg. He hardly knew his sister, as Irma had visited Traunstein House very rarely since their mother's death.

Georg and Andreas followed her down the corridor to the salon. Outside the kitchen door, Georg set down a basket of food.

"Mathilde sends her love. She's put together some produce for you, though the estate can't spare too much. We still have almost fifty refugees."

"Thank you, Father; it's very kind of you. But we're not starving yet. Our arrangement is that each of our guests brings something," Irma said.

Marie came out of the salon. "Not knowing what's going to be there is an adventure in itself. In any case, our stores are always well stocked."

Georg and Marie shook hands in greeting.

"Will you have a cup of tea with us? Hello, Andreas."

She led father and son to a group of blue silk-covered chairs. Like the rest of the furniture, they were new. It seemed the young women were doing well. At least the salon, which was open to all from early evening onward, was now more tastefully appointed. The eclectic mix of styles and colors had been replaced by cool functionality in the choice and arrangement of the furniture. It looked very much as though Irma had helped her sister redesign the interior. Georg recalled when Konstanze first moved into the castle, how she had had the upper floors renovated to her own taste.

Andreas was staring, openmouthed, at two brass Buddhas positioned between the windows.

A maid brought tea and cakes.

"Please, could you look after my son for a moment? I need to talk to my daughters alone," Georg asked the young woman.

She held out her hand to the boy. "Come with me, Andreas. Let's make a mug of cocoa."

"What's the big secret, Father?" Irma sat next to Marie on the sofa.

Georg cleared his throat. "Your mother, Irma, was the author Lina Stein."

Irma looked in bewilderment from her father to Marie, who raised her eyebrows in amusement.

"Would you believe it! So that's why she shut herself away in her room for hours on end," Irma said in amazement. For a moment she remembered her nanny keeping her away from the sewing room, as her mother had instructed. She thought of the light she saw burning in her mother's room whenever she woke in the night and went to look for her. Irma remembered the absent look in her mother's eyes when she emerged from her rooms after hours on end. As a little girl, Irma had always longed for her mother's attention, but she had eventually given up on ever gaining it.

Georg continued. "In her last novel, Lina Stein tells the story of a young bride who discovers that her husband has an illegitimate child, and she can't bear to think about it."

Marie looked at him.

"She describes how she asks her father-in-law for help. He hands the matter over to a pimp, who abducts the child with the intention of selling her on the streets."

"You mean she tells Marie's story?" Irma asked, astonished.

Georg nodded. "She goes on to tell how she suffered for her actions when they heard about the girl's disappearance. Back then, there was a superstition—"

"Please!" Marie broke in before he could finish. "That's so typical of your wife. She always had to be the center of attention. And now she's claiming responsibility for my abduction?"

Marie laughed with amusement, though whether it was laughter of relief or aggression, Georg was unable to tell. "I survived the crypt. And I want to leave it at that."

The tone of Marie's voice left them in no doubt about her disinterest in any further revelations about Konstanze's novel. Her expression silenced Georg.

Irma looked from one to the other. She had no idea what her mother was supposed to be guilty of—telling the story of Marie's fate in a novel, or actually being responsible for it?

The doorbell rang, and the maid showed Lechner in. Georg had not seen the agent since Vincent Zacharias had been sentenced. It seemed that Lechner had come through the war well.

"Oh, you have visitors," Lechner said jovially, as though he were master of the house. Georg stood and called for Andreas. He had said all he had come to say, and had no desire to continue the conversation in Lechner's presence.

"There's no need to run off on my account, Herr Traunstein." Lechner relished the fact that Georg was no longer allowed to use his title. "We could have a chat about the new times," he said pompously.

"I heard you've been promoted to superintendent," Georg replied.

"It seems our young lady 'Republic' doesn't only want to be sweet-talked by old men but also wants some young blood to take her by the arm."

Georg took a step toward him. "Your corrupt services for the old regime haven't been forgotten. You have my word on that!"

Lechner bowed to Georg. "The old ties need to be broken; otherwise nothing new will ever grow. You have my word on that!"

They glared into each other's eyes.

Georg took his son's hand, and they walked to the door. Irma joined them. Marie followed, calling as she left, "Ask the maid to get you a cup of tea, Fritz."

Georg thought about how Irma now lived in the company of these people. "Do you have any plans for the future, Irma?" he asked at the door.

"Maybe I'll write for the newspaper," she replied enthusiastically.

"Irma's got a real talent for leading discussions. Why don't you come one evening—you'd be surprised," Marie said.

He should have accepted her invitation a long time ago, an omission that moved him to embarrassment. "Gladly." He saw in Irma's eyes that she did not believe him, and confirmed, "I'll make the time."

Georg kissed his daughter's brow. He could rely on her self-confidence, her decision-making strength, and her sense of justice—things she had learned under his roof, or so he hoped.

He offered his hand to Marie. She bent down to Andreas. "Well, little man!" She looked at the boy.

"Marie," he said. He liked her.

Irma stopped her father once again. "What do you think, Father? Could Mother really have done it?"

"I don't know, Irma." He hesitated. "I never tried to get to know your mother properly. I truly regret it."

When the sisters came back into the salon, Lechner was sitting in the place Georg had vacated. He remarked caustically, "He may have had to relinquish his title, but he still thinks he's a cut above."

Irma hated it when Lechner made nasty remarks about her family, and sprang to her father's defense. "Every person is special. Ultimately, we live to change ourselves for the better."

Lechner enjoyed seeing the "Princess," as he liked to call her, get angry. "I don't believe people are capable of changing," he said provocatively.

"Because you spend all your time searching for the bad in others, Herr Lechner," she replied.

"Enough, now!" Marie had enjoyed her father's visit. There was no doubt that he belonged to a dying breed.

She stood by the gramophone, searching the records for a suitable piece of music. "Don't get bogged down with the old," she said as she put the record on. "Something completely new will come." Irma looked at her sister in admiration.

After a few crackles and scratches, the music began: Liszt's *Les Préludes*.

Lechner surrendered himself to the music and prepared himself for the time when men like him would hold this city firmly in their hands.

61

They met that afternoon in the Sacher. Love was wearing a simple black dress. His shoes were worn and his suit threadbare.

While she sat on her usual seat in the foyer, tapping her foot as ever, he, Death, strode through the corridors of the hotel. Some of the men who lived here, their homes gone, called after him. This war had been wretched, and there was no such thing as a hero's death.

Death had roamed the battlefields tirelessly in order to bring souls home. Many of them had refused to follow him, remaining instead where they had died so inhumanly. Others returned to their families because they had unfinished business from their lives there. Unintentionally or deliberately, they prevented their loved ones from living. People began to deny themselves happiness. Illness and epidemics spread.

Love had to keep track of all the connections made and broken. These were difficult times.

~

Johann set Martha's suitcase down. Back in the hotel uniform, he had his left sleeve pinned up.

Martha looked around her old room. Flora hurried up to her.

"Frau Aderhold, how lovely to see you here again." They shook hands. Flora showed Martha her wedding ring, a narrow gold band that was so new it still gleamed brightly. Martha wished them luck and gave Johann a tip.

Death leaned in the doorway and watched the three of them. There was nothing to do here, not for now, in any case. The crippled bellhop was enjoying good health, and his wife was no longer of an age to put her life at risk through pregnancy. Some situations did have their good side.

Martha sat down at the desk where she had written so often while staying here over the years. Time had left its mark on the furniture and walls. The mirror by the desk showed a woman of almost fifty.

For a fleeting moment, she believed she saw death flit across her face. The encounter did not unsettle her. There were some things still to be done, and she did not intend to go before they were complete. Martha thought about Maximilian and the fact that it was the war, of all things, that had enabled his talent as a writer to blossom.

~

Love stopped tapping her foot when the door opened and the doorman greeted some guests as they entered.

"It's good to see you again, Mayr—and in such good health!"

Georg was at pains to achieve an air of relaxed civility, which was not something Mayr would ever consider. The doorman executed a series of bows, so happy was he that everything would soon be as it had always been.

"The pleasure is all mine, Excellency. I hope you had a good journey, Herr von Traunstein."

"We're supposed to be called simply Traunstein now," said Andreas, who clearly understood more of the circumstances than people expected of a child his age.

"Nonsense!" Mayr replied cheerfully. "You're the von Traunsteins, and no official decree will change that, my little Prince von Traunstein."

Anna Sacher came over to meet the newcomers. "Oh, Andreas! You look just like your papa."

The adults exchanged a knowing look. Andreas looked up at his father and protested, "But everyone says I'm just like Mama!"

They laughed.

At that moment, Martha emerged from the elevator.

Georg went to meet her, took her hands in greeting, and turned to Andreas. "Andrasz, come and let me introduce you."

The boy approached hesitantly. Martha saw his resemblance to Maximilian as she bent down to the boy. "Hello, Andreas."

"Hello, ma'am." He looked in fascination at the stone at Martha's throat.

She unfastened the chain and refastened it around Andreas's neck. "For luck."

Martha thought about Maximilian and how the lapis lazuli had always perplexed him.

Andreas placed his hand on the stone. "It's still warm," he said. "Soon it'll be my warmth. Then I'll give it back to you."

Martha nodded, struggling to hold back the tears.

Anna Sacher came over. "Andreas, why don't you come with me? Let me show you where my Sacher boys always used to sit."

She took the boy's hand. Andreas looked up at his father.

"Off you go with Frau Sacher. We won't be far away."

With this reassurance, the boy found his sense of adventure and went with Frau Sacher.

"Let's have a drink together," Georg suggested, leading Martha to a table.

Love followed them.

Georg took Konstanze's manuscript from his bag. Martha looked at the familiar paper. *A Story of Seduction* was written in a sweeping script on the front page. There was a dedication on the second page. Konstanze had never before used quotations or prologues, but had simply launched into the story. This time there was a simple, measured dedication.

For Martha. For the one I love.

Was this a volume that would hold them all together? Even now, after the deaths of Konstanze and Maximilian? Did Georg and

Martha deserve to build their happiness on ground prepared by the other two?

The unconscious creates destruction and pain.

Maybe in the end it isn't an entanglement, but the next stage in the course of life, Martha thought as she held the manuscript in her hands.

Georg laid his hands on Martha's. "Life is giving us a second chance. What do you think?"

Martha felt as though they had known each other for an eternity.

Death looked at Love sitting near the couple. And he saw the space she had reserved for him. It gave him certainty. For what would *he*, Death, be without *her*, Love?

Love felt his gaze on her.

EPILOGUE

Little Andreas was sitting in the place where Vincent Zacharias had written his doctoral thesis, eating Sachertorte. Anna Sacher smoked her cigar, deep in thought, and smiled when she looked at the boy. Her old world would probably soon vanish. But the Sachertorte . . . no one could take that from her. It would tell of a world in which people tried to relieve their pain with sweetness.

The end of the story?

No! A BEGINNING—life never stops offering us second chances.

AUTHOR'S NOTE

The Aderholds, the Traunsteins, Johann and Flora, and of course Marie Stadler, Würtner, and Lechner are fictional characters. I gave myself every freedom in shaping them.

I drew my portrayal of Anna Sacher from the many anecdotes readily available to me and from the few photos that exist of her. I wondered what lay behind her decisions and her life. The way I have portrayed her character is therefore my highly personal view. The same applies to Franz and Eduard Sacher, the Sachers' children, and also to Julius Schuster, Mayr, Katharina Schratt, and the head waiter, Wagner.

HISTORICAL CHRONICLE

1832

While working in the kitchens of Prince Klemens von Metternich, the sixteen-year-old confectioner's apprentice Franz Sacher invents the Sachertorte, which became world famous and is still made according to his secret recipe.

1854

Franz Josef I, emperor of Austria, marries sixteen-year-old Elisabeth, known as Sisi.

1876

Franz Sacher's son, Eduard Sacher, opens the Hotel de l'Opera in the immediate vicinity of the Vienna State Opera. Subsequently renamed the Hotel Sacher, it was to become Austria's most legendary luxury hotel.

1880

Twenty-one-year-old Anna Fuchs and thirty-seven-year-old Eduard Sacher marry in spring of this year.

January 30, 1889

Crown Prince Rudolf, son of Franz Josef and Sisi, commits suicide with his lover. Franz Ferdinand of Austria-Este, a nephew of the Emperor, becomes the official heir to the throne.

1892 (the story begins here)

After Eduard's death, his thirty-four-year-old widow, Anna Sacher, takes over management of the hotel and obtains a license to operate as Purveyor to the Imperial and Royal Court. The Hotel Sacher is one of the most important meeting places of Vienna high society.

1897

At the age of fifteen, Annie Sacher, Anna's daughter, marries the son of the administrator Julius Schuster.

September 10, 1898

The Empress Elisabeth is murdered in Geneva.

1900

At the turn of the century, both the high point and the beginning of the decline of the Habsburg monarchy, Vienna enjoys a cultural flowering.

The Wiener Moderne—the Viennese Modern Age—sees the births of psychoanalysis and coffeehouse literature along with the rise of the Art Nouveau and Secession movements, twelve-tone music, and science.

March 22, 1902

Annie Schuster, Anna Sacher's daughter, dies.

March 11, 1907

Franz Sacher dies in Baden.

June 28, 1914

In Sarajevo, a Serbian nationalist shoots the Austrian heir to the throne, Franz Ferdinand, and his wife. The assassination incites Austria-Hungary to declare war on Serbia, which leads to the outbreak of the First World War with the involvement of the German Empire.

November 21, 1916

Emperor Franz Josef I dies at the age of eighty-six. His death, and his country's military defeat in 1917, lead to the downfall of the Dual Monarchy of Austria-Hungary, which is ultimately dissolved in the autumn of 1918. Julius Schuster does not live to see the end of the war.

1919 (the story ends here)

The nobility is abolished in the newly created Republic of Austria. The nation suffers, as does the former German Empire, under the consequences of losing the world war.

February 25, 1930

Anna Sacher dies in Vienna at the age of seventy-one, having been legally incapacitated by her son the previous year. The hotel is taken over by the Gürtler family in 1934.

ABOUT THE AUTHOR

Photo © 2017 Ev-Katrin-Weiß

Rodica Doehnert studied directing at the College of Television and Film in Potsdam-Babelsberg and has worked for twenty years as a screen-writer, producing complex, thoughtful screenplays. Her three-part television series *Hotel Adlon: A Family Saga* won the 2013 Magnolia Award for Best International Miniseries at the 19th Shanghai International Television Festival and has been seen by more than thirty million viewers in over twenty-five countries.

ABOUT THE TRANSLATOR

Alison Layland is a novelist and translator. A member of the Institute of Translation and Interpreting and the Society of Authors, she has won a number of prizes for her fiction writing and translation. Her debut novel, the literary thriller *Someone Else's Conflict*, was published in 2014 by Honno Press to be followed by her second, *Riverflow*, in early 2019. She has also translated a number of successful novels from German and French into English. She lives and works in the beautiful and inspiring countryside of Wales, United Kingdom.